THE HOUSE

WITH THE

BLIND GLASS

WINDOWS

Herbjørg Wassmo

Translated by Roseann Lloyd and Allen Simpson

my friend, ⬛⬛⬛⬛⬛⬛, friend

SEAL PRESS

Copyright © 1981 by Gyldendal Norsk Forlag
English translation copyright © 1987 by Roseann Lloyd and Allen Simpson
Cover Illustration by Kris Wiltse
Cover design by Clare Conrad

All rights reserved. No part of this book may be reproduced in any form, except for the quotation of brief passages in reviews, without prior written permission from Seal Press, 3131 Western Avenue, Suite 410, Seattle, Washington 98121.

Published by arrangement with Gyldendal Norsk Forlag, Oslo, Norway. Originally published in Norwegian as *Huset med den blinde glassveranda*.

Publication of this book was made possible in part with support from the National Endowment for the Arts and the Norwegian Cultural Council.

Library of Congress Cataloging-in-Publication Data
Wassmo, Herbjørg, 1942–
    The house with the blind glass windows.
    Translation of: Huset med den blinde glassveranda.
    I. Title. II. Series.
PT8951.33.A8H813 1987   839.8'2374   87-16704
ISBN 1-878067-59-1

Printed in the United States of America
10 9 8 7 6 5 4 3 2

Distributed to the trade by Publishers Group West
In Canada: Publishers Group West Canada, Toronto, Ontario
In the U.K. and Europe: Airlift Book Company, London, England

ACKNOWLEDGEMENTS

The translators thank the following people for their assistance in bringing this novel from North Norwegian to American English: Kristin Elsbak, Gunhild Ramm Reistad, Susan Hill Oppegaard, Lillian Wikstrøm, Kari Gade, Kaare Strøm, Brigitte Frase, Liv Dahl, Scott Thoe and Katherine Hanson. And we thank Barbara Wilson for her valuable insights into the delicate art of translation.

THE HOUSE WITH THE
BLIND GLASS WINDOWS

Chapter One

SHE DIDN'T KNOW WHEN SHE FIRST BECAME AWARE OF it: the danger. It was long after she moved into the pantry behind the kitchen, because her mother thought she should have a little room for herself. It was long after she started waking up at night because of the loud voices from the living room where Henrik and her mother slept. She woke up in the night and felt sweaty. As if she were coming down with a fever. And she wanted to cry out for her mother, feel her there close to her. But she couldn't get a single sound out. Everything was hopeless and strange and the darkness was unsafe. It happened more and more often. Mostly when her mother was working the night shift at the fish packing plant and didn't get home until late.

So she had to force herself to wake up completely, even though she didn't want to. Sit up in bed and be like an empty shell. It felt like her head was swollen up and held that empty shell afloat in the room. Her ears were like the doors on Almar's boat house in Hestvika—their hinges so damaged that the storms whistled through and tore at them.

She'd been up to Horse Crag once. All the way to the top. There was nothing there but stone and heather. Henrik had grabbed her by the shoulder and held her all the way out over the edge. The cliff plunged steeply down to the ocean, with a horrible slope covered with rocks and boulders. As they stood there, she heard the same whistling in her head. She couldn't move. Her mother's voice sounded scared when she begged Henrik to move back. Tora couldn't remember the words.

That was when she'd understood that Henrik was the strongest. Because he laughed.

She could hear the echoes tumbling beneath her on the rocky slope every time he took a breath to send another burst of laughter into the abyss.

The kids at school taunted her sometimes, saying they could tell by the smell where her mother worked.

But everybody smelled like fish, Tora thought. She didn't much care what they did. As long as they didn't grab her.

Hands. Hands that came in the dark. That was the danger. Big, hard hands that groped and squeezed. Afterwards she barely managed to get to the bucket before it was too late. Sometimes she didn't know if she dared to pee in the kitchen, where they kept the bucket.

Instead, she would pull on her boots and put her coat on over her nightgown and run outside to the outhouse, summer or winter. The yard was big and safe and there was a hook on the outhouse door. She could sit down there a long time. Sometimes she stayed until she was stiff with cold or until she heard her mother's footsteps on the gravel path.

Henrik was almost always out on the nights her mother worked.

Tora woke up whenever the door opened and one of them came in. Her mother had footsteps that sounded tired but light. She opened the door gently, as if she were afraid it would fall apart. Henrik didn't worry about doors or door frames. He didn't have footsteps either, he just shambled in. But Henrik had other footsteps in the house, when he wanted to. Steps that almost couldn't be heard. Silent, but full of rough breathing.

One day Ingrid began to question Tora. Asked her what time Henrik came home. How he acted. Tora smelled the sickening odor of carnations and the palms of her hands got clammy.

After that she began to get up and help Henrik to bed when he came home, so her mother wouldn't find him on the couch in the kitchen. He smelled disgusting, and sometimes he was simply too heavy. But he never touched her while she was

4

helping him. He just wiped his nose with the back of his hand now and then. He didn't even look at Tora, just squinted into the dark room. That way, things stayed quiet and peaceful until her mother came home.

Even so, one night everything went wrong. Henrik hadn't turned the light on when he came in around eleven o'clock. In the darkness, he'd bumped into the dishes left on the counter to dry. A couple of glasses and cups were knocked off the counter and smashed all over the floor.

Tora woke up when the avalanche started. She heard him fall down out there and heard him swear. She didn't dare go out right away. Her heart was somehow hanging outside her body. It took a while for her to get it back inside again.

But then he shouted, hoarse and rasping, and Tora was afraid that Elisif would come down from upstairs and discover the whole sinful room. Then Mama would die of shame.

She felt the thin small slivers of glass working their way into the sole of one of her feet as she went out into the kitchen. She had to go all the way over to the entryway door to find the light switch.

He was sitting in the middle of the floor, crying.

A strange figure wrapped in Henrik's skin.

Tora found the broom and dustpan and swept a rough path over to the sink. When she went back, she could see the trail of blood she'd left. The harsh light from the ceiling made a lonely slash over the miserable figure on the floor. She avoided thinking about it, just got a kitchen chair and propped him up on it.

His crippled shoulder drooped even more than it usually did. It looked as if somebody had stuffed a jacket sleeve with wool but didn't have enough to fill it up. He held his damaged arm like a precious object that had to be protected from bumps and blows. His good hand was bleeding but he didn't pay any attention to that.

His crying had subsided. He head had sunk down on his chest. It was as if he didn't see her.

She washed off the fresh blood on his forehead too. There was a glistening redness in the gaping cut over his right eyebrow. The dripping of the faucet and the last of his hoarse sobs were the only sounds in the room.

Then the entryway door opened and Ingrid was standing there. Her eyes were two dark pools in pearl-gray fjord ice.

Tora seemed to shrivel up beneath her stare.

The whole room was rocking gently.

She realized that Mama *saw* them. Henrik and her. She saw herself and Henrik dissolve before her mother's eyes. Like soap bubbles scattering out the kitchen window. Falling, weightless and worthless.

Mama was God, who saw them. Mama was the pastor or the school teacher. Mama was Mama—who SAW! Tora was guilty. She was in Henrik's picture, caught within Henrik's power. She was lost.

Ingrid sat down on the old kitchen stool that always creaked. The sound cut to the bone.

Then Tora went out of her body and will, hauled Henrik up out of the chair and stood a moment, swaying slightly with him. She gave him a firm tug and managed to get the two of them balanced on four legs and moving slowly into the living room.

Ingrid was still sitting there when she came back. Her eyes were fixed on the floor, and that was almost worse than having them staring at her, Tora thought.

"So this is how it is around here when your poor mother's at work!"

Her voice came out, abruptly and unrecognizably, from within her coat collar.

"It was just tonight," Tora answered.

She was so terribly happy that her mother had said something. But Ingrid didn't say anything else. She hung her coat up on the hook in the entryway and closed the door gently behind her as she usually did.

But she didn't touch the coffee that Tora had made and put in her thermos, and she didn't even glance at the slices of bread on the plate. She shook her head when Tora wanted to finish sweeping the floor, just nodded silently at the door to Tora's room.

Only then did Tora notice that something in her was crying. Something as empty and sad as a worn-out wish.

She crept into her little room, put a dirty sock on her foot so she wouldn't mess up the bedclothes with blood, then crawled deep into herself under the comforter. Trembling, she caressed herself all over with her cold, clammy hands. It was strangely quiet that night. Like an evil omen. Then she was alone in the world. There was only Tora—who existed.

Smell of dark night, dust and bed. It was like coming in to a bowl of soup after a long day out in the rain. Sleep wouldn't come and her foot throbbed a little. She could still feel a sliver of glass in it.

Just before dawn, the warmth finally spread over her, the girl with the sopping wet face turned to the blue light. Inside her head there was a rustling and a whistling, like the wind through the big yellow aspen swaying in the pastor's field.

Chapter Two

T ORA COULD CLEARLY REMEMBER THAT ONCE SHE'D
climbed up on a stool and was fumbling with a black knob
next to the door. An impatient voice had said:
  "No, you have to *turn* it! *Turn* it—like this!"
The voice was deep and hard and made everything around
her so strangely empty, made her whole world dead. The big
hand pressed on the back of her hand. Her fingers hurt when
it twisted so that both her hand and the light switch had to
obey.
  Then the sharp light flooded into the room. It filled all the
corners, made her eyes ache, hurt so much that something
whistled inside her head. It reminded her of the times she'd
held the really big shells up to her ears to try to hear the
ocean's roar from the fairy tale, the way Grandma had taught
her before she died. But there was only a kind of hissing in
there, a harsh, complaining sound that kept her from what she
was searching for. The fairy tale stayed far away, behind the
hissing and the ocean waves.

That was how it was with the light that the electric switch and
the big hand controlled. It never became warm and familiar
like the light from the kerosene lamp on the breadbox way up
on the table. Tora didn't know if she was friends with the light
from the bulb in the ceiling after that first time with the
switch, or if she just accepted it because it was useful for many
things. Her mother packed the kerosene lamp and put it
away.

Light! She felt it on her eyelids in the spring, before the snow
melted. It flashed and sparkled. And she still thought she was

8

standing on the stool with her weak hand on the knob and didn't know that you had to use all your strength if you wanted light even though you were small. Otherwise the big hand would come and take everything from her, make everything strange and painful like sunshine in April, when you'd been in bed for a whole week with the flu and suddenly you were supposed to be well enough to go outside.

When the ancient mountain ash trees outside the kitchen window were red and the berries hanging so you could stick your hand out through the window and grab a cluster, it was time to make soup. As far back as she could remember, there had been a galvanized steel tub upside-down on top of the cupboard in the entryway. Her mother used it to carry potatoes and vegetables in from the garden. She walked in her cut-off rubber boots down all the steps, out the door and behind the house, where the path went down to the fish racks and the communal garden.

Sometimes Tora got to go along. She watched the hoe between her mother's legs. It stuck out and was a part of her mother in an odd way. The handle tussled with the hem of her skirt and dug its iron nose into the dirt out in front of it. Now and then it hit a potato unexpectedly and hacked it in two. Then the potato sighed and the hoe paused a moment as if it were sorry. And her mother said, "Oh, would you look at that." And went on hoeing.

The taste of carrots when her teeth had ground them up and they lay in her mouth like a sweet, coarse mush—that taste was somehow Tora's alone.

She gnawed on potatoes too. With peelings and sand. She must have been awfully little and dumb then. But she could remember it clearly.

The soup kettle on the table. The fat that floated around in circles and bubbles. The colors were nice and delicate.

She liked *looking* at the cooked vegetables the best, because they tasted awful. But the deep voice forced into her mouth so and so many bites of cooked carrot and at least one leaf of cooked cabbage. The potatoes were all right—she was used to them.

The meat was all right too, but it was disgusting to look at

9

when it was cooked. And it was tough when you chewed it. It somehow squirmed before her very eyes and ruined everything. But before it was put into the kettle, it was brownish red, with a membrane all the colors of the rainbow. Tora didn't think anything had as pretty a red color as the raw meat on the cutting board.

Sometimes there was blood on it. Her mother cut it slowly, into bite-sized pieces. And the colors changed with the shadows and motions her hand made.

The knife always glittered so nicely and so dangerously when she was cutting.

Then it was finished and her mother took the whole cutting board over to the stove and scraped the meat into the kettle with deft, quick motions. That was the end.

Tora knew that the pieces would become gray and knotted-up and not much to look at. On the other hand, the carrots, cabbage and rutabaga would glow down in the broth and hold onto each other's colors so they'd make a beautiful combination.

She was allowed to sit a little while and just look and smell while she waited for the soup to cool. Then the voice would order her to eat her food and she would let the despised cabbage sail past, spoonful after spoonful, before she finally put it in her mouth.

Tobias's shack had been there forever. Tora knew that. It was old and chilly and there were rags in the hole in the window and a warped door that creaked horribly when anyone came in or went out. It was only used for storing boxes and odds and ends, or for card playing on Saturdays if the weather was warm enough and you were a man.

The shack was a large, low-ceilinged structure that stood by itself and didn't have steep steps like the fishing shacks down by the wharves. It was easy to enter and just as easy to stumble out of.

Once, a long time ago, Henrik had taken her along to Tobias's shack because her mother had to go to work cleaning someone's house. That was a long time before Tora could stay home alone and before her mother started working at the fish packing plant.

Henrik had been sitting there with a glass in his hand, telling stories. Sweat dotted his forehead, the way it always did when he was drinking and caught up in a story. Henrik had been out in the world, out where things *happened*. When he was telling stories from those days, he seemed to forget the damaged shoulder he usually tried to hide under his jacket.

The other men sat with their legs sprawled and their chests looming over the table. Henrik always sat slumped with his crippled shoulder hanging down, as if he were a cormorant with a broken wing.

But he knew how to tell a story.

Sometimes, it was as if he drew strength from the expectant faces around him, so that he could get his shoulder up for a moment, using his weak elbow for support.

The strange and frightening thing about the upper part of Henrik's body wasn't the crippled shoulder. It was the good one!

It writhed and heaved under his clothes. The hand and arm were a single knot of angry muscles in restless motion. But on his left side, his crippled hand and arm hung passively, an insult to Henrik's entire being.

That day in Tobias's shack the smoke from the pipes and hand-rolled cigarettes swirled thickly around the lantern that hissed up there in the rafters like a drowsy animal being teased. The mantle inside the lantern glowed maliciously and flickered like lightning across the shiny metal handle.

Tora needed to go to the outhouse and she tugged on Henrik to tell him. But his face was so far up and she was so little and way down on the floor.

He raised his glass in his big good hand and went on with his story. He was Samson and he didn't see her.

Then it began to soak right through her clothes. At first it was warm and she could stand it, but she knew it was terribly naughty. One of the men saw what was happening and told Henrik. The other men started laughing. They pointed at Tora and slapped their knees and said that Henrik wasn't cut out to be a stepfather. Their laughter got louder and louder. After a while it filled her whole head and seemed to come from another world.

She crept into her shame and was completely alone against them all.

But that wasn't the worst.

She dirtied her pants. It just happened. She couldn't hold it. She felt how it pushed and then it flowed out. The men laughed even more, sniffed and wrinkled their noses and made fun of Henrik for not being able to handle Ingrid's kid.

Someplace inside her she was trembling. But on the outside she was rigid.

It ran down her white wool stockings and all the way down to the floor. Runny, runny shit.

She'd disgraced herself in Tobias's shack and so she only went there when she had to. She had to sometimes, when she was sent there on an errand. Then she would get the bursting feeling again, as if something inside her would never stop breaking. She could still smell herself and see the brown-stained stockings. And the memory of the brutal laughter coming from the big, gaping mouths around the table would fill her with shame.

Elisif who lived in the attic upstairs was religious and she'd told Tora that shame was invented by God. That made everything hopeless because then there was no way you could escape from it. God had made the world so that some people would *have* to feel ashamed, because it would be good for them, sinners that they were.

And Tora understood that she was one of them.

She told lies when she thought lying would be the easiest way out, and she took more than her share of prunes when her mother wasn't looking.

Even so, it amazed her that some people looked like they'd never been ashamed of anything in the whole wide world, even though they were so unbearable.

Chapter Three

TORA STOOD BAREFOOT AT THE WINDOW IN HER ROOM
and saw that the heather was brown and withered. Patches of
mist from a rainy night hung like washed-out ghosts over the
two mountain peaks, Veten and Horse Crag. The mist, lifeless
and eternal, stretched all the way out to the mouth of the fjord
behind Dahl's wharves. Rowboats in the bay looked as if they
were sketched in with a gray pencil and then smeared, and
Tora knew that the plump currants in the parsonage garden
would have big drops of water clinging to them. The old rain
gutter gurgled.

She saw the road make a sudden turn around the farms
highest up on Veten before it came running down the hills,
stopping at the farthest edge of the wharf.

A handful of houses were flung along the road, down the
slope towards the ocean and harbor. Mostly old cottages with
low roofs and modest little windows. Bleached and faded like
forgotten paper flowers. A couple of garishly painted box-like
houses stuck up here and there. Some had rough foundations
that clung to the clay soil with a stubbornness you had to admire.

Like a warning and a reminder of where the good comes
from, a golden stripe shot abruptly out from a tear in the
clouds. The sun. It gilded the branches on the birch-lined
drive to the sheriff's house.

Tora followed the gravel road with her eyes. Began all the
way up at Bekkejordet and went down past the fields and the
heath with its cheerful fall colors, past the marshes and the
stand of birch, past the fish-drying racks and the huge barn
that nobody used anymore—where the wind-blown, fallow

earth changed to rock, seaweed and living, wet ocean. To the left, where the road to the wharves forked, her gaze came back to her window and was home. In the big, old house called the Tenement.

The house was quiet a moment longer.

Then the racket started above her head. It was Elisif's kids, tumbling out of bed and running across the floor in an uneven rhythm.

The sounds were neither good nor bad. Scraping sounds, light footsteps, and Elisif's religious voice that Tora had learned wasn't the least bit mean, no matter how much Judgment Day there was in it.

She heard her mother filling the coffee pot out in the kitchen. Henrik wouldn't be getting up yet. It was only her and Mama before she went to school. If her mother was at work, Tora was home alone with her slice of bread and the clock on the wall.

Tora knew that the strongest one was the one who made decisions and was right about everything.

It was important to know who the strongest was.

Henrik was the strongest.

Even though he had one shoulder that people laughed at a little and that wasn't a real shoulder, he was horribly strong in the other one. And he talked in sudden bursts with his mouth big and open.

When he laughed, it wasn't real laughter. Instead, it sounded like he was aggravated. Like a kind of gurgling or a storm against the rocks along the shore. Henrik had bad days sometimes. Then he didn't go to Dahl's warehouse.

Mama's days weren't good or bad, Tora thought. She always looked the same, just a little paler sometimes.

Usually Mama's eyes were large and greenish, with a thin, opaque curtain, just like Aunt Rachel's summer curtains. But suddenly they could change color, open the curtains and let her see inside.

Then they were full of life! Looked like green trees in summertime, full of little birds and soft, quick shadows. Everything flickered and was alive there, among the leaves. That was almost always when she and Tora were all alone.

14

Henrik hit harder than anybody Tora knew. With his good hand. Sometimes Mama swatted her on the bottom with the palm of her hand. A little swat. But that was because she wanted Tora to know she was aggravated. The swats never hurt. Mama didn't hit her often. Only when she had to. Tora wasn't afraid to cry when Mama hit her.

When Henrik hit her, Tora shriveled up. Seemed to hang around his fist like a rag.

If felt as if she no longer had feet, and an intense pressure built up so that she almost wet her pants. So far, she'd managed to get through it, because she always remembered Tobias's shack.

She became like the alley cat that the boys in the village had tortured to death because nobody owned it.

They had crucified it on a picket fence.

It shriveled up too. At the end, it was only fur and claws. On the first day, the crows quickly pecked out its eyes. Tora sometimes wondered if it had been the same for the cat as for her, that there somehow wasn't any room for crying. Something just burst and burst but nothing came out. Everything was too tight.

Her mother told her often that Henrik wasn't bad. Tora had never said or thought Henrik was bad, so she didn't understand where her mother got that idea.

It was as if she looked sternly at Tora and admonished her: Henrik isn't bad!

But for Tora, Henrik wasn't bad or good, he was Henrik.

Tora pulled on her stockings and skirt. It was cold in her room even though the fall sun was doing its best. But a new day had arrived. All she had to do was run her face through the cold water from the faucet. Tora waited until her mother was busy out in the hall. That way she wouldn't have to fill the washbasin. Ingrid was strict about washing.

They didn't talk much while they were eating. But the silence wasn't threatening, the way it was when *he* was there.

When Henrik ate with them, Tora always kept her eyes on the table. She knew that he watched her, waited for her to tip something over or do something wrong.

She'd made it a habit to eat only what she absolutely had to when he was there. And she never put sugar or jam on her bread. She might spill. Cheese was all right. It stuck in the butter and she could trust it.

The milk glass was a constant ordeal. It seemed to spill if she even thought about it. It seemed like Henrik's eyes could *stare* her hand into knocking anything over.

But today it was only Mama and her, so Tora took her time and let her eyes wander wherever they wanted to go.

On mornings like this, Ingrid would pass her hand gently over Tora's shoulder when she was ready for school, her knapsack on her back. Then she would stand at the window and watch the thin knot of a girl, her red braids swinging behind her, disappear at the crossroad together with Elisif's kids and Rita from the first landing.

And Ingrid would feel a kind of vague powerlessness about everything.

Tora and Sol liked to sit in the blue outhouse late in the afternoon, after dinner, when the grown-ups were taking naps or otherwise preoccupied so that their trips to the outhouse dwindled. The girls talked and read old newspapers.

"The Phantom rides his white horse through the jungle, searching for Sala. The drums have told him where she is," Sol mumbled to herself, her index finger struggling with the piece of newspaper and nature right below her chubby bottom. The wind often blew hard down there. At high tide, small waves came smacking up over the rocks and the turds fell straight into the sea.

When the tide was out, dull thuds interrupted their reading and paper fluttered around homelessly down there before making up its mind and setting off to sea.

Tora couldn't afford very often to tear off pieces of newspapers that weren't at least a week old. They could be used for many trips to the outhouse. There were various realms and worlds that had to be investigated before they were scrapped. Mysterious ads for feminine hygiene. Gabardine coats at reduced prices. But above all, the Phantom and Sala.

And Tora would fold the newspapers carefully and put them at the bottom of the pile on the shelf. Under the ancient magazines too stiff to wipe with. Under the gaudy summer magazine covers and an issue of *Allers* magazine from way back at Easter, with its picture of an enormous baby chicken torn in half.

Now and then they tore out a picture and pinned it on the wall. But there was always a shortage of thumb tacks.

Once, in the distant past, the outhouse had been painted white and had had two doors with triangular windows at a decent height that prevented anyone from peeking in but were necessary for light and air.

You can tell by looking at an outhouse what kind of people use it. Originally, the parsonage outhouse and the Tenement's had been equally white and distinguished. Now there was a melancholy, faded glory about the latter, which anybody who had ever used a better outhouse would notice at once.

One of the doors was for men and the other for women and small children.

Once in a while, the men's side was hosed out with a hose from the fishing station. It was stretched, with a great hullabaloo and much arguing, up the gentle slope from the wharves to the Tenement. It didn't happen very often and never until it got so bad that the men wouldn't go inside voluntarily.

The women had a torn curtain in their window and a mat made out of sacking on the floor. Sometimes in the summer there were bluebells and daisies in a tin can on the shelf over the seats. There was one little hole and two big ones. Now and then all three were used at the same time. Especially on late autumn evenings and when the winter storms and the arctic night had taken hold of mind and body.

It was as if the cold had less of a grip when another naked bottom and a voice were there beside you in the darkness. Even if it was just the smell of another human being, and the warm steam from what was inside and hidden, still it was a comfort and created a kind of companionship that you didn't have to talk about or make a fuss over.

You just knocked discreetly on the door across the hall, whispered a few words, and the pact of sisterhood was sealed, the trip to the outhouse set. Whispered philosophies of life, confidences about the hormonal world or the heart's uncontrollable madness were often a part of these outings. It wasn't only nature's discharging of waste that took place there. As much spiritual care and comfort filled the cold outhouse all through the long arctic night. People didn't notice so much the ocean's cold blasts through the open holes when several bottoms were sitting on them.

The men had a lonelier outhouse experience. But they had a different kind of fellowship, from which the women were mostly excluded: talking and drinking in the fishing shack lofts and loafing around in the village on weekends.

They weren't as open about their fear of the dark, not them.

The day Einar moved into the garret above the sun porch, he opened first the one outhouse door and then the other. And since he could easily see that the women's was the homiest and the most inviting, that's the one he went into, closing the door securely behind him. That was the big mistake Einar made at the Tenement. He was never really forgiven.

When he came back out onto the outhouse step, his trousers still not properly buttoned in front, three pairs of shutters facing the yard had already flown open.

Three women's faces came into view, one angrier than the next. Elisif was the first. She clutched her sweater tightly over her ample bosom and made her mouth into a pointed funnel. Her white, store-bought teeth glittered threateningly and the sound of her voice cracked like a whip in the light blue day.

"What're you doing in the women's, if I might ask?"

Einar was standing half turned away on the crooked wooden steps, his right hand on his fly and his left on the door hook. His lower jaw seemed to come off its hinges for a moment when he turned and caught sight of the women's heads against the dirty wall of the house. Three uncompromising, white-chiseled faces against the dusky-gray background.

Einar swallowed. Then he came to his senses and, quick as a flash, took his right hand from his fly and put it behind his back. He didn't even dare to stuff it into his pocket, he was so surprised at this enormous cuckoo clock of a house with three cuckooing heads sticking out at the same time, their beaks wide open. He swallowed again, before anger spread over him like frostbite and made him hoarse and short of breath. "What the hell are you squawking about up there? There's a law against doing your business here?"

"You were in the women's. I saw you all right!"

Elisif was merciless. A punishing voice of thunder in a very high register.

But Einar had won back his self-confidence. "There's a difference between her-crappers and him-crappers here? It wasn't that fancy where I come from, at the parsonage. The parson's women's butts weren't so damned refined that they had to have their own outhouse—the way you women here at the Tenement do."

Paying no further attention to Elisif's cackling, he strode across the yard and into the middle entrance. He closed the sun porch door with a slam and stomped angrily up the old wooden steps so heavily that the brass fittings rattled on their exposed positions on the edges.

In a little while, Einar was sitting on his couch and squinting belligerently at the wall. A hell of a bunch of women! He wouldn't admit to himself that his heart was still pounding in his chest.

He never used the women's outhouse again. Still, whenever he was out in the yard answering nature's call, he would glower up at Elisif's windows. And whenever he heard her thin, high voice anywhere in the house, his heart would begin to pound uncontrollably. This enraged him. For Einar was master of his own fate in all respects here in this world. He feared neither pastor nor woman.

Chapter Four

THE TENEMENT! THE BIG WOODEN BUILDING FROM THE turn of the century bore the signs of past glory and human folly.

You could see both clearly on the old, peeling eaves. There was an aura of old money made in fishing about the place, all the way from the tiled roof covered with moss and gull droppings to the thick foundation of handcut stone with roots three feet below the earth's surface.

The house had three stories and a basement and a large number of tall, drafty windows.

Its gazebo had become a moss-covered trap where Elisif's child, her fifth one, had fallen through and broken his foot one summer. But on clear, cold days the smoke still hung grandly over the patched roof, rising from three chimneys at once.

A sight like that could still command respect.

But there weren't many of the fishing tycoons left. They'd disappeared in the bad years of the '30s. And then the house stood there alone with its decay and its wounds inflicted by the common folk.

Because the poor came to the Tenement. Those who had heavy burdens to bear and were poor in earthly goods. A few of them might even have been poor in spirit.

They crowded together around the three entrances and were of use when a gap opened in society. On the wharves, in the baiting shacks, or under the stained ceilings of their betters on housecleaning days.

The people in the Tenement didn't dwell on the fact that they were going to inherit the earth for their meekness. That was the farthest thing from their minds.

But in the late fall, when the moon was high in the sky over Veten and Horse Crag, and the mothers had nagged their oldest children into digging the potatoes from the common garden, and the annual feud about where Elisif's boundaries ended and Arna's and Peder's began was over, then they all settled down in their own way under their lamps. Or else they drifted around down in the village if they were young, or played hide-and-seek in the dark basement if they were even younger.

The moon scattered its profusion of silver over the old dragon head on the top of the south gable (the one on the north gable had fallen off before the war) and spirits in the Tenement rose above their customary gray meekness.

In February, when the sun returned above the snow-covered, old tile roof, the men came home with cod and roe. Potatoes were brought up from the basement and the building was filled with the steamy, comforting smell of simmering cod liver.

Then they shouted the winter darkness out through open windows and the women helped each other push wheelbarrows down to the mouth of the river where they spread their ragged, winter-yellow sheets to bleach on the rocks and old drifts of snow.

Poetry lay in ambush in the details. In the blessed dripping from the broken rain gutter, for example. But it was as shy and as forgotten as a wretched child that nobody would nurse or love.

The magic of being alive seldom occurred to any of these poor folk. For that, heavy gales and shipwrecks, at least, were needed.

That happened sometimes.

An old widow had lived in the garret at the top of the stairs in the Tenement for many years. She knitted for the children in the building and whacked them when they got into mischief.

She threw rocks at stray dogs and scrubbed the steps whether it was her week to do it or not. In that way, the people who lived in the apartments off the middle stairway were lucky. But then she started washing her dish towels in her chamber pot and forgot to wash both herself and the steps. Finally she had to go to the old folks home at Breiland. She was there exactly twenty-four hours. That was the end of her.

That's how the garret was available for Einar when he was thrown out at the parsonage because he stole eggs from under the hens and salt pork from the storehouse. The garret was built over the old glassed-in sun porch. There wasn't much glass left in the porch windows, however. Storms from the southwest had played havoc with them and taken one small pane after another. Now there were only two whole windows left. They faced the woods and Veten, where the winter storms couldn't reach them. The men had nailed boards and sheets of wood on the southwest side to keep out the storms and wind.

When the outdoor light was on, glittering on the white-capped, angry sea, the glass sun porch looked like a blinded eye. Only on the southwest side had two small panes escaped. They squinted in defiance and astonishment up at the enormous sky.

The floor of the garret at the top of the stairs was quite cold. By way of compensation, there wasn't much of a draft. The little window in the roof didn't have that defect, at least. But it wept.

When snow or rain blinded it, the window leaked.

Einar quickly learned the same trick the old widow had used. He put his washbasin under the leak.

On the floor beneath the window there was a blurred circle of rust left by the widow's basin. Einar grasped immediately its significance and he put his basin there the first time it stormed. Through that blessed window in the roof came God's ancient, depressed sky—if the weather was in that mood. No curtain was needed to keep the glances of the curious out, and there was no window sill for potted plants. That suited Einar just fine.

Tobias A. Brinch and Waldemar E. Brinch once owned everything that lived and moved on the island. They steered from afar every fishing boat south of the bay and they steered the profits into their own pockets too.

Long ago, orders that could mean life or starvation issued from the two Brinch mansions, with their servant girls, balls and festivities of every kind. The parsonage was the third center of power and it still held its own all right, even though money was never mentioned there.

At the end of the '30s, the incomprehensible happened: the Brinchs went bankrupt. The wharves and the fishing station, the houses and fields—the entire village turned out to have been mortgaged and in hock. Bad times and bad investments, they said—those who were in the know about such things.

The estate belonging to the eldest brother, Mr. T. A. Brinch, was the largest. It stood arrogantly down by the beach, with its carved gables and its glassed-in sun porch.

First a gentleman had come from Bergen and administered the estate for one winter and one summer. But he was just employed by a firm in Bergen to keep the wheels turning, and apparently he thought it was too lonely, being a bachelor and all, to play the big shot way up here under the northern lights and the cries of the gulls. In any case he disappeared one spring day and never came back.

Today the mansion sheltered such a multitude of vermin and garbage that it was called the Tenement and rightly so.

Farther up the hill stood the other brother's house, called the Manor, less extensive than the Tenement, to be sure, but it still had more than enough authority left beneath its facade of white paint. It was used as a school and was heated and looked after by old Almar from Hestvika.

The Germans discovered the Manor during the war. The old hinges were oiled and the faded wallpaper painted over. And then coarse laughter and shouting could be heard under the ceiling beams and the smell of leather and wet uniform jackets was left forever in the rooms.

A year of peace had to pass before it was found morally defensible to send innocent children up to the house, but people had been spawning as if possessed and the old schoolhouse down on the spit was getting too crowded. So the children and Almar came and made the Manor theirs. But for the old people, who clung to the era of the fishing tycoons, it was an evil sign that the Manor passed from hand to hand. And they would no more let the word "school" cross their lips in connection with the Manor than they'd ever called the place "barracks" or "German camp" during the war.

But Almar wasn't hampered by nostalgia. He'd got a secure livelihood at last.

People were producing kids left and right, and there had to be heat if the miserable wretches weren't going to freeze to death in the winter.

But the summers, bless them, he had to himself, out on the fjord fishing for coalfish.

Throughout the school year, Almar kept the fires going in the three-foot-high stoves, emptied the outhouses, and picked up trash.

In the large, drafty classroom on the second floor, a big, rickety, black iron stove brooded over the grandeur of the past.

An icy draft from the open sea swept across the floor and at face level the heat burned like red-hot iron. The children were runny-nosed no matter whether they sat by the stove and their heads sweated or they sat by the door and froze all over. It was as if the stoves didn't have the sense to send their heat downwards, Almar said, on the rare occasions they complained.

So instead they thawed their feet in their school bags.

Tora sat right in front of the teacher's desk.

Miss Helmersen wore big felt slippers and sat high over the children like a pink and gold flower above her varnish-encrusted desk.

Miss Helmersen's name was Gunn and she was very young. Younger than any of their parents. She had dimples and lots of big, white teeth. They looked absolutely real.

Gunn was beautiful, Tora thought. Prettier than her mother even, because she was happier.

Her hair was blonde and curly and thick like the big color picture of the angel that Tora had in a frame over her bed.

The children called Miss Helmersen Gunn and their eyes became gentle when they talked about her.

A lot of their fathers' eyes did, too.

She was a certified teacher, even though she was so young. People felt they owed her a huge debt of gratitude because she'd left the mild climate of the south, and religious parents, to come up here to the island, to the cold and the dark. In Elisif's opinion, it was the Lord's doing that they got to keep her for a second year.

The children made excuses to go up to the Manor in the afternoons, after school. They pestered her with questions and brought her cod tongues and home-baked bread.

At night, when she was alone in her room and couldn't sleep, Tora would sometimes see Gunn.

She always saw her with a large, open mouth and with the deep hollows in her cheeks. It looked as if somebody had pressed an index finger into her cheeks and left the impression there forever.

Tora dreamed that she was Gunn. Sometimes she tried to undo her braids and comb her hair straight up so it would look like Gunn's. But hers was an entirely different color and an entirely different head. She climbed up on a chair and peered into her own reflection over the utility sink.

No matter how much she brushed her hair or how big she made her smile, it never did any good. Tora's face was, and remained, thin and sallow, with a narrow mouth and a nose that was too big. Brown freckles were scattered thickly across the bridge of her nose. Her hair was thick and unmanageable and completely without curl. The ends of her braids brushed around her face like the bristles on a worn-out brush.

She was Tora. Nothing could be done about it.

Elisif had told her more than once that she couldn't understand how a person as beautiful and shapely as Ingrid could have had her. It must have been the foreign blood and the wages of sin that had done it.

Tora figured out finally what she meant and blushed all the way to her earlobes.

The foreign blood was the worst, it was connected to the war and was what her mother never talked about. The wages of sin didn't weigh so heavily on her. The wages of sin—that was something you could get around, from what she'd seen.

But if the mirror over the utility sink told Tora who she was, she could still live her own secret life under the covers. In the dark, alone with herself, she was whoever she wanted to be. There beneath the comforter with the small flowers, she shed her outer self, warmed herself with her own cold hands, cuddled herself while conjuring up another Tora. If she happened to be alone in the house, she could forget the real Tora completely.

For a time everything that gnawed at her stomach during the day would vanish as if it had never been there at all.

The danger?

That also vanished.

She was nice to her thin body until it began to glow and tremble and she grew warm all the way down to her feet. She was free of all the voices and all the eyes and could decide for herself who she wanted to be. She knew that she shouldn't really do "that" to herself. But if she did it without giving it too much thought, it couldn't really be so bad.

Chapter Five

EVER SINCE THE DAY OLE FROM THE VILLAGE HAD TOLD her she'd come out of her mother's cunt, Tora almost threw up whenever she remembered that people did that. . . .

That her mother and Henrik . . . or the pastor!

Why didn't they die of shame, when they knew that everybody else knew!

The pastor had four children!

And Elisif, who was so religious, let herself be led astray by Torstein so that a new baby came every year!

It was better to do it yourself and forget the danger. Even so, she could lie for a long time in the darkness of her room and try to figure out how they managed it—what Ole said they did.

Once she had been with Jørgen and some of the other kids on the other side of the hill and watched the horses that were pastured there.

The pastor's stallion went completely wild and got into the mares' pen. Tora couldn't understand why the pastor's horse wasn't better behaved. But at the same time, watching it had a strange effect on her.

The stallion had made his thing swell up and Tora sensed the danger and felt a kind of insistent curiosity at the same time.

The horses ran wildly around in the pen for a while, but as soon as Tora realized that it was serious, she pretended to hide her eyes in her sleeve. She could have saved herself the trouble, however. Nobody had time to pay any attention to what she did. They were all standing with their mouths open and their eyes moist and staring at the horse's cock.

When the stallion made it disappear inside the dun mare and neighed and snorted, she could clearly see that Jørgen, Elisif's boy, kind of sagged at the knees and that Rita pushed the tip of her tongue out one corner of her mouth.

Tora knew suddenly, in a flash, that they were all standing around the pen staring at the stallion pumping in and out of the mare and they were feeling the same strange, secret hollowness in their bellies that she was. They were there and they had something in common without being able to talk about it, without daring to look at each other.

Tora tried to imagine how it was to be the mare right now. First she just stood there, quivering. Then she just stood there. She was somehow not really involved. Was she ashamed, maybe? That's what it had to be!

She surely didn't like them all standing there and staring. The big, swollen cock must hurt terribly bad.

No, it didn't look like that, either. The mare wouldn't just stand there, if it did. Hot and cold chills ran all through Tora.

It was like running so hard and so long that you started to taste blood in your throat, it was like playing hide-and-seek during the dark fall evenings. Yes, this was almost better than riding ice floes in the bay.

Finally the stallion collapsed over the mare and snorted through his nostrils. He threw his head back so that his mane flared out from his neck.

Then he slid weakly off the mare and his cock followed. It happened too fast for Tora. First she'd thought everything was beautiful. The stallion throwing back his big, brown head and the mane flying in the wind.

Now the stallion was acting ashamed and useless. His cock swung limply from side to side and started shrivelling up right in front of the kids' eyes. It dripped a little.

Rita's light blue eyes went on staring, long after it was all over. Then she burst out, "That pig! He pissed in the mare!"

Jørgen gave her a contemptuous look and then said, in between two gobs of spit, "That's sperm—anybody knows that, you ninny!"

Then he gave a short lecture on various matters. And Ole chimed in and said that they'd all come out of their mothers' cunts and it wasn't anything to be ashamed of.

Afterwards they never talked about what they'd seen to any of the grownups. And they never asked about what was on their minds.

Sometimes they sat on the stone fence by the church, quarrelling over what it really was they'd seen so close up, that time in the pasture.

Jørgen always wanted to describe the stallion's cock as having been much bigger than it was.

Once Rita accused him of lying. She measured the length in the air with her hands, but Jørgen insisted he was right. He finally pushed her off the fence.

It might have ended disastrously, if it hadn't been for Lina, closemouthed and shy, who suddenly said that she'd seen a real man's cock.

Their eyes rolled in her direction out of sheer attentiveness. Their mouths opened. They were simultaneously thrilled and horrified.

"Yeah?" someone said skeptically.

"Whose was it?" Ole asked.

"I'm not telling. But it was blue."

"Who? The man?" Tora asked in disbelief.

"The cock, of course, you dummy!"

Lina tossed her head back triumphantly and grabbed a stick and scraped some dirt out of the worn tread on the bottom of her boots. She pursed her lips. Her mouth looked like a little beak and she stared out into space and wouldn't look at them.

Jørgen snorted. "You're a liar. They aren't blue. You're crazy!"

He was indignant. Ole and the girls looked at him. They realized that he was ashamed on behalf of his species, and that he was declining the honor of having a blue cock hung on him. Ole gave Jørgen his cautious support and sneered at Lina. But Lina wouldn't budge. "A boy's cock isn't the same as a man's. Don't you know that?"

No, Ole and Jørgen didn't know that.

But they gradually turned to other subjects, for their arguments were all used up and they really liked talking about things better than being enemies.

But Tora brooded anyway on what Lina had said. At night, beneath her comforter, all her fantasies took on a blue color and her imagination gave her the shivers.

The repulsiveness and the danger lay over all of it and created havoc.

All the whispered conversations between her mother and Aunt Rachel, all the sounds from the living room when they thought she was asleep.

All the half-spoken jokes down at the shacks where the men gathered, all the stories that weren't meant for her ears.

She couldn't make heads or tails of it, couldn't figure out where she belonged in it. She didn't know if she was repelled or. . . .

Sometimes she was ashamed of what she did and was glad no one could see her there in the dark.

She no longer recognized herself, somehow. The tender bumps on her chest felt as if they weren't really her. She hunched over, so nobody would see them. Wanted to hide them inside, somehow.

But it didn't help much. They made all her clothes too tight across the chest. She wished she were a boy. Lina and Rita—they were still flat. Could still jump and skip wearing just their underpants, last summer down on the beach. Tora had made up all kinds of excuses to avoid going along.

It wasn't just her breasts that made her feel shy. She thought hair was growing all over her body. And sometimes both her body and her clothes smelled like old carnations. It reminded her of funerals. A kind of sickly sweetish odor every time she was hot or nervous. She went around with Sol, who was almost two years older and had already filled out substantially.

On Saturdays, Tora lit the stove in her room herself and brought in wash water and towels.

The winter before, she'd still bathed in the tin washtub in

front of the kitchen stove. But then she'd rebelled against her mother and refused. Somebody might come in. Once Henrik came in while she was still in the tub.

He looked at her. She couldn't stand it.

She stayed where she was until he left. He'd seen the body that wasn't hers.

Then she refused to take a bath for several weeks. Her mother got irritated and said worms would start growing in her ears. Finally she suggested that Tora could heat up her room and bathe in there if she wanted to.

Tora felt a kind of gentle, warm gratitude to her mother for saying that. She wanted to hug her but couldn't bring herself to do it. There seemed to be an ocean between them—when it came to hugging.

All spring and summer she'd washed in her room, a knife stuck securely in the crack between the door frame and the door. That was the only lock she had. It would be easy to work the knife out from the other side. But it was a barrier of sorts, an unspoken warning that she wanted to be alone.

She could also be alone in front of the big teacher's desk at the Manor. There she only had Gunn in front of her.

All the eyes were behind her. She could sit there and pretend she was listening to what Gunn was saying but really be thinking her own thoughts. She could fantasize about the most marvelous things in peace. Gunn was strict about keeping the classroom quiet.

She had a remarkable power over her flock of children that even the old teacher envied. And she left children like Tora in peace with their thoughts.

It was hard to understand her authority because it was so wholly different from the angry scoldings and smacks they got from their fathers when they didn't behave. Gunn's method was especially confusing to the older boys. She *looked* at them. *Held* them with her stare.

Sometimes she came over and put her warm hand on a boy's neck. She lifted his head with a firm motion and looked him in the eyes until the classroom quieted down and the trouble-maker gave in.

But it never took long before Gunn's dimples reappeared, like signs of well-being, and everything was all right again.

Tora liked school. She liked the smell of dust and chalk. All you had to do was the work you were assigned and then you were left in peace. At least during class.

You could ask Gunn about everything—almost.

And you got an answer.

But the pastor's stallion and the danger were among the things nobody could ask any grownup about. And you couldn't always ask other kids either. Only sometimes, if it happened to come up. Like the time in the pasture.

This past fall Tora had moved up to the same class as Sol. The last two years of school were combined.

Sol was a year ahead of Tora but she never rubbed it in. A kid from the Tenement could rarely afford to sacrifice a friend for something trivial.

Tora no longer looked up to Jørgen the way she had ever since she was little. Daily life and the years changed them. And Jørgen poured water in their shoes and hid Sol's school books, swore when his mother wasn't listening, and he was always loafing around down on the wharves.

Sol was quiet, but she had a handle on most of what went on behind closed doors and what was hidden in life's many labyrinths. She was the oldest of Elisif's seven children and more or less against her will she'd had conceptions and childbirths up to her ears, as the weeks and the years crept nightly over the Tenement roof.

But Tora couldn't ask Sol about the kinds of things kids talked about, because Sol might think she was just a little kid herself.

Chapter Six

GERMAN BRAT!

She'd heard those words sometimes. There was something evil in them. A judgment.

Henrik had used those words too. Not to her directly, but they had come to her through the thin walls.

She wanted to ask her mother what they meant, but they were a part of the danger. So she deliberately forgot about it because she couldn't stand it. Weeks, sometimes months, could pass without her hearing anybody say those words.

But they always came back. Then it felt the way it did that time when the kids in the village had tricked her into skiing down a steep hill and she didn't know that they had made a ski jump out of snow in the middle of it and made it icy below the jump with several buckets of water.

There was somehow no escape, once you were in the air. Just a great hollow feeling and emptiness all around. And the only thing you knew for sure was that you would have to land.

The road had its own code of law. That code wasn't always the same as where the grownups were. And by no means the same as in the kitchen.

But it wasn't bad except for brief moments. Just like scrapes and pinched fingers. Hurt so the tears ran at the time. But it passed. And there was no need to be bitter about it, because everybody got a turn.

Ole was the strongest and the biggest, but not the worst. He had his weaknesses. He wet his bed. And sometimes he smelled when he didn't have time to wash before he left for school. The big boy!

Tora collected weaknesses—in others.

She didn't say anything to them, for that would just cause trouble. But she considered it.

Now and then she dreamed that someday she'd pay them back, and just where it would hurt the most, too. But nothing ever came of it. Tora was thin and scrawny and small. The only thing she had power over was her rubber ball.

She could run faster than anyone when it was necessary. Or else she would sneak away without anyone noticing it.

Then a blush would spread across her sallow cheeks. She got her share of beatings out on the road. But they were nothing like the kind she got from Henrik.

On the other side of the bay, on the heath where the heather and the scrub timber grew lush and dense right up to the sides of the road, Tora could see the old youth center. It wasn't *really* old, just so sadly neglected. Once it had been red. Before the war.

A long time had passed since the war, but Tora knew that she was a part of it.

She'd heard many stories about it.

From everything she heard, she had a sickening feeling that Mama was also a part of it.

When Henrik talked about the war, Mama went to the other end of the room and always turned her back on whoever was there. Henrik cursed the war more than anybody else because it had almost pinched his left arm off and partly collapsed his lungs.

"Goddamn German devils!" he said and deep wrinkles appeared between his bushy eyebrows.

Everybody agreed with him, even though they looked away and gave Ingrid strange glances when they were there during Henrik's outbursts. Mama never talked about the war.

Aunt Rachel had once hinted that Tora's birth was the death of Grandma. That wasn't meant for Tora's ears, so she couldn't ask any more about it.

Tora thought it was strange that she should be blamed for Grandma's death, because she could clearly remember her as a pale and gaunt face against a white pillow, in a room in Aunt Rachel's and Uncle Simon's farmhouse up at Bekkejordet.

Tora knew everything had been rationed, so people didn't have much to eat or wear. Maybe she'd heard it wrong, maybe her aunt had said it was the rationing that had killed Grandma.

Tora usually imagined Almar from Hestvika wandering naked and starving on the deck of his square-shaped motorboat in the middle of the rationing. It must have been a cold and strange sight. It was always Almar she saw, never any of the others.

Anyway, the youth center was on the heath. It, too, was a part of the war.

There they'd once cut off Mama's hair, all the way down to her milky white scalp.

Tora had heard about it in many versions and from many mouths. But she trusted Sol's version the most: They'd cut off her mother's hair because Tora was born during the war.

All the same, Tora thought it was because they were jealous of her mother. Because she could clearly see that her mother's new hair was also unusually dark and thick. She had the most beautiful hair in the whole village.

But how could they have been so bad?

She'd asked Aunt Rachel once.

Then her aunt had given her a big hug and told her that the war had made many people crazy and that she shouldn't pester her mother and ask about things like that.

But every time Tora went past the youth center, she felt as if invisible hands were reaching out after her and wanted to hurt her.

The house had frightened little eyes for windows, and a crooked pattern on its faded curtains, so it was odd that she felt that way about it. But she simply couldn't imagine that any of the people she saw on the road, at Ottar's store or on the wharf, would ever have been capable of wanting to hurt her mother so much that they would cut off her hair. So it was better to blame it on the building.

That's where it had happened. And it could just stand there alone, in plain sight of anyone, with its unpainted walls and its wire fence up against the disgusting marsh.

Her mother never took her there.

Tora didn't take part in the 17th of May* celebrations or Christmas parties there, the way the other kids did, until after she started school.

Tora imagined that if the house hadn't cut off her mother's hair, it would have reached all the way down to her hips. She could envision her mother at the river, bending over in the wind, washing clothes. Her hair was flowing between the rocks and right out into the ocean.

She told Sol about it.

But Sol was almost two years older and she laughed it off. "Nobody's hair gets that long. That's only in fairy tales."

Sol and the rest of Elisif's kids lived right above Tora's head. Every morning the water pipes up there gurgled loudly for a long time. There were a lot of them who had to fill the tin basin and wash up, bent over the peat box by the stove, with Elisif's reproving eye on them constantly.

Things scraped and thumped up there and kids coughed and cried. And you knew it was supposed to be that way.

But of course there was no shortage of people who thought it was a shame, all those kids of Elisif's.

Their father was a small, grey man who never slammed doors or raised his voice unnecessarily. A kind of mild shadow to whom nobody paid any attention next to the strong, domineering Elisif.

Meanwhile, the men hanging out in Ottar's store sneered and wondered aloud if a new one would be coming along at Elisif's before Christmas this year too. It didn't always happen. Jørgen, in any case, was born on May 18th. It consoled Tora, the idea that it was bad for a new Elisif baby to be born every year. It meant she wasn't alone in her misery.

When Tora was little, she sometimes sat on the beach and watched the light that was rising from the grey and the blue and spreading its glow right into the sky.

* *The day on which Norway celebrates the signing of its constitution in 1814.*

"No, it's the sky that gives light to the earth and the sea," Ingrid said, when Tora tried to get her to understand what she saw.

They usually sat at the mouth of the river and ate their food while the laundry was heating up in the huge wash tub on the rocks. "Coffee Hole," people called the place because you could get fresh water from the river for your coffee pot and at the same time have the open sea right before your eyes.

Tora didn't really believe what her mother said about the light and the sky. Because the sea, after all, was so endlessly deep. It could hide whole ships and multitudes of people as if they were nothing. And still it was so huge that there was room for all the rest, the fish and seaweed and fishing gear and rocks.

But she didn't contradict her mother, just looked in wonder at the sparkles down there on the water, let her eyes follow the river's currents and the eddies out to where they met the grey sea water and turned into green glints with tops of shimmering foam.

Tora had once drunk salt water because she hadn't realized there was a difference between sea water and river water.

She never forgot the taste afterwards.

It made her afraid of swimming in the ocean. She preferred the pools in the river, even though they were colder. And whenever she heard that someone had drowned in the ocean, she always tasted the salty, nauseating water.

So she knew a little about dying.

Chapter Seven

FALL WAS THE TIME FOR HEATING WITH BRUSH AND peat.

People were getting ready for the winter season and did their work indoors.

They were all waiting more or less for the great surge of activity when the fish were brought in off the boats.

Then their nerves and limbs were strained to the limit and nobody asked whether it was night or day or whether they were eager to work or exhausted. Some stood in the midst of fish guts and sea spray and worked. Others stood at their kitchen window or with their ears close to the speaker on the radio shelf. Children cried and animals had to be fed and cleaned up after, even though the wives were home alone. They didn't complain. The important thing was to dig as much as possible out of the fishing season. Many got only this chance to make some money. That was it.

Ottar and Grøndahl would have to be paid for the food that might already be manure on the little plots of frozen land or floating in secret, out-of-the-way places among the clusters of seaweed at the high-water mark.

The children would have to have new boots and ski pants and dress-up clothes for Christmas.

Peat was only for kindling, so the coal dealer had to get his payment too. People with sheep in the barn for slaughter later in the fall might be well off, but people who had to buy their meat would bleed. You might as well just stretch your neck over the block and chop away. And maybe the Devil ate pork.

For only the big shots and those with industrious wives at home raising pigs got that.

Simon Bekkejordet maintained that a good wife was worth half a year's groceries.

There was a lot of truth in that, thought people who knew Rachel.

Everybody knew there was more to her than just good looks.

Rachel managed Simon's property and Simon's debts. She fiddled a little with the books now and then. But not because she was malicious. Just so he wouldn't have to listen to her fuss and nag him for money for things he absolutely couldn't understand were necessary.

Rachel had her little emergency cashbox in her desk. With time, however, it wasn't all that little.

If she had to take from it, well, then she *had* to and she didn't worry about it. But she never left herself with nothing. For Rachel had gone through harder times than those she'd known living with Simon.

Simon allowed himself the luxury of smiling at Rachel's desk, but he never stuck his nose in her business. She, on her side, never let on that she knew anything about the fishing business, boats and crews.

But there was a hidden well at Bekkejordet too.

Once Simon had come very close to drowning in that well. Then Rachel had come out from the warmth of the living room and snatched him out of the cold.

In his heart Simon knew that Rachel would be the last to go down, if worst came to worst and they were shipwrecked.

Rachel's strength confused him and surprised him, precisely because it wasn't in her hands. It was of a more unassailable kind.

He realized that fully the day she came home from town and told him she couldn't have children.

She'd stood there in a new plaid coat with big checks and threw out her arms.

The doctor had said it. After seven years of marriage: no children to hope for. So she might just as well buy herself a new coat. She said this as tearlessly and firmly as when she mopped the floors after Simon's workers during the potato harvest.

No children! She had a defect.

She'd stood there in the blue office doorway down at the fishing station. In his realm she'd taken upon herself something he knew was his fault.

For there was no life in Simon Bekkejordet's sperm.

He'd been on the verge of telling her that many times but somehow couldn't get the words out.

Of course he knew how much she wanted a child. He thought through everything he should say. But when the opportunity came, it remained unsaid anyway.

He failed time after time. Finally it affected him so deeply that he began staying away from her bed. He found one pretext after another to stay down at the fishing station until she was asleep when he came home.

Maybe that was why she'd unlocked her desk and taken that trip to town.

Rachel managed what Simon didn't have just as well as what he had, it seemed.

So she'd stood there in her new coat and lied straight into his face with the sincerest expression he'd ever seen.

"I can't have children, Simon. We're going to have to get along some other way, or do without them."

That night he made love to her, at first a little shamefully, like a grateful dog. But she let him know that that wasn't how she wanted him. And then he buried himself deeply beside her and felt the security of having someone by him who was at least his equal in body and in will.

They were awake together until morning came and the workday lay in ambush with its sledgehammers beyond the edge of the bed.

Each of them lived for the other, warmly and closely.

Both knew.

Rachel got herself a cat.

The rain took them by surprise, and below the steep mountain crags the mist lay, as thick as ancient evil.

40

The mountains to the south didn't belong to the visible world.

People lit their stoves, closed their front doors and grumbled over the draft from the windows. They brought out their wool underwear and stockings and dreaded the necessary trips to the outhouse.

You buttoned up everything you had on when you went out.

When you passed people on the road, their faces were white and luminous in their bundles of clothing.

For the most part, people clustered together under their own roofs. Kept their distance from everything outside.

The time for calling over dilapidated garden fences and rusty, squealing metal clothes poles was over.

The potatoes were in. What few currants were left, the birds could have in God's name.

An occasional sheet or pillow case hung among the underwear out there and danced in the wind. But late at night they crackled as they hung in a row, stiffly fluttering. They swung like abandoned corpses in a cold wind.

There's a great difference in the underwear of a person from the north in the winter and the same person in the summer. The winter person is significantly smaller on the inside but much larger on the outside.

Life on the wharves went along sluggishly. It was as if all fuel, human and otherwise, were being saved for the winter fishing.

The men walked around the boat hatches with long faces.

Big, open hands hung helplessly alongside oilskin trousers or fiddled with pipes or hand-rolled cigarettes.

Now and then they made an effort and flapped their arms furiously in front of their work shirts, until they glowed with the increased circulation and the cold.

"What're you hanging around here for?" the men might snarl at one of the kids who was sneaking around in the shacks or behind the boathouses and didn't show enough respect for the sou'wester.

But some of the men could be good-natured at this time of the year too and hadn't forgotten that they'd once been green behind the ears.

These men often had little mocking gleams in their eyes and flung teasing words after them when Tora and the Tenement gang came by.

Rain-soaked, flushed faces and gurgling shoes one day, frostbitten fingertips and running noses the next. That's how it was.

Galoshes that had to be held on with canning-jar rings one day, and mukluks the next.

The good Lord had sunk all of October and November at the bottom of a sea of fog, but the nights were ice-cold and bitter anyway, with an irritating moon that promised a bright tomorrow and lied. Because long before the hens started poking around over in Anna's shed, believing just a little in the day, the rain would be pouring from a life-hating sky. It gurgled down the Tenement's decaying rainpipes.

The men gathered in the new shop at North Bay or at Ottar's old, dark general store. They shot the breeze and loafed around. After a few hours of that, one of them might even remember that he was supposed to do some shopping. That made the time pass too and there wasn't any hurry.

Ottar stood behind the counter, doing a little weighing and measuring.

He calculated prices and took part in the grumbling about the weather when he didn't have anything better to do.

"The Devil can take this weather," he might say, frankly and bitterly, when he had to put on his sou'wester to go out to the storehouse on the wharf for herring or syrup or whatever it was.

For Ottar had a stylish haircut.

His thin hair of no particular color was carefully combed with a part on the right side.

That's how they did it in Bodø back when he worked there as a clerk, he explained proudly.

Naturally he didn't have time to be always fixing his hair on workdays, so he put on a large, yellow sou'wester when he had to go out. It hung in readiness on the peg made from a spool, over by the door with the oval, spotted enamel sign that said: PRIVATE.

But the sou'wester was troublesome, both the one raging

outside and the one hanging on the peg.

Sometimes he got all the way out on the wharf before he remembered his headgear. If there was any wind, and there usually was, his hairdo went to hell.

Then the only thing he could do was rush back to his private quarters and fuss with his hair while precious business minutes were evaporating. But the little secret bald spot had to be camouflaged, whatever the cost.

A poor fisherman couldn't even sneak out in search of a bit of dinner! It looked as if the powers that be thought they should sit out here with their hands in their pockets and starve to death, with a pantry right off the edge of the wharf.

The men spat into the big, stained bowl over by the door, whether they chewed tobacco or not, and they all had the same opinion.

Tora sat on a small barrel over in the darkest corner and waited. She had the list of what she was supposed to buy clutched in her fist. Her wool stockings itched. Mama had made her wear them this year too.

Every time somebody came in or went out, she felt the draft steal up and find exactly the place where her pants cuff had pulled away from her stockings and her skin was bare because she'd grown so much last summer that her stockings had become too short.

She didn't feel it right away, it sort of snuck up along her thighs, like needles of ice.

She dreaded the moment when Ottar would nod to her that it was her turn, because she hadn't brought any money today either. Just a note, moist from her sweat and the rain. In Ingrid's handwritting, it said:

½ *lb. coffee*

2 *lbs. margarine*

4 *lbs. flour*

1 *package yeast*

1 *bottle corn syrup*

Would you please put this on my account until I can come down?

Ingrid

Ottar's face wrinkled the wrong way and darkened a little bit when she gave him the note. He cleared his throat and got the groceries for her.

Then he got out the long, thick book that had once had a marbled pattern in all shades of green.

Slowly and somberly, his index finger pointing threateningly, he looked for Ingrid Toste's name. Then he added the new sum to the many that were there before it. Last of all, he closed the book with a slam and sighed under his breath.

Tora had been standing there, shifting her weight from one foot to the other and feeling as though she had ants between her clothes and her body.

She always felt like she had to pee. Even though the last thing she did before she went into the store was to squat down behind the tall wooden fence.

But she always got what she went for.

Nobody had ever heard of Ottar refusing anyone the ingredients for baking bread.

Tora sneaked among the men, their faces floating together high up there. Eyes and more eyes. Mouths that chewed and mouths that clamped pipestems between yellow teeth or gaped half open and curious above her. The tiny jingle of the brass bell over the door could be either a good or a bad sign for Tora. It depended on which way her toes and nose were pointing. In or out.

Trembling and out of breath, she stopped as soon as she could behind the wood fence and relieved herself. Then she flew over the road and down the hills to the Tenement. She jumped over mud puddles, the groceries bumping against her legs. The old, black raincoat billowed like a sail behind her because she hadn't taken time to button it.

She didn't really know what would happen if she couldn't get out as soon as the groceries were written down in the book. Her fantasy stopped there.

But Ottar the storekeeper was like Jesus and God and the pastor and the old teacher and Henrik all rolled up in one.

She couldn't stand it! She had to run from it!

When she came home, her mother didn't bawl her out because she stomped up the stairs or kept her boots on all the way into the house. She just took the groceries and touched Tora for a second with her free hand. She smiled faintly as if she wanted to say something.

But Tora ran down the stairs and out into the road to the other kids with her stiff red braids flying behind her like rope ends and a strange, fugitive happiness inside.

She was somehow saved. This time too. She could put the next trip to the store out of her mind with a clear conscience. Push it down into her stomach!

Of course she felt it gnawing like a rat now and then as the day approached. Especially when she was lying in the lonely, warm darkness of her bedroom. But at the exact moment it was over, she had no more worries.

In the evening, when she came home with numb hands and fire-red earlobes, the smell of bread floated all the way down the hallway. Her mouth watered and she ran up the stairs.

Her two thin, straight legs could move unbelievably fast when they wanted to. The loaves still sat on the counter, steaming.

Nothing could compare to the smell of her mother's bread. Even Henrik's face became almost kind when he picked up the scent of it. Sometimes he sat down at the counter and puttered with something or other. He was remarkably capable with the one hand he had control over, and he helped out with the other one as best he could. But only when he, himself, wanted to.

Aunt Rachel thought he could easily make a living mending nets, as dexterous as he was, if only he didn't have a wife so willing to drudge for everything they needed. But Ingrid never answered such remarks. She simply pretended she hadn't heard them. Tora knew that if it hadn't been for Aunt Rachel, things wouldn't have looked very good for them the times her mother was out of work.

This evening they were alone, she and her mother. Henrik was down at Arntsen's shack. She'd heard his voice through an open window when she'd flitted by while they were playing hide-and-seek among the barrels down there.

It was Saturday and some of the men were down there passing the time.

Tora hung her wet clothes up to dry by the stove. She put in a couple of shovelfuls of coal, just to show her mother that she wanted to help.

Ingrid was sewing. She sat bowed over the old, dark sewing machine she'd inherited from Grandma.

Now she got up slowly and stretched, her right hand pressed into her back for support. She looked pale and tired, but she smiled. It was a real smile, as if she were thinking about something good. Then she went over to the counter and tested one of the loaves of fresh bread. With quick, practiced strokes, she cut through the soft bread, which gave each time she pressed the knife through the golden crust. It was crunchy, and with every slice it made a noise as if pleading for its life.

Ingrid buttered a piece thickly and let the sugar spoon tremble above it so the sugar sprinkled evenly over the entire slice.

"What did Ottar have to say?" she asked, sprinkling sugar on another slice.

"Oh, nothing ... I mean, he just talked to the men who were there."

Tora hesitated just long enough so that her mother turned and showed her the face Tora least wanted to see tonight.

"Why do you say it like that? Why don't you say it the way it was?" Her mother sounded irritated and anxious.

"What should I say, then?" Tora's voice was tiny, but she reached for the slice of bread her mother was handing her.

"Sit down at the table and don't spill the sugar all over the place!"

Tora sank down at the table and put a small plate under her bread, the way she knew her mother wanted her to.

Why did she always have to say something that ruined her mother's good mood? Why did she always have to do something wrong? It was just her luck! And why tonight, just when they were alone and could have had such a good time together!

46

"Ottar didn't say anything to me. That's the truth. If you mean did he say anything about putting the groceries in the book, well he didn't. Honest!"

Silence fell between them. Ingrid had turned back to the counter again. The sugar crunched between Tora's teeth. She couldn't help it, because it tasted so good and she was hungry.

The rain was drumming against the window panes now. It shut them in together. Mama seemed to realize it too, that they only had each other, for she turned suddenly, gave Tora a friendly look, and said, "No, I guess not. Ottar's all right. Besides, you can take him the money next week. I'll be getting a little something for the extra cleaning I did at the sheriff's place. And I'll be getting my wages too, you know. You'll be able to take him his money."

Tora chewed and smiled. In her mind's eye she could see at least ten items in Ottar's book. But she didn't say anything. She just fidgeted uneasily and licked up the sugar that had fallen on her plate. She licked her finger and pressed it hard into the grains of sugar so they stuck until she got them to her lips.

"Don't do that," her mother said. "It's disgusting when people lick their fingers while they're eating!"

Tora lowered her eyes and stopped licking up the sugar. She felt a knot in her stomach, and the second piece of bread her mother handed her was much too big. She felt so miserable that she couldn't think of anything else to do except smile at her mother again. But it wasn't a real smile, and her mother didn't see it anyway because she had turned back to the counter to put the food away.

After a while, Ingrid went over to the table where she kept the sewing machine. Always with her back turned.

Tora felt the emptiness.

It was as if Mama's back were enemies with her the whole time.

"Should I make coffee, Mama?" she asked tentatively a little later.

Ingrid turned slowly and looked at her daughter as if she'd never really seen her before. Squinted a little as if she couldn't see very well after her eyes had adjusted themselves to the

47

sewing machine's bright light and then had to look into the darkness all of a sudden.

"No, dear ... But you can help me fit this jacket. The sleeves are giving me trouble. Rachel's smaller than me. Narrower in the shoulders. See? But the altering went just fine. It looks like new."

She held up Aunt Rachel's made-over jacket for Tora to see. Tora wiped her mouth quickly and rushed over to her mother.

"Yes. What do you want me to do?"

Her mother explained and directed. She put on the jacket and turned around in front of the mirror that she had brought in from the living room and leaned up against the back of a chair. Tora put in pins where Ingrid told her to. The naked light bulb made a cold halo around the two heads bending over together.

The fitting was over a short while later and Ingrid sat down at the sewing machine again. It hummed when she pressed her foot on the treadle. Tora leaned over the edge of the table and watched. She could risk that now. She'd moved her chair as close as she could and she could watch the whole process. Her mother was pleased. The jacket was turning out fine, and she could see an end to her work. The deep furrow between her eyes disappeared. Smoothed itself out in such a nice way that Tora began to feel warm inside.

Then her mother asked her to warm up the coffee after all. And they talked together about how surprised Aunt Rachel was going to be when she saw how nice the jacket had turned out.

They weren't finished yet when Henrik came home.

They hadn't paid any attention when the entrance door opened and closed downstairs, because they didn't expect him home this early on a Saturday night.

He wasn't as drunk as he could have been, Tora saw. He sat down at the kitchen table and wanted to talk.

Once he handed Tora the scissors that she'd left lying on the table after she'd cut off some thread ends for her mother. Tora didn't think the scissors felt the same, somehow. They were colder. Alien. In an odd way it was disgusting to take them from him. That's why she did it properly and calmly. Without looking at him.

She said aloud, "Thanks!"

Later he asked her how things were going at school. But by then he'd already become somewhat sleepy and Ingrid got up from the sewing machine and helped him to bed.

When her mother and Henrik had gone into the living room, and Tora could see them through the half-open door, together, a sudden nausea overwhelmed her. She hurried into her room and carefully closed the door after her.

It was cold in there. But it was also quiet and nobody saw her. She stood for a while in the middle of the room and felt sorry for the angel that hung in the glass and the frame on the wall. Her cheek was resting on one chubby hand as she stared at nothing.

The angel was completely alone.

Chapter Eight

TORA HAD GOT A SUCKER FROM JENNY AT THE NEWS-
stand because she had gone to get the *Lofoten Post* bundle
when the mail boat docked.

Now she was strolling slowly home.

She saw that the cloudless sky was a miracle and that the
gulls were putting on a show for her above the fish drying
racks. Their cries made such lovely echoes in her head. She
could hear the gulls crying whenever she wanted to, wherever
she was. She carried those sounds with her.

But sometimes they were brighter and friendlier that usual.

Today was a day like that. A day to begin all over again. A
day to think about good things. A day made for running really
fast, laughing really loudly, or just for strolling along by yourself with a sucker. Going no place in particular, even though
you were walking home.

Jenny was nice. She was sometimes gruff and could swear a
blue streak. But she was nice. It was her eyes, probably. Narrow chinks with something greenish in them. Full of life,
whether she was happy or mad.

Jenny's cheeks were somehow related to her apples. Red.
Her yellow and brown striped apron was never completely
clean. Spots from her indelible pencil on the pockets. Always.

The door to the apartment was open. But no one hollered out
that she should take off her galoshes. Tora suddenly stood
still. Her stomach shrivelled into a hard knot. Somebody was
there, but there wasn't anybody there.

Could Henrik be drunk in broad daylight?

Ingrid was sitting at the kitchen table when she came in. In her worn, brown coat. She didn't look up, as if she didn't notice Tora had come in. She was sitting there in her scarf and mittens too!

Her face was a blur. Her nose was an ink spot that somebody had tried to erase but only smeared.

Some of her dark, thick hair stuck out from under the scarf and in contrast to the rest looked oddly alive.

"They won't let me work. They say I'm putting on airs because I didn't want the night shift anymore. I don't have a job, Tora!"

Ingrid's voice rang out shrilly in the room. There was a kind of helpless rage in it that didn't dare show its strength, as if it were afraid it wouldn't be strong enough.

"I don't know what we're going to live on," she went on, subdued and whining now, the way Tora had heard her sound before.

"Do you want me to put on the potatoes, Mama?"

Tora slipped the words breathlessly out.

If she pretended she hadn't heard anything, then maybe it would just be something she'd made up. If she could count to a hundred while she ran down to the basement to get the potatoes, then maybe it would just be something she'd dreamed and her mother would be there as if nothing were wrong and would make brown gravy for the fish cakes when she came back up.

But when she got back to the kitchen, she'd forgotten to count and her mother was still sitting there the same as before.

"If only you were able to take care of yourself at night," her mother complained, "then I'd still have my job!"

Tora felt the words like a blow across her back. She made the water splash into the sink full force, so she wouldn't have to hear any more. She sloshed her hands around in the sandy tub of potatoes as noisily as she could. Pressure was building up behind her eyes somewhere. But she went on washing the potatoes as if her life depended on it. As if she were trying to show that she could take care of herself alone for as many nights as she had to!

But the accusation became important and true, because Mama had made it.

True! If only she—Tora had been. . . .

A strange skinlessness began to spread over her whole body. And she didn't dare turn around. Her face was too naked. It started with her eyes and then she felt it in her fingertips. It spread fast, reached through her whole body. It was a clammy and cold feeling, like touching her grandmother last year after she was dead.

Maybe she'd also begun to die in some way?

The smell of carnations?

Whenever she had to stand up in class, recite something with everybody's eyes watching her—even though she knew that she knew the lesson—her hands slowly became clammy and her armpits wet. Then she caught the sweetish smell of death and carnations.

Ingrid wouldn't stop talking now. Talked her way all through the dinner preparations. Wandered absently around the kitchen, still in her coat and scarf. Tora didn't listen to what she was saying, or she deliberately forgot it as soon as she heard it. It was best that way. For both of them.

She was already at work fashioning a plank on which she could float for the rest of the day. She'd do her homework first and then race straight down to Jenny's newsstand and help her with the pricing.

She'd already promised!

She was going to make herself invisible today.

But first of all she'd clean up the kitchen properly so her mother could take a nap.

If Jenny didn't want her all day, she could go to the warehouse attic where she kept her notebooks.

In Uncle Simon's warehouse attic there was a small window with four dirty panes in it. They let sunlight in to her, if there was any to let in. Showed her a tiny piece of the sky. There wasn't any other light.

Sometimes she played with the idea of taking a candle up there but resisted the temptation.

Ingrid had impressed upon her how terrible it was when fire got out of control. So she couldn't read or write if it wasn't

52

light outside. But nobody could stop her from sitting under the big, tattered piece of sailcloth over in the corner below the window and listening to the mice scurry around in the walls. The ocean and the gulls could always be heard too.

There were herring boxes, barrels and all kinds of junk in there. She could make so many kinds of strange furniture out of it.

She was really much too old for that. But nobody saw her.

Tora never took anybody up there with her. Not even Sol. Sol was no doubt too grown up for that, so Tora didn't think she was cheating her out of anything.

She had an old, ragged wool blanket up there too. For use on cold days when she could see her breath like spooky and lonely smoke rising from her mouth. It was as if she were an ogre or a dragon under a spell who became itself only when it was alone. But she was still Tora.

She had more stories in her head that she could remember if she just sat there a little while. Some of them were unbearably exciting. Some of them had the same beginning but ended differently.

Sometimes she tormented herself by letting them end sadly. Then she cried down into her wool blanket, without tears. It was so hard for her to get tears out. They were locked in somehow and didn't want to come out at all.

Her stories waited there for her, by the walls, in the shadows of her furniture, among the beams across the ceiling.

The finest ones always had a father who came back.

Some had a sick mother who died. And when the father heard about it, he came from a foreign country and got his daughter, even though he'd never seen her. Easily and without guilt, she let the mothers die. It was clear they were better off in heaven.

Alone.

The thought was a lovely secret.

She kept her treasures under an upside-down margarine crate. Three noteboooks that Gunn had given her and an indelible pencil. But it wasn't often she took the time to write down any of her stories. Often it was too dark, or else the story went so fast she didn't have time to find words for it.

Sometimes she thought it looked so clumsy, when she saw it there in her notebook, that she scribbled it out.

It was better when her thoughts just floated beneath the blanket and out in the air. Her thoughts in themselves were so big. They were the finest things she knew. It couldn't be helped that some thoughts were unbearable.

Tora had a fine story about walking along a road with a key in her pocket. The key to a little, locked room. Locked to people. Then she always came to a certain place on the road where she turned and went home to the room, no matter where she had been going. She unlocked the door, went in, locked it behind her.

There were no voices.

The danger? The danger couldn't get into a room like that.

If anybody happened to mention *his* name unexpectedly, the danger could suddenly turn the whole day grey and dark, even though she'd practiced not thinking about it.

If he suddenly came into a room where she'd been alone, it could feel as if someone had thrown a dirty, clammy piece of cloth over her.

Then she just stood there, stiff as a post, until something happened to break the spell.

She saved herself sometimes by putting herself into the fairy tale, quick as lightning.

She was a bewitched princess and something terrible had befallen her. But if *that* or *that* happened, then the spell would be broken and the danger undone.

Sometimes it could plunge a whole good day deep into the muck at the bottom of the sea if he just hung his outdoor clothes next to hers in the hall, or if her plate got stacked on his when the table was cleared.

At other times, when she believed she was thinking of something else entirely, she could inexplicably become sick to her stomach just by seeing his shaving soap floating around in the washbasin.

Outside, life was mostly good.

It was a different kind of life. You could run! Run from whatever came up.

If there were a storm and enough wind, she felt as though she were flying. She just put on extra speed, took extra high leaps. Then, all of a sudden, she was Tora who could fly!

"When you get big enough!" Aunt Rachel and Mama often said.

Tora knew that she was starting to get big enough. Because the danger had come so close, closer than ever before. It wasn't just dreams and daydreams, it was inside her. And she would have to deal with it. It was her business.

That's how it was.

In the meantime she ran as fast as she could. And nobody could run as fast as Tora.

She got to play ball with the big boys in the village when she wanted to. She scooped up the ball and threw it, hard and accurately. If she were in a good mood, she could put a curve on it that everybody admired.

Nobody's throw stung as hard as Tora's when she threw you out, even though she looked as if she might break in half at the waist any moment and distinctly smelled of fish!

Her sharp little chin jutted out as her bony, stone-hard hand closed on the rubber ball and she held it a moment before she let it fly. At the same moment it left her hand she could feel all the wild power she had within her. Her body was like a tight spring. It filled her with such furious joy!

Then the ball flew, and she was left behind . . .

But it stung—wherever it hit you.

Chapter Nine

THE AFTERNOON LAY SNUG AND BLUE AGAINST THE WIN-
dowpane when Tora pulled the curtain shut. She'd filled the
biggest tin basin to the brim with lukewarm water. Now it was
on the stool at the foot of her bed, a joy in itself.

She'd kept a fire going in the stove all afternoon, ever since
her mother left for work. She wasn't supposed to. Ingrid
thought that a couple of hours of heating up her room before
washing was enough. Coal was expensive. They couldn't
really afford to burn coal. Einar, up in the garret, often said
they should eat it instead.

Tora had put the big, sharpened table knife on the bed.
They usually used it for peeling potatoes. The blade glittered
in a friendly but dangerous way.

There was only one key to the apartment, and that was to
the big, brown front door. That door had two solid panels
with lots of coats of paint, and it was set into an even more
solid frame with even more coats of paint on it.

The big, old-fashioned key was used if they went away.
Otherwise it hung by the light switch on the kitchen wall. In
each room, a spare table knife served to keep people out.
More as a warning than as a lock.

Tora had brought out her new, white cotton undershirt, the
one she'd only worn for good until now. Her mother said she
might as well wear it, since she hadn't had time to wash
clothes in two weeks.

Joy came over Tora. Of course she could wear it!

For that matter, all of her clothes had become too tight for
her this year. It was a real pity, the way her stringy body had

56

filled out in every possible direction.

It was shameful of her to grow so much that her mother had to spend lots of money on new clothes, when the old ones weren't worn out. It took a long time for Tora to realize that it didn't do any good to draw in her chest, duck her head and feel ashamed.

She caressed the new, white undershirt. It had a bluish tint in the glow of the lamp on the night table. It was so much better and whiter than her old one.

She'd taken off her clothes. Was standing by the small, black stove feeling the warmth coil around her body. Good.

To be able to go without clothes all the time. In the warmth of the stove. On the rocky shore. In the sun. Just be the way you were, without anybody thinking it was strange or bad.

It dawned on Tora that that must be the finest thing of all.

Her long, wiry braids tickled up and down her back when she moved.

There was a distinct crack around the door and an ice-cold draft blew suddenly around her naked body. She shivered and plunged her hands down into the basin to let the warm, soap-scented water stream slowly over her body. Her braids kept wanting to fall into the water, but they'd have to wait until another day. Her mother usually helped her with her hair. Rinsing was hard. It required so much water that she had to do it at the kitchen sink.

To be naked . . . always . . . it was almost a nasty thought. She must never tell it to anybody. Not to Sol or Aunt Rachel even.

But it was a fact that Aunt Rachel talked openly about a lot of things that her mother never mentioned.

When they were sitting in the kitchen, talking—just the three of them—Ingrid would sometimes purse her lips and say, "Oh, Rachel, remember the child!"

Aunt Rachel was different.

But she could afford it, of course, with a husband who owned a boat and a fishing business, a little white house right up under Veten and a barn with sheep in it. It was easy for her to laugh.

Aunt Rachel was a big kid, her mother often said. But Tora

couldn't understand why she cared if Aunt Rachel was a big kid since, after all, there weren't any children at Bekkejordet.

Rachel knew how to laugh. Like a big avalanche.

You were surprised, the first time you heard it. An unbelievable amount of laughter came out of her mouth and, at the same time, a chuckling inside her belly. And her red hair with the permanent was like a cloud when she threw back her head and laughed at the top of her lungs. There was a story that she'd laughed so uncontrollably at her own wedding that Simon had had to say "I do" for both of them, in church and right in the middle of the ceremony. And all because the pastor had got a new set of false teeth and wasn't able to speak clearly when he asked them if they would take each other to be man and wife.

Tora suddenly heard footsteps on the stairs.

She came to her senses immediately and stuck the knife between the molding and the wall, against the door. It wasn't certain that anyone was coming to their apartment. She listened, holding the piece of soap tightly to her chest with both hands. Water dripped rhythmically and almost soundlessly from her throat and nose down onto the wooden floor. An occasional drop fell on her small breast and made her nipples taut.

Someone opened the kitchen door. Him!

But he was supposed to be working down at Dahl's warehouse for several more hours! She sank down in the corner at the end of her bed.

If anyone tried her door, they could open it a crack before the knife stopped them.

It was possible to work the knife free from the other room. Now she could hear him creeping along the kitchen wall.

"Ingrid!" he shouted out into the empty kitchen.

So he was drunk, and in the middle of the day too.

Now she could hear him in the corner of the living room. He groaned and tried to pull off his shoes.

If he just went to bed, he'd fall asleep almost at once. She'd hear groans and snores through the thin wall. Then she could finish washing, down below and her feet. She couldn't get up or wash until he was asleep.

He shuffled in to his bed. So far, so good.

Tora crouched down, stock still in her corner. It had grown dark in the chinks around the door in the stove, but she couldn't make herself get up and put more coal in.

Something told her she shouldn't let him know she was home. She shouldn't be there. She should be out in the street, at her aunt's, in the village. Anywhere but here. Until Henrik fell asleep.

Once he went to sleep, she'd have the whole house to herself. She could pretend he didn't exist. She could close all the doors and sit on the peat box in the kitchen and feel clean and fit and brand new. Or she could turn on the light over the kitchen table and read in the beautiful, sad book she'd borrowed from Gunn.

The world could still be good.

Her thighs felt stiff from squatting, the water on her body had evaporated and she was shivering. She still couldn't hear any snoring. Maybe he was so drunk he couldn't snore? Maybe he was dead!? Would she mourn, she wondered? She supposed so. Because Mama would.

Henrik *was*. She couldn't waste time wondering about that. She called him Henrik. Other kids called the man who lived in their house papa. Tora was suddenly happy that she'd never called him papa. She didn't really know why. It had something to do with hard hands, something to do with dreams and reality spun so tightly and darkly together that she couldn't stand it.

A heavy knot, a wild pressure all the way down into her crotch.

She wanted it to be summer and light all day and night when she felt that way. At the same time she wanted to conceal herself in the winter darkness in the most deeply hidden corner she could find.

Surely she could heat up the stove. Henrik had to be asleep by now.

Only coals were left, so she raked up some scraps of wrapping and threw some peat on to make a fire.

The room had grown chilly and she was shivering because she hadn't dried herself off.

Soap lather was floating in the basin like a congealed clump of frog's eggs. The water was cold. She wrung out the wash cloth and washed her crotch and bottom anyway. Quickly, quietly and almost without breathing. She broke out in goose pimples wherever the wash cloth passed. Then it was time to do her feet.

Her mother was always so strict about how you had to wash properly. Face, ears, neck, chest, arms, back. And then down below, as she called it.

Last of all her thin legs and then her feet. All the way up under her knees, and it didn't make any difference to her mother that it was late fall and weather for boots.

She never dared try to cheat.

It was as if her mother could see the kind of washing Tora had done right through her clothes.

She'd moved the basin down onto the floor and stuck both feet in. Then she heard him at the living room door.

Her head seemed to expand. Grew big and formless and floated away so she couldn't control it. Not another thought!

The veins in her throat pounded and her tongue seemed to swell up in her head that wasn't there. Filled her whole throat.

"Tora. . . . " he said, his voice hesitant.

She didn't answer. There was no one in the whole world whose name was Tora. She had flown into nothing. There was only an immense stillness.

The knife under the molding began moving slightly. She watched and watched. Watched the door open. Watched him stumble in like a huge, shaggy mountain. She held the piece of soap tightly against her body. Tried to cover herself with two thin arms and a piece of soap.

Then there was only breathing in the room. Breathing was the night sound of the house. It was daytime now, but. . . .

The man had no face. The basin tipped over. The good arm was willing to do the work of two.

Once she heard a voice someplace close to her head,

"You don't need to be scared. I'm only . . . I'm not going to stick it in all the way . . . I'm only. . . . "

The skinned cat in the road.

There was no longer any use, hiding in any corner. There was no place to hide.

It was the same hand that had saved her from the edge of the wharf, the same hand that had held her out over the edge of Horse Crag, pushed her in the swing between the big birch trees behind the house, the same hand that had beaten her and helped her with many things. It surrounded her, grew around her, in her. Became a shapeless and burning swarm of jellyfish that clung to her and was everywhere.

When he went back to his own room with his clothes flapping open around him, he still had no face. Only a fixed grin that hung in the air between him and the bundle on the bed.

Tora understood that she was dead in some way.

But she used the wash cloth and wiped off the half-congealed traces on the woollen blanket. She rubbed and rubbed as hard as she could to get it all.

The skinned cat. Bertelsen's dog had caught it anyway. Dragged it a long time through the mud and filth. Afterwards, it lay a long time in the ditch.

It had to be the cat's own fault. Because nobody owned it and took care of it. It affected people in such a way that they skinned it. Affected dogs in such a way that it got dragged around in the shit.

That's how it was. Somebody had decided it a long time ago. There was no getting around it.

Chapter Ten

Simon's farm Bekkejordet lay right under Veten, with the scrub birch and the wild moors close up to the upper fields. The farm buildings in the middle of the slope were well cared for and painted white, with large double hung windows in both the kitchen and the living room. The barn stood out conspicuously, red and with a fan-shaped window up in the hay loft.

It was said that Simon's uncle had gotten the pretentious idea once when he'd been down at his sister's in Gudbrandsdal, and he modelled his barn window on the ones he'd seen there.

Simon had inherited the house and the land and the wharf. He wasn't exactly overbearing, but he never approached anybody with his hat in his hand, either. He hired people during the haying and plowing seasons and kept up his small farm.

He could afford it, people muttered. Simon made good money. He didn't even have to go out fishing himself, but instead hired both captain and crew. He stayed at home with his papers and his fish buying and contracts. He hopped too lightly somehow from one thing to another without ever getting his feet wet, in the opinion of the villagers. That Simon Bekkejordet and the pastor, they could both afford to hire farm hands! Well, you had to give Rachel credit for the miserable, dirty potatoes, of course. She did everything but plow. While the pastor had a host of milk cows and a regular hired man, Simon had a barn full of sheep that he fattened up in the mountains in the summer. After all, there had to be some difference between Simon and the pastor. Absolutely!

Nobody could accuse Rachel of twiddling her thumbs or

sitting around drinking coffee with the other wives on week-days. She took care of her sheep herself and had a name for every single one. During the slaughtering season in the fall, she hired the best slaughterer from Breiland. She stirred the blood herself as she sniffled and cried and drove away with threats anybody who came too close.

Late every winter she was down on her hands and knees in the clean-swept sheep pens, dragging the poor, slimy crea-tures into the world, crying the whole time and wiping her nose with the back of her hand. Rachel had her own fasting time. Contrary to any known tradition, she didn't eat lamb in the slaughtering season.

Up in the loft, where the plan had been that her children would eventually reign, Rachel kept her loom. It was big and green and absorbed her completely when she climbed onto its seat.

Every year there was great excitement over who would win Rachel's contribution to the big Christmas lottery for the ben-efit of the sailor's mission. This consisted of several yards of woven rug. All in one piece. Nicely harmonized colors, not everything in a gaudy disorder of random scraps the way it usually was when other women put together a rag rug. No, like a work of art in color and design, mixed squares and stripes that repeated themselves exactly after so many wefts.

Before electricity came to the island, two lanterns hissed si-multaneously up there in the loft in winter. People who took the shortcut to the village through the farm could hear Rachel joyously and merrily weaving up there.

Sometimes the loft was silent but the light was shining just as brightly from the big windows. That meant Rachel was standing over her boxes of scraps, holding one ball of yarn up to the other and carefully choosing color and thickness.

If she couldn't find exactly the color or thickness she'd got it into her head she had to have, she'd run from farm to farm and beg and swap. Or else get the big tub from the basement and furiously start dyeing.

She'd bawled out poor Ottar at the store more than once be-

63

cause he hadn't gotten around to ordering the colors she needed. Sometimes he got angry about it, but he didn't say anything until Rachel and her shopping bag were safely out of earshot.

"She expects a lot, that wife of Simon's," he might say.

If any customers happened to hear those words, it didn't take Ottar long to undo the damage. "She's not outright snotty, though. Lots of times she can be helpful and friendly. But she's got a sharp tongue. That's not right for a person who got everything handed to her on a platter, like Rachel did. And she doesn't even come from good family. But of course that was a long time ago. Far be it from me to dredge up all that German stuff. Poor Ingrid... a long time ago. And *Rachel* pays in cash! But she really chews out the fisherman down at Simon's fishing station, let me tell you! Just because they don't wipe their feet before they come into the office. She says they're a pack of assholes and asks them if they were born in a Lapp hut! Can you believe it? That's not right, I say. And Simon, he just stands there grinning and tells them they'd better do what Rachel says because she's the cleaning boss. Only the fish are my territory, he says. Can you believe it?"

Snow whirled up in drifts around the buildings and light from the windows lay blue and lonely on the snow crust as soon as the stingy daylight disappeared.

The cold had finally taken hold of the Tenement too. It had invaded the halls and gusted up at you from the outhouse hole. Everybody forgot how they had longed for it when the fog was at its thickest in the late fall. They rejected it, now that it was here. They huddled up and shivered and went down into dark cellars after more coal.

Just before Christmas, Rachel hired Tora to help her with the baking.

Tora buttered the fluted forms for the tart shells. She was flushed and happy. The aroma of the tall sugar cake cooling on the counter, still in its pan, filled the kitchen. It was for the second day of Christmas. That was when Rachel put both leaves in the dining room table and served a lavish buffet for family and friends. People came and went all afternoon, depending on when they had to do their chores in the barn, or bathe and put their little ones to bed. It was mostly friends who came, of course, because family was just Tora and Ingrid. *He* was never there.

Tora thought he was afraid of Aunt Rachel and that he didn't like Simon because Simon had two good arms. But she wasn't absolutely certain.

Tora made sure the forms were buttered properly. Traced the grooves in each one with buttered paper before going on to the next.

"I'm thinking I ought to invite Jenny this year. She's just sitting up there in that attic of hers in the Tenement and doesn't have anybody to talk to that I can see. She's no monster, even if she has gone and got herself a little bastard."

Tora's cheeks burned. *Bastard!*

"I think she's taking good care of herself. At least she doesn't depend on welfare for everything."

"How come?" Tora finally got her voice back.

"She earns money herself, at the newsstand."

"Wh—where did she get the bastard?"

Rachel laughed and gave Tora a quick glance.

"I guess he came with a squirt of love medicine, like any other kid. Just that the father wouldn't marry Jenny."

"Why wouldn't he?" Tora asked unsteadily.

"You ask so many questions! He was already married, I suppose. They say he's not from around here. They say he's the one who travels around with the district moving picture shows. Could be. I'm the last to hear loose talk. Nobody comes running to me with such stuff. They must know . . . "

Rachel broke off abruptly and began energetically to rearrange the forms Tora had buttered.

The coziness and warmth at Bekkejordet flew suddenly out the window, Tora thought. The word and the shame had followed her right into Aunt Rachel's kitchen.

The shame! The shame that gave the other kids the right to shout after her in the road, "Her hair's on fire, her hair's all red, her mother slept in a German's bed!"

German was the worst word in all the world. Worse even than being from the barracks at Nordsund. Worse than being a "lush" in the fishing season. Worse than being Jenny's bastard kid.

It was the cold itself.

Apparently, of all the people on the island, Tora was the only German.

Once Ole had gotten mad at her because she wouldn't let him borrow her new eraser. They were doing dictation.

"Stingy German brat!" he'd flung at her.

Then they suddenly heard Gunn's slippers coming down the aisle between the rows of desks. The sound stopped between Ole and Tora.

Gunn didn't say anything and she didn't even look at Tora, but Ole's ear got a fiery red pinch mark and the hair on his neck stood straight up for a long time.

However backwards it seemed, it wasn't until that moment that Tora fully realized how bad it was to be a German brat. Because she'd never seen Gunn that way before. It was enough to make you shrivel up inside.

Rachel looked at the girl across the bread board.

Then she said gently, "It didn't hurt your feelings, did it, child? . . . That word I used?"

Tora felt her eyes brimming with tears. Because of the concern in her aunt's voice, somehow.

Words flew out of her instead of tears. They seemed to have been lying in front of a locked door, ready to spring out as soon as someone opened the door just a crack. "Who was he, my father?"

Her voice wasn't the way it was supposed to be, it sounded much too breathless and worn out.

Rachel stiffened, as if somebody had turned her off. Not even her breath, which whistled faintly from the corner of her mouth whenever she was preoccupied with work she liked—not even that could be heard.

"Wh—what'd you mean?" she finally managed to say, mostly just to stall for time.

"I mean him—my real father."

Tora had set out on the open sea, now it was just a matter of staying afloat. There was no time to turn back. Rachel dried her hands carefully on the snowy-white baker's apron and sank slowly down onto the nearest chair.

"Hasn't your mother ever told you about your father?"

Their eyes met, testing, each pair as uncertain as the other.

"Oh... well... Mama, you know, she has so much—she's so busy. She doesn't have time!"

The last sentence came out fast, a piece of driftwood Tora had found to hang on to.

No matter how much a betrayal of her mother it was, she had to know. Had to have the strength it gave to know—when all the insults were hailing down on her and she couldn't do anything about it.

Rachel sat there, her eyes on Tora the whole time. She seemed to force herself not to look away. Then it came, "All right! Take the cake out of the oven, Tora! And then come over here and sit down. This is going to be more than a day for baking."

And Tora did what Rachel said, while her arms felt as if they were fastened to her body with loose string. Her feet bunched up the scatter rugs as she walked.

"Your father," Rachel began hesitantly, "your father was an ordinary man with black hair and blue eyes and broad shoulders. A fine man. He and your mother fell in love. He wasn't an ordinary soldier."

Rachel came to a stop. She shifted her glance to the stove, to see if it was drawing. But then it burst out of her, fast and decisively, "But he was sent here to conquer us, so he *was* an enemy! No matter how he behaved or how he looked or who he became the father of! At that time he was the enemy! Even though he fell in love with your mother and... Your grandfather never had a happy day afterwards. He got tuberculosis and died, you know. The spring the war ended. Your grandmother cried and everything was in confusion when it was clear you were on the way. You have to understand, Tora! It was a difficult time, in a lot of ways. There was so much hatred. People had to learn to hate and to survive. Later, when peace came, then people found scapegoats for their hatred. Your mother got all mixed up in that, and I don't know if she's really come out of it yet."

The last words were barely audible.

It was quiet in Rachel's kitchen a moment.

"But who was he? Where—where is he now, Aunt Rachel?" Tora asked in a whisper.

"Wait a minute." Rachel cleared her throat. "He and your mother were supposed to go to Oslo where he had friends she could live with while she was having you. This was no place for you. They believed the war was coming to an end, like everybody else. Then they were going to go to Berlin where he had family and a home."

"And?"

"They didn't get that far. In Trondhjem they did away with your father, Tora . . . "

"Did away with! Who did?"

"We've never found out. It wasn't important to find out things like that after the war, how the enemy was done away with. The main thing was that they were gone! But it might have been his own people . . . just as easily . . . "

"His own people?"

"Well, he didn't have permission to do what he did. He just left, to take your mother to his friends. That was no joke for a man in a German uniform. Your mother got a letter, stuck under the door of the boarding house where she was staying. Full of ugly words and telling her that he was—dead."

"Dead!" It was as if it hadn't hit Tora until then.

"Yes, Tora. And so your mother had to travel half of Norway to get home again. Mostly on her own two feet. For *he* was the one carrying the money. And you were in her belly and I don't suppose the sun was shining much. . . . "

"But is he dead, Aunt Rachel? Is he *still* dead?"

Rachel stared at the girl in disbelief. Then she got up and came slowly around the table to Tora.

"Dear Tora, sweet darling! You know we love you. Grandfather, poor man, was dead, of course, but you remember your grandmother. She was kind, Tora. Wasn't she? Nobody was allowed to hurt a hair on your head."

Rachel smiled searchingly. But she couldn't seem to reach Tora with what she was saying.

"Your grandfather wasn't a bad man, you know. Ingrid herself was the one who wanted to move away from here. The gossip hurt her so horribly. I've wondered many times how things might have turned out if your real father had been one of Vilar's sons, as Simon is. Had been Norwegian and everything."

Tora didn't hear a word. She just saw Rachel's mouth moving at breakneck speed. Faster and faster. It was as if she would suffocate by watching.

So it was something she'd dreamed up in the warehouse attic after all. Made up and dreamed. Given him a name. A face. Everything.

Papa.

There wasn't any Papa. Had never been one. He was dead before she was born!

Wasn't she supposed to have anything? Was that the idea? Her mouth twisted, as if she were going to cry, but nothing came out. Then she got up from the chair where Rachel was standing with her arms around her, went quickly across the room to the door. She didn't remember that her jacket was hanging in the hall, she struggled out into the blowing snow and closed the door behind her.

A big hole had opened in her. It didn't do any good to crawl up into the warehouse attic and daydream it away.

DEAD!

For Tora it was worse than the danger this time. Because something good had been lost—for always. Everything awful—you could force yourself to forget that. You could run from it, fly across the parsonage fields like the wind, shout joyfully into the wind like a crazy person, play ball, throw so hard that the kid you hit moaned—even if you didn't come up to his shoulder. She could sit snugly in her blanket up in the warehouse attic with all the dangers in the world, stare into the grey sky until everything disappeared and became blurred and irrelevant. But she couldn't cope with this. This was her happiness, the only thing she really cared about having, dead and gone forever.

Tora felt a painful, heavy desire to have something to hit. Kick, squeeze the life out of. *Them*—the ones who had done this to her!

And she suddenly realized that there was no use blaming an old youth center for what was or wasn't. It was people! They were the ones to blame. It was people you had to be afraid of and run from.

It was people who made everything dead.

Rachel found her crouched against the barn. Like a forgotten sack of hay. The snow and hail stung horribly. Whipped their bare hands and faces. Stuck in their hair only to be swept away by another icy blast.

It was a storm. It cut right through them. But those two didn't notice *that*. They had other things to think about.

For the first time in a long time, Rachel didn't know what to do.

They were both silent. Tora was led in, thawed out, and dressed. Rachel held her tightly the whole time.

The road to the Tenement was a long one.

"There's just us three women left in the family," Rachel said with authority.

She knew that if anybody were going to say anything, it would have to be her.

"There's so much we should have talked about."

She poured the coffee she'd made herself, and passed around Ingrid's precious Christmas cookies, right from the tin. Ingrid didn't say a word. She'd seen that something was wrong as soon as the girl and Rachel had come in the door.

Henrik had gone out, as he usually did when Rachel came over. It was Rachel who had gotten Tora under the comforter, made coffee and served coffee and cookies at Tora's bedside.

"I don't know if I've done anything wrong today, Ingrid, or if you're the one who's been negligent and didn't have the sense to tell the child who her father is. But now she knows, as far as it's in my power to tell her. And I'd like to hear with my own ears that you agree with what I've said, so later you can't say I lied. Because you're her mother. You're the one who has to tell her that we've struggled our way through this problem together and she doesn't need to go around feeling ashamed of the father she should have had if things had gone the right way. And that the Lord, men and the Devil are in charge of war and things like that in this world. We women don't have that to be ashamed of. We're not the ones who have to hang our heads. We're the ones who have to see beyond lies and silence and support one another instead. Do you hear, Ingrid!?"

When Simon came home late that night, wet and tired but with the Christmas halibut, the boat and the crew safe and sound, Rachel was still in the kitchen baking, for the afternoon at the Tenement had gone on a long time.

Her red hair stood defiantly out from her baking scarf. Her face was covered with flour and hard at the edges. Her small half-moon-shaped mouth was thinned out into an involuntary grimace as she looked at her husband.

Simon saw that the mood in the kitchen was close to the breaking point, but he crept up to her from behind anyway, to cheer her up with one of the little "fishguts hugs" he liked to tease her with before changing out of his fishing gear.

"Scat out of here! Today I want to puke when I see a man! I'm doing the Christmas baking and I'm going to go on doing it until I see things differently!"

Simon laughed a little, but the outburst made him uncertain. Something big must be up. He knew Rachel.

He pulled off his wet clothes, filled the big galvanized steel washtub and carried it in to the pantry they'd made into a kind of washroom. They had a modern porcelain sink with hot and cold running water. But when a bath was called for, they brought out the galvanized tub. He was even thinking of having a bathtub installed next summer. Not many people in the village had one. But you didn't need to advertise it, of course. . . .

Simon scrubbed himself thoroughly and was careful not to ask for a back scrub or a change of clothes. Then, he carried his dirty clothes to the box in the hall. When he returned to the kitchen, he told Rachel about his catch, as though he hadn't seen or heard anything from her since he returned home. But she went angrily on with what she was doing and pretended not to hear. Then he mentioned something about that damned big rusty fish hook he'd been dumb enough to catch in the palm of his hand.

Rachel spun around and then rushed out of the room and came back with iodine and bandages and bandaged his wound as if Simon were a little boy.

Rachel's *Berlinerkrans* cookies were so burned that Simon and the cat got the whole batch with their bedtime coffee.

And while all this was taking place, the dam burst in Rachel. Simon heard the whole unhappy story and all about the child's strange behavior by the barn wall too.

And Simon forgave her immediately for choosing him to be the scapegoat for all the world's war and misery and paternity. Even though the latter was what he wanted most of all.

When they finally went to bed, Rachel was like a trembling meadow of warm, steady spring rain, earth and flowers. And Simon accepted it all and filled his rough hands and his wounded palm with all the glories the earth had to offer. Even though it was the middle of Advent.

Simon was a happy man.

Chapter Eleven

In the Tenement each sound and rhythm always had its audience.

You could never be absolutely certain what turn the sounds would take. There were always surprising elements and uncertain factors. There were often secret urges and concealed meanings in the sounds of the evening and the night. You could be very much mistaken, sometimes, if you tried to interpret sounds not meant for you.

Laughter and crying were easy. Swearing and hymn singing too. Faucets and footsteps, hushed conversations and scrapings on the floor and walls—these were harder to figure out.

Some of the occupants had little to hide, it seemed. They let their sounds escape freely into the stairwells and out through the windows. These people were usually responsible for the sounds of the day.

When the lights were turned off on the long nights before Christmas, a muffling wool blanket seemed to spread over the sounds.

One night around eleven, someone suddenly opened the front door with a bang and walked up the stairs with firm, quick steps. Whoever it was made no effort to move quietly. It was the middle of the week and some of the men were away at extra jobs or down in the village somewhere.

Tora and Ingrid were home alone. Ingrid was sewing a new dress for Tora. It was for Christmas. It was being made over from Rachel's hand-me-downs. But the color was warm and green and Tora thought she would like it even though the material was itchy.

It had been so quiet at Elisif's all evening. So they told each other that no doubt Elisif was at one of her meetings and Sol had put the little ones to bed early, as she usually did when she was alone with them.

Tora peeked cautiously out the door, even though Ingrid told her to get back inside. She easily recognized the trim on the old midwife's coat and the rubbers she wore over her slippers.

So Elisif was about to have her latest baby! Torstein—who was the father—had gone out a little while before. But nobody had paid any attention to that.

Ingrid sighed and looked anxiously at the ceiling as the groans up there grew louder and louder. Elisif was normally not one to carry on much in childbirth. She had the routine down, poor thing, Ingrid thought.

She'd been converted since the last baby. A Pentecostalist, and received into the congregation by the grace of God, bestowed only on the chosen. Baptized in the river at Hestvika in glory and amidst great rejoicing. On the old oak bureau she'd inherited from some relative, she had a green glass bowl where she kept her "manna seeds" safely out of reach of her youngest children, who were always underfoot. Every day she drew out a manna seed with a reference to a passage of the Bible printed on it and then put her household in order as the Bible passage directed. It was really bad when the passage was from the Old Testament. Elisif tried now and then to explain to the Lord that she couldn't read about fornication, stonings and the Devil's work out loud to her poor innocent children. It sometimes seemed as if the Lord could temper justice with mercy, for she chose a new seed in His honor and opened to another passage as fast as she could.

Tora had often heard Elisif say that she put everything in God's hands. But it was easy to see that if it hadn't been for Sol, God would have had a lot of dirty work to do. Because there was enough to do at Elisif's.

Tora just couldn't understand how anybody dared to put such disgusting things as childbirth in God's hands and then not think any more about it.

Apparently Ingrid thought it ought to go through women's

hands too, because when the midwife came rushing down and asked her to help out, she put on a clean work apron and ran up the stairs.

Those who helped Elisif that night could tell how she'd prayed her way through many hours and through even more labor pains. Prayed for a handsome boy, big and healthy and dedicated to the glory of God, so she could send him as a missionary to the heathen.

But around six a.m. the air was torn by an animal scream. It went through every head in the Tenement. And they all had their own thoughts.

It was Elisif, who couldn't trust in the divine any longer. She had to let out the only thing she had that could help her. The primeval scream. The first real scream in the history of the world. Air being forced from a creature in great distress, a human being abandoned by God, alone with her pain. The battle that is not recorded as anything special, because the leaders of armies never scream for new life.

She gave birth to a stillborn, blue little girl with a misshapen head.

Everyone moved about quietly when they heard the news.

For Pentecostalist or not, Elisif was one of them. They wished better for her after her battle. They invited in the seven who were living, made cocoa with water and asked them if they had been given sweaters or anything like that to wear for Christmas. And the poor things shook their heads, and ate and drank and let themselves be dressed from whatever closets and cardboard boxes had to offer in the way of surplus.

The morning that Torstein walked out the front door with the little wooden box for a coffin on his shoulder, the children and the women who could get away followed behind him. They were silent. Not a single hymn was sung until the pastor started singing. He stood on a frozen pile of dirt in black shoes that were much too thin and sang the first few stanzas all alone. Then the women seemed to come to their senses and they joined in with a low-pitched, murmuring noise that sounded less like a hymn than like an empty threat against a force that was much too powerful.

Chapter Twelve

INGRID WAS GIVING THE KITCHEN A THOROUGH CLEAN-
ing. Tora was in her room with the door open, answering
twenty-five questions on "Asia's people, animals and culture." Steam from the scalding hot water seeped in through
the open door. She smelled the sharp odor of ammonia and
the fine, safe scent of green soap.

Ingrid was standing on a stool in the middle of the kitchen
table. Her hands were flat against the ceiling with the grey
dishrag between them and the dirty yellow surface. There
were some conspicuous stains and a distinct difference between the surfaces where soap had done its work and where
half a year's tobacco smoke, cooking odors and coal fumes still
clung.

"How can just three people get things so dirty?" Ingrid
sighed and stretched her back.

The stool and kitchen table rocked threateningly when she
took a little step forward. Then everything steadied itself and
she got both herself and her scaffold back in balance. Only the
wet smacks of the dishrag could be heard, splashing rhythmically. Now and then she wrung the rag out, or changed rags
and went over what she'd washed with rinse water. Then her
movements became quicker and lighter and seemed to have a
sigh of relief about them because now one more area was spic-
and-span.

Tora couldn't get going on Asia's countries and people and
culture. Finally she stole a glance at her mother and pulled the
big reference book out of her knapsack. Gunn had let her bor-

row hers. It covered A and B. So it was natural to ask to borrow it for today.

But Tora didn't look up Asia. She had already stuck in a little bookmark at B.

The book lay in front of her and was strangely alive, but at the same time distant and unfamiliar.

Her index finger traced the boldface type until she found what she was looking for, the heading with several columns that included maps, pictures and a lot of tiny print. Berlin. "The former nation's capitol city is in Brandenburg, on the rivers Havel and Spree," Tora read.

The map was a loud pattern in three shades of grey with a lot of foreign-looking names. She put her finger firmly on an area on the outskirts, Schönhausen, and settled on that one spot with all her imagination. Grandmother's house was there. Right there, like an invisible dot on the paper. Exactly halfway between Frankfurter Allee and Greifswalder Strasse. Tora smiled.

She formed the difficult, foreign names in her mouth with great care, but not a sound slipped out.

Then she let her finger slide along the lines of text. Read about buildings and streets. She was thorough and looked them up on the map afterwards. Then she closed her eyes and thought about something else. After a while she opened them again and tried to find the name on the map quickly, and rattled off to herself what the text had said.

Grandmother had come to her the day before as she was sitting in the warehouse attic chewing on her indelible pencil. It was while she was thinking about the night she'd found out Papa was dead. It had come out that he was from Berlin, that he'd talked about a brother and a mother. Beyond that, Ingrid didn't know anything about his people, or even his address. He'd told her, but Ingrid couldn't remember.

Rachel had suggested that they could track down his relatives. She knew that others had done that. After ten years of peace, it was about time, in Rachel's opinion.

But Ingrid shook her head and stared down at her hands.

"They have their life, I have mine."

It came out hard and bitter and without hope.

"Henrik's with me now," she added. "I'm not sure he'd like it...."

"Yes, but Ingrid, there's nothing strange in the child wanting to know something about her own family on her father's side! The kind of people she's from! I think we could try to help her, so she gets some straight answers."

"No!" Ingrid's voice was like a shout.

Rachel straightened up and pressed her lips together.

"I hope you don't live to regret this!"

Tora had been sitting under the comforter, watching the two women. She couldn't help it that she felt more pleasure when she looked at her aunt than when she looked at Mama.

If she looked at her mother, a lump worked its way from her stomach and all the way up to her throat. A kind of pity.

It made her feel confused and insecure.

That's how it happened that Tora had to live with insecurity, for there was no getting around her mother. But if the girl did find a tiny bit of security on her path, she picked it up with gentle hands—and knew that it was on loan for just an hour or two.

At Tora's bedside, the night she found out about her father, it was Rachel who had plunged her into the sea, but it was also Rachel who had pulled her up again, into a kind of open boat of safety. Because you could talk to Aunt Rachel!

And Grandmother was alive!

She came, large as life, in between the roof beams and began talking to Tora. She also grieved for Papa. She'd never forgotten him. She was going to send Tora a ticket to Berlin as soon as she finished school. Because it was best that she attend school where she knew the language. Tora agreed with that. Besides, there was so much to arrange. That was the best time she'd ever had up there in the warehouse attic.

When she walked home in the dark, she knew exactly what Elisif meant when she talked about the peace of the soul.

It didn't occur to her for a moment to bring God into it.

Tora helped her mother wash the walls. She rinsed and dried, following her mother's terse directions. Asia's land and people were finished, although not very thoroughly.

"Aunt Rachel said I'm going to get some head cheese for Christmas!" she chattered.

Her mother turned away. There wasn't much left to do now.

Sweat was running down her forehead.

"She said I'm getting it as payment for helping with the baking!"

Too late, Tora realized she'd mentioned *that* night.

Ingrid hadn't said anything about Tora's father since then. A scab seemed to have formed over it. And Tora couldn't bring herself to ask any more about it. She was afraid the scab would come off and the wound start bleeding.

But no one could stop Tora from saying "Wilhelm" to herself. She held that name close, close—as if it were a wounded baby gull that nobody must find out about because if they did they would kick it to death.

At last Ingrid and Tora were sitting at the kitchen counter, drinking tea. Silent and content, with red, swollen hands and tired eyes. Steam from the newly cleaned room seeped out through the window that was open a crack. Floated out into the cold night and gathered under the eaves in elaborate, wavy little patches. The building creaked delicately and mournfully when a cold wind was gusting and it was growing late.

The lights went off in the Tenement one by one. Tora lifted her sharp little face with the big nose and her eyes met Ingrid's. They'd accomplished a lot. The room smelled clean and there was a well-earned doughnut on a gilt-edged saucer in front of Tora. That was enough for tonight. For it was such a long way to Berlin.

Chapter Thirteen

It seemed that Elisif couldn't comprehend this business of the baby. She refused to pump her breasts, bursting with milk. Ingrid and the other women of the Tenement took turns going up to her place to try to talk sense into her. The old midwife tried outright to pump her by force. But Elisif moaned and held on for dear life to the sour-smelling rag she'd put under her nightgown so she wouldn't flow away. The Lord's gifts mustn't go to waste, she wailed. But there wasn't any sense in those words, because the gifts were overflowing abundantly. For the children who had to go on living, however, there wasn't much of anything.

And she wouldn't let herself be washed, either. She wouldn't even get up. The midwife pretended to be angry and tried to frighten her by telling her that she'd get gangrene all through her private parts if she didn't take proper care of herself. But Elisif thought that the Lord gave and the Lord took away, and His name be praised through all eternity!

Meanwhile, her wool rag became more and more sour-smelling and her hair crusted around her dirty face. Internally, her body seemed to be cleansing itself in the midst of all its suffering. She bled freely. First the bedclothes turned red. The color gradually spread over the whole greyish sheet, which then became a darker and darker brown in color. Closest to her body there was always a spring of fresh, red blood. It was as if her body, despairing, tried to keep the channels open. Elisif got sores and praised God. She didn't shed a single tear. And she insisted that she didn't need to eat.

After about a week, the midwife came suddenly into Ingrid's kitchen and was like a Fury.

The stitches had become inflamed. She'd had to hold Elisif down by force just to see that much when she was trying to take them out.

They used force against her—Ingrid, Johanna and the midwife. There was no other way.

The midwife did what she needed to do, and the whole mattress had to be burned, down on the beach.

But when it was over, they all cried, except Elisif. For none of them had ever seen such a childbed.

Torstein went around like a whipped dog. After a while, he couldn't bear to go into the room where his wife was.

It was Sol who went in with food and drink and calmed her mother down and tricked her into taking enough nourishment so that she wouldn't die. Each time she opened the door a crack, the sickly-sweet smell of fresh and old blood assailed her. It was mixed with the raw stench of urine and sour milk.

On Christmas Eve Sol and Tora were in the outhouse together.

As they sat there, the church bells rang, announcing Christmas. Sol was crying a little, but without enough spirit to really sob. Tora sat on her hole and didn't say anything. It was too much for her that Sol was crying.

Finished, Sol blew her nose in a piece of old newspaper that she didn't even crumple between her fingers first.

As they were on their way across the yard in the snowy weather, Tora touched Sol's cold arm. And when they were standing on the porch and brushing off the worst of the snow, Tora said firmly, "You come down, you and Jørgen, when the little kids are in bed. I'll light the angel candle in my room."

Sol brightened for a moment or two, then the light went out of her again. She shook her head and quickly went up the stairs. When she was on the curve of the last landing, she turned and looked helplessly down into Tora's pale face. The garish light from the ceiling ate into each of Tora's features but left Sol's face up there alone in the dark shadows.

The rumors about Elisif also reached the pastor.

One Thursday morning there was a clear, mild southern dialect on the stairway. Tora recognized him by his accent. So did Sol. Einar up in the garret expressed himself by slamming his door harder than necessary, so he must have recognized the voice too.

Elisif had been in bed for almost three weeks, and the calendar was torn off far into January. Back when Elisif was young and worldly, she'd given birth to a girl whom she'd named, simply, in honor of the sun: Sol.

But there wasn't much sunlight in the fourteen year old's life. It was dark outside, and at home pitch black.

The pastor greeted them and sent Jørgen after Torstein. When he saw their important visitor, Torstein stood in the middle of the kitchen, silent, ashamed, twisting his cap in his hands. He couldn't even ask the pastor to sit down. His cap was turning like a wheel now. He stood there with all the things he wanted to tell the pastor, who had turned up now in the middle of their troubles. But it was as if his words couldn't make their way up and out. And he wasn't so sure that a wise and educated man would understand, anyway.

"It's all this religiousness of hers, this conversion. Take it from me, pastor, that's what all this madness is."

Now he'd said it, but the result was just what he'd feared: the pastor didn't understand the hint.

"Your wife is surely a good person and a devout Christian, I have no doubts on that score," the pastor said absently.

He'd been in and out of the sickroom quickly. Sickrooms were women's business. Of course he'd given what spiritual consolation he could, but the woman wasn't overly cooperative. She'd sung hymns the whole time. The pastor was understandably confused.

Finally he took Torstein out into the hall and closed the door behind them. He wanted to talk to Torstein alone.

The children would have to be sent away, the pastor asserted.

"But where?" Torstein worked up the courage to whisper.

The pastor hadn't figured that out yet, but a way would be found. That was a matter for the child welfare council. He, speaking as pastor could only make house calls and ascertain a great need for, and an absence of, a firm guardian's hand. A foster home was a necessity for a time.

Then he went back in and spoke kindly to the children, patted Sol on the head and asked her when she would be coming up for confirmation.

There were wide cracks in the doorways on all the landings, and ears and eyes in every corner. So in less than half an hour Torstein's and the pastor's conversation was well known throughout the Tenement. Torstein went back to his net mending and was grey from emotion under his stubble.

Tora and Sol finished the dishes.

They had a galvanized wash tub on a bench. On a big bucket lid on a stool up against the wash tub, Sol piled the scalding hot dishes, her movements calm and slow.

Tora wiped the plain dishes with a worn-out dish towel. It had been soaking wet a long time, but she made herself as invisible as she could and didn't want to ask for a dry one. Something told her that there probably wasn't a little pile of clean towels in the kitchen drawer, as there was downstairs in her mother's kitchen.

Sol's face was expressionless, the way it usually was when she had too much to think about. There were deep lines beneath her stringy bangs that were trimmed almost to the hair line. Her hands were unnaturally large. And that was a good thing.

Sol spent ages just on the laundry. She was the oldest, a girl—and nice besides. That was her curse in Sodom. She couldn't say no. Wasn't capable of real rebellion.

Tora put one of the little kids to work sweeping the floor.

He did it in his own way, but nobody scolded him on account of that. Tora cut some dried mutton into small pieces over on the counter, and Sol changed the smallest child.

Almost no words were spoken.

The hymn singing in the living room had stopped. So apparently she was sleeping.

Jørgen and Tor came in, ashamed and silent because everybody in the Tenement knew that the pastor had been at their

83

place. Finally Sol got all the little kids playing with the box of kindling, and the five older ones sat down at the kitchen table and shared the shame with one another over a big, hand-painted board game. They found buttons and broken matches and played partners. Sol and Tora won every time and that made Jørgen mad. That put some color in his face and gave him something to think about beside the fact that he was going to child protection.

Tora sat there feeling strangely content. Almost happy. She wasn't the only one who had a defect.

That night, when Tora and Sol went down to the village to buy milk, each with her swinging pail, Sol said in a confident voice,

"It's not going to happen!"

"What do you mean?"

"We aren't going to be sent away."

"Oh?" Tora was uncertain and didn't know what to say.

"Nobody'll take us, there's too many of us!"

"That's for sure!" Tora agreed.

They looked at each other. Then Sol started laughing. She laughed a kind of heartfelt laughter that surprised Tora. But she joined in. She could do that much, at least. And they swung their pails and ran down the hill.

The milk truck hadn't come, for snowdrifts had closed the roads over the mountain pass.

They stood in a crowd. All the kids and some old people. Huddled up against the wall in order to be in shelter. Above their heads was nailed a home-made sign: MILK OUTLET.

They pushed and shoved and gradually began to shiver, but thought up practical jokes to make the time pass. There were lots of people. Six just from the Tenement.

They waited and they froze—together.

Finally the truck arrived. The children from the Tenement had a remarkable talent for being first in line when the milk was dispensed from the top of the huge transport cans. Because the cream was at the top. The kids from the Tenement knew that without anyone having to tell them directly.

They paid from swollen hands or had the milk written down in the book that lay on the unpainted shelf of rough wood directly above the milk counter.

Chapter Fourteen

Sol was right.

There was no way to find foster parents for so many. At least not in the winter and on such short notice.

Four grown women turned and washed Elisif by force. But she wouldn't get up.

One day Ingrid sat down at her bedside and tried to talk to her about the dead baby. Elisif's eyes began to glow and she praised the Lord for His wisdom in that matter, so that cold chills ran up and down Ingrid's spine. The only person who could reach the poor creature beneath her pious surface was Sol.

A splashing thaw set in at the end of January. In the spring and fall there was always a great pushing and shoving for shoes and boots in the hallway outside Elisif's place. But this year it was just their luck that mild weather put an end to dry snow and mukluks in January!

Elisif stayed blissfully ignorant. Some mornings Torstein took a hand in distributing the shoes, but the results were rather poor. All four children could never be at school at the same time during a thaw. Sol saw to it that the absences were fairly evenly distributed. And she helped Jørgen, the slow learner, with his homework so he could get his share of Gunn's wisdom.

Otherwise, whoever was unfortunate enough to be last out of bed had to stay home in disgrace. Because one pair of adult shoes and two pair of cut-down boots were all the four eldest had at their disposal. The small kids were lucky enough to have inherited hand-me-downs, so they could get outdoors. But the big kids had four pair of equally big feet and three pair of shoes in all. Three of them went every day to the Manor and to Gunn's red correction marks.

Then Sol began staying home voluntarily, to do the housework and take care of the three small children and her mother. Torstein had his steady job mending nets and was seldom to be seen on the stairs.

Gunn never said anything about absences. But one day she arrived unannounced with her backpack full of books and assignments for Sol. In the long run that turned out to be the most practical solution.

She stayed in the stinking living room with Elisif a long time.

The next day Gunn made it clear, to the pastor, the child welfare council and to anybody else the village had in the way of well-meaning and competent men versed in law, that it wasn't the children who had to be taken away, it was Elisif who was sick and needed help.

What the midwife had called "witchcraft" and the pastor "an otherwise good woman's weakness with respect to her children," Gunn called a nervous breakdown, without even raising an eyebrow. She wrote formal letters, talked on the telephone—and got her way.

They found a place for Elisif somewhere in Bodø. Nobody said that place's name aloud.

But at Ottar's store, good people agreed, as they went about shopping for their margarine and coffee, that poor Elisif was crazy and had to be taken away.

They blamed the evangelist for it. He was probably going around someplace else right now, driving other simple women crazy. It was a shame that such people were allowed to run loose!

The day arrived. And Elisif had to be dressed and taken forcibly from her bed. Her shrill curses hailed down on Torstein, Gunn and Ingrid. Threats that the Lord would punish whosoever laid a hand on one of His children.

The nurse from Bodø had apparently seen worse cases, for he was as calm and as firm as a mountain and didn't acknowledge her with so much as a word in reply. Securely strapped into the transport basket, she broke down and started crying.

Sol had stayed out in the kitchen with the small children, but at the sound of her mother's crying she came into the living room. She stood for a little while in the middle of the room as if struggling with herself and then she went over to the basket. Bent over close to Elisif's face and whispered, "Mama, everything's going to be better for you where you're going. There are people there who have time to sing with you and read the Bible all day long. You'll be allowed to pray in peace, without anybody making fun of you, Mama. And when you're well again, we'll... we'll come and get you. Honest! Here's your manna seeds, Mama.... "

She slid a greasy grey paper bag under Elisif's blanket and held out her hand to say goodbye. She had a closed, old woman's face as she stood there. You couldn't see a smile or a tear.

The grownups turned away for a moment. They'd watched and listened to a fourteen-year-old adult, with eyes that were much too old and a name that taunted her. Sol!

Chapter Fifteen

ONE DAY GUNN SAT AT HER DESK AND TALKED about—hate. Tora tried to feel hate.

It wasn't in her. Not the way Gunn described it. Where hate was supposed to be she felt only emptiness. Emptiness—like staring at the brand-new sun until tiny blurred circles flickered in front of her eyes and the sunshine turned white and meaningless.

Gunn talked to them about war.

Tora cringed and got busy rearranging her pencil box, her head bent over. She waited for the German word. Only wanted to get it over with.

"Atomic war!" Gunn said. "That's worse than anything else mankind has ever done. All grownups who keep up with what's going on in the world are afraid that there's going to be an atomic war."

And she held forth about atomic explosions and their horrible effects. One atomic explosion had glowed as brightly as a hundred suns. Had hung like a fireball against the sky 15,000 meters above the Nevada desert. And everything around it grew radioactive!

Tora let her body relax at the old desk she shared with Sol. She put her damp palms in her lap and felt unspeakably relieved.

Atomic war! That was much worse than the Germans! Gunn had just said it so everybody could hear.

Without any reason at all, without even being really hungry, Tora looked forward to the food in her blue tin lunchbox and the swallow of milk in her bottle. Became so warm and light inside, whenever she looked at Gunn.

The same day Ingrid told her she'd been rehired by the plant on condition that she take night shifts again, Gunn mentioned that the cod had arrived at the fishing banks at Vesterål. At Øveregga they'd already got a fine catch.

Then Tora realized that her mother would be working long night shifts. . . .

She stared straight into her teacher's face until she saw Grandma's aristocratic head float right into the collar of Gunn's blouse.

Tora sat stiff as a post and stared until she was able to believe that the day had a little warmth in it after all.

Nobody's cat.

Nobody cared.

The cat was lost in its own shame.

Finally it was dragged down into the ditch.

Chapter Sixteen

THE MEN IN OTTAR'S STORE WERE SWEARING THAT NOW there'd have to be tax-free gasoline for the fishermen.

Several of them had set themselves up as big shots by buying fifteen or twenty nylon nets, confident that the fish would come.

A third of the fish caught in nets were brought up in nylon nets last year.

Almar dragged thoughtfully on his cigarette, squinted straight at the shelves, and said savagely, "Well, there won't be much to fish for anyway, pretty soon. The purse seiners have been fishing up all the mature fish for years, there's just immature pollack left. They've scared the cod half way around the ocean, so they don't dare open their mouths to swallow the bait. The purse seiners have got in the way of the poor long liners, they've split the cod shoals into bits, so the other fishermen haven't been able to find anything but scraps."

Almar took another drag, loudly and meaningfully.

"But they're not letting the purse seiners in Hopsteigen," Ottar put in cautiously.

"Yeah, so the little guys, who can't scrape up the capital for a sixty-footer with purse seine and echo sounder, they'll be able to fish to their hearts' content, just like in a fairy tale. Huh! In an area the size of a postage stamp!"

Two of the men from Simon's crew got busy carrying out the box of provisions. They couldn't waste time arguing with the old man from Hestvika when he was in that mood.

But one of the men couldn't restrain himself anyway. When he came back to get the oil can he wasn't able to carry on his first trip, he flung through the partly open door, as he left, "Almar, of course, can go on strike! What's to stop him? Then he can live off the interest he gets from what he earns at the school. *He* doesn't have to invest an arm and a leg and then bleed when the fish vanish!" The other men left Almar in peace after this outburst. They turned dutifully to the counter and Ottar and started gossiping about other things.

"Dahl's going to need more workers next week. He's expecting a boat that's taking on fish for the U.S.A."

That was good news.

But the hand liners scowled, even though they didn't take up arms openly. And bitter words passed across the oilcloth in the shacks. The fight spread all through the village, even into kitchen corners. Wives took sides, kids flung dirty words and noses bled as it gradually became apparent that there were two sides. On the one hand, those who sided with the purse seiners. On the other, all the rest.

It got serious sometimes. At the youth center you didn't dare even mention fishing on Saturdays, because it could so easily result in a fight.

Meanwhile, 783 purse seiners received licenses for the season, and the drift netters, long liners and hand liners carried on like yeast without dough to work in. They threatened to stay home in comfort with their wives if the authorities didn't postpone the date for legal purse seining.

The men had big, restless hands in their pockets. The times were uncertain. Even so, a few of them went so far as to purchase a radio, wherever the money for that came from.

The wind increased steadily and the good Lord arranged shore leave thanks to the bad weather, with plenty of time for radio listening. Even though it wasn't exactly welcome for those who were looking to make a profit.

Opinions were divided as to whether it was the Good Lord or the Evil One who was responsible for the price of fish. Someone blamed it on a couple of big shots down in Oslo. Cod from Lofoten was getting sixty-seven øre, while pollack and haddock were still bringing only sixty-one.

The women sighed over the price of coffee. But they were

grateful, as long as the storm didn't take lives or boats. In Finnmark, six boats had disappeared.

Good Lord! You shouldn't complain about prices. . . .

Down at Dahl's plant, everything was going full speed ahead. Dahl wasn't a hard taskmaster. But he liked the work to move along. It was best for all concerned. Especially for those who sat at the packing table and got paid by the piece instead of the hour. He never neglected an opportunity to let the foreman remind "the ladies" of this fact. As for himself, he kept in the background on such occasions.

Cross-eyed Håkon, the foreman, didn't relish the task much and didn't carry it out too sternly. He was a sociable man and well-liked. He consoled and cheered the women up when the work slowed down for some reason or other and their output fell so that they earned less than thirteen *kroner*.

The men got their fixed salary of fifteen *kroner* and fifty *øre*.

But the wheels turned—that was the main thing. And the women who'd managed to get their boot-warmed feet in the packing room could count themselves lucky. Frida, Greta, Hansine and Ingrid knew it. They took turns washing their hands in the cracked basin. Worked the soap in thoroughly to get rid of the worst of the smell while they ate their sandwiches.

An entire, precious half-hour!

The lunch room had just enough room for the six tube chairs and the big, square table with the plastic surface. There was a washbasin and mirror by the door. They saw a kind of grey, formless shadow of themselves in it when they put on their white caps or ran their combs through their hair at the end of their shifts.

The light over the table, on the other hand, shone on the defenseless, pale faces and turned every line into a poorly-healed operation scar, and every pimple into a loathsome, unappetizing challenge.

Ingrid pulled off her cap and sank down on the bench over her dented thermos. She listened absently to Greta's coarse bantering with Frida.

Chewing. One-syllable words. Wrap both hands around the grey bakelite cup to warm them.

The first few minutes there wasn't breath enough for anything else.

The four hours, with short five-minute breaks, had lodged in their shoulders and necks and lay like a film over their eyes.

After a while, Frida spoke a word or two. Dahl wasn't the worst, she said. And he didn't pay the worst, either.

Half the lunch break was over. The draft from the doors and small windows stung their legs. Greta was much too lightly dressed, Ingrid thought contemptuously. She liked to show off her figure.

Hansine went to the toilet. Greta mumbled something about how they should get someone who could work faster on the shift.

Hansine slowed up the work, lowered everybody's earnings.

The other two exchanged glances, chewed, said nothing. Voices could be heard from out in the hall, some of the men came in. Ingrid felt an enormous relief. She wasn't up to listening to Greta's attacks on Hansine today.

The fish lay in piles and were there to be packed, that was the important thing for Ingrid tonight. It didn't help much that it was Saturday and the men could get off work.

Ingrid knew that she wasn't the only one who had work waiting at home.

Frida mentioned that she hadn't managed to do her laundry before she left because one of her kids had got sick to his stomach and she had to take care of him. She had her sick mother living with her, and her husband was out fishing.

Hansine had a cow with inflamation of the udder. She lived on the other side of the bay and her old bike had a flat tire. It was going to be a long night for her if she didn't get somebody to row her across.

"We're going to earn a lot this time."

Greta was chattering with the men. Crossed one nylon-covered leg over the other and stuck out her breasts. She always removed her woolen long johns during the breaks. Ingrid sat there, wondering where she got her zest and stamina. Good Lord!

But she was the only unmarried one among them. She had a child, but he lived with his grandmother at Breiland. Greta was free as a bird.

The words stabbed Ingrid: "Free as a bird!"

"Tomorrow I'm going to take the morning off, damn it, see if I don't! With coffee and Danish! Anyway, I should have been a man!" Greta was in top form tonight. She inhaled her store-bought cigarette with great energy and looked meaningfully at the youngest of the men.

"What do you mean?" he asked.

"I'm thinking of the fileter—who doesn't have to slave away on Saturday nights with the taste of blood in his mouth for miserable piecework pay."

"Are you starting in on that again?" said Hansine, who had just come back in. She stood leaning against the wash basin because there wasn't a chair for her. One of the men offered her his knee. Hansine laughed and refused.

"You'll have to get yourself some different equipment above the knees and quit dolling yourself up like that. Then Dahl might think you're a man and give you men's work to do," said the oldest of the men with a grin.

Greta's face stiffened for a second. Something hard and ugly spread over her features.

"Sure, you think it's right that only someone with a pouch hanging between his legs gets an hourly wage."

There was a drop of spit in each corner of Greta's mouth. Her eyes were flashing. She completely forgot to stick out her nylon-covered legs. She ground her cigarette out in the tin ashtray so violently that the ashes flew over onto Hansine's cheese sandwich. The men got up and went out laughing.

"You ought to get yourself a steady man. Then you wouldn't have to work for a living and take the place of someone who *likes* to earn money!" came a voice from out in the hall.

Ingrid saw to her amazement that Greta was close to tears.

"What Greta says is true," she heard herself say. "It's us

women who sit here with the fish when the men take a day off. There should've been five of us packing."

"Yeah, but there *are* only the four of us," Frida said wearily.

"Is that something to just accept?" Greta replied angrily. "Don't we have a foreman we can complain to?"

Frida got ready to go. Their break was nearly over.

"We're not organized. He doesn't have any obligation to represent us," said Ingrid despondently.

"You let yourselves be bullied, just like idiots!" Greta said with a snort.

"Don't you?" snarled Frida.

The room became silent.

"If you'd only stop sucking on those butts, so the rest of us could eat our sandwiches without ashes and having to listen to you mouth off, then things would've gone a lot better for us with the packing."

Greta turned to her quickly, her face oddly vulnerable. But she didn't say anything else.

"I think we're tired. It'll be better if we keep quiet now. We have to pull the load together, no matter how much we snap at each other. It mustn't come to such a point that we use our breaks to go for each other's throats."

Hansine looked imploringly at the others.

Greta was the last one out of the lunch room.

"Men aren't chased away when there's no fish," she called after them.

"Men are the breadwinners," Frida hollered back.

"So am I!" yelled Greta, and got the last word.

Then she took revenge on the cigarette butt she'd already put out. She ground it, crushed it, crumbled it down in the tin ashtray.

When Ingrid came out into the hall, she realized that it had been warmer in the lunch room than she'd thought. The draft out here came from everywhere. Icy-cold and clammy.

It made her angry in a way she couldn't understand. She stood there and waited for Greta just out of spite. Felt miserable and discouraged. But deep inside she was climbing up onto a plank of fury. *That* was Greta's doing.

"I just want a bit of life too," Greta explained when she caught up with Ingrid. "Can you understand that, Ingrid?"

"Yes, I understand it. And so do the others. It's just that they don't have the strength. I'm a breadwinner too, you know," she added quietly.

Greta was stunned. Such confidences didn't come from Ingrid every day. She gave Ingrid a friendly nudge in the back and said firmly,

"It'd be nice if we could see each other outside of these walls too, Ingrid. I think we're birds of a feather."

Ingrid smiled.

"Maybe so. . . . "

"I want a life and a little luxury. I've been thinking of buying a fur coat. Yes, I mean it. Then I'm going to walk through the village in a fur, one I've bought myself! Then they'll see, those lice! I've seen them advertised in the newspaper. 'Brown and black silk-seal coats: 400 *kroner*. Highest quality: 850 *kroner*.' It'll have to be one of the cheaper ones, I suppose," she added.

Her face was glowing and her glance slipped away from Ingrid and drifted off on a daydream.

The *Torstein Jarl* lay at the dock for loading. Ingrid glanced out there as they hurried past the last window in the narrow hall. So *some* of the men at least would have to put off their Saturday night plans.

Chapter Seventeen

ALMAR FROM HESTVIKA WAS THE OWNER OF A TWENTY-two-foot motor cruiser.

He'd had it for many years and learned that it was a precious everyday instrument in the wet hands of the Lord.

It wasn't exactly spic-and-span at all times. But the motor was always kept in running order.

Almar fished a little on the side. You couldn't keep body and soul together just being custodian at the Manor.

In Almar's opinion, he who earned his bread working for the village wasn't meant to eat it too. You should put away what you got for Christmas one year so you'd have something to eat the next.

Thanks anyway, Almar said, and fished.

Besides, the boat was a good thing to have if anybody had to go into Storøya or over to the mainland on the days the mail boat didn't run. Sometimes babies came out of their mothers feet first, or in some other position the old midwife couldn't handle.

Then faithful Almar was of use. It wasn't a good idea to count on what you didn't have until the mail boat arrived, he thought, and started up his motor.

He'd thought for a long time that he should buy a new and better boat, but money didn't grow on the bushes in the garden, so nothing came of the idea. But it was a great shame that the superstructure was so small and open that women in labor often had to lie with their feet sticking out of the narrow cabin door in the cold breeze.

Down below was the rank odor of diesel fuel, boiled coffee,

grease and an evil-smelling ship's stove.

On the trapezoid-shaped table in the bow, with the narrow brown-painted benches on either side, the oilcloth was scarred and cracked. You could just barely make out that once it had had a dense pattern of roses on it. The outer layer had flaked off so that the weave in the cloth made its own dirty brown pattern here and there.

Over the stove hung the same red-checked kitchen towel—always. It had acquired the colors of life's trials and was a part of the boat's inventory.

Nobody ever said anything about it, except Rachel.

"I gave you a new kitchen towel for Christmas, Almar. What've you done with it?"

"Well," Almar answered, "It was so nice that I've got it at home, in a drawer."

"Yes, but it said on the box that it was for the boat!"

Almar hemmed and hawed. "That's what it said all right, but...."

"I'm not drinking coffee on this boat if I can't wash my cup and dry it. With a clean towel! You can see that, can't you?"

"*I* don't give a damn!"

"You're not mad that I said it, are you Almar?"

"Huh!"

"You are getting mad, I can see it in your eyes. Don't be silly!"

"Huh!"

Rachel tried to make things better again. She promised a towel for the drawer and one for the boat. She would even sew a monogram on it, she joked.

But Almar started his engine with an angry jerk and headed out of the bay at full speed.

They had come all the way to the farthest buoy before he turned and hollered down into the cabin.

"Have you got the kettle on, Ingrid?"

He didn't look over to where Rachel was sitting.

Rachel peered up at him, trying to needle him,

"You've got a big piece of ocean to be gruff on!"

Almar ignored the remark and turned the wheel, aggravated. Tora was no longer enjoying herself. It wasn't a good idea to tease Almar, she knew that from before.

She didn't want anything to ruin this trip.

Rachel was going to Breiland to have her teeth fixed, and she didn't want to go alone. Ingrid didn't have work the rest of the week anyway, and Rachel was paying for the trip. She'd spoken with Gunn and got Tora excused from school.

Her aunt was wearing her wide coat with the big checks. She looked fine, Tora thought.

Then she glanced quickly at her mother's old-fashioned made-over coat. It was newly ironed and the spot on the hem had been carefully removed the night before. But it was somehow still there anyway, Tora thought. As if everybody they'd meet at Breiland today would surely *see* the spot and think, "Wasn't there a spot, right there?"

Rachel had stylish rubbers on over her shoes. "Polars," they were called, and they were green. Her mother was wearing boots. Wide and short and with wool linings. The same ones she used at the packing plant. Tora thought people would be able to smell them a long way off.

Was she ashamed? Of her mother? No! But she felt weak inside when she saw the difference between her aunt and her mother.

Tora had a homemade jacket on over the dress she got for Christmas.

Her dark-blue wool long underwear had idiotic seams on the inside and hung in pleats like an accordion down her legs, even though she had hitched it up all the way under her arms.

It didn't make much difference. There wasn't anybody to compare herself to in Almar's motorboat.

But she could wish that her mother dressed nicer. Could wish that she had a mother like—Aunt Rachel.

Sparks seemed to fly around Aunt Rachel. It wasn't just her clothes. She was so full of life, always. Whether she was angry or in a good mood. She radiated energy. All eyes turned to her when she came into a room. Tora had seen that happen more than once.

It was unfair! Even though she wished the best for her aunt. If only her mother were a little bit happier....

Was it really that simple? Did happiness make people beautiful?

They'd come out as far as the small islands now. Almar lashed the wheel and came down the steps to get his coffee.

The boat rocked violently.

The coffee cup was big and deep and only half filled, but it slopped over onto the oilcloth anyway.

Almar picked up a lump of sugar between two rough fingers that would never be the color of skin again. He'd stoked and oiled all his life and he'd taken on the color of it, body and soul.

The snow-white lump of sugar looked strangely foreign between his stubs of yellow teeth. But it quickly took on the same color as the man, for he sucked his coffee pleasurably through it with a mouth like a greedy funnel.

Tora sat there staring until Ingrid nudged her with her elbow. The others also got their share of the bitter coffee. Almar stuck a rusty spoon in the can of powdered milk and, with a generous hand, sprinkled a lot of the strange, white powder into Tora's cup.

"Reserved for young ladies," he joked, half-opening his mouth in a smile.

Then he disappeared back up to his helm and had his hands full. The two women could finally talk undisturbed, under cover of the motor's roar.

Tora supported herself on the bench with her palms flat against the hard wooden seat and her fingers turned out. That way she could keep her balance in the steadily increasing roll. The rhythm seemed to spread to her thighs and her hands and held her safely in place. Her feet reached all the way to the floor this year. Last year, when she went with her mother to Vestbygda, she could remember that she'd had to stretch her toes to reach all the way.

The rush of water past the bow and the monotonous pounding made her sleepy. It was just dawn, not yet six. The bus was what determined when they should start. And Almar always gave himself plenty of time. He was slow and thorough. Would sooner sit half an hour out on the water, idling, and wait for the bus, than damage the engine by driving it too hard.

In this way he had to be both chauffeur and waiting room.

Because ashore there wasn't even a shed to hide behind as you searched the road for the red monster of a bus that would take you further.

Almar had already been up a long time, lighting the school stoves, by the time he came down to the boat.

Gunn had agreed to get up a little earlier and take over the job of keeping the stoves going through the morning. She was better about things like that than the old teacher. He'd been so sickly and delicate all his life that it wasn't fitting to ask him for a helping hand with anything that didn't have something to do with reading and writing. Mostly he just walked up and down the rows of desks and blew his nose in clean hankerchiefs, in Almar's opinion.

Now two women had taken over from the old teacher. It was because people were starting to reproduce so prodigiously that one teacher wasn't enough any more.

One of the two ladies seemed to have been cast from the same mold as the old teacher. Not much for talking to. But then they'd also got this fine girl from the south. Always smiling. Small and plump and funny. She came right out and laughed! He'd even heard that she laughed when she was in the classroom with the kids!

Sometimes she was walking around wearing nothing but her nightgown in the cold hall when he came out after starting the stoves.

But she called "Good morning!" just as if she were fully dressed in both skirt and sweater.

She was blessedly down-to-earth in that way.

Almar idolized her in the depths of his heart and he guarded that feeling carefully so that nobody could take it away from him.

He brought her rosefish and cod, depending on the season. Once she'd called him in and asked him to teach her how to cook fresh fish the Nordland way. Almar never forgot that moment. It stayed like a colored picture inside the rough hide of his head. Yes, it even passed through his well-worn circulatory system and all around in his thickset, tough body.

And he didn't blab much about it, except to mention it, more or less in passing, to acquaintances. But he avoided making anything special out of it, just as a good hunter doesn't mention the good grouse thickets by name.

Gunn was to Almar like a Sunday in summer. He needed her.

Almar felt far from old. He was forty-seven last October, and he could stand in his own boat and think his own thoughts.

It felt like riding a horse.

Tora followed the rocking with her whole body. She leaned heavily back against the sloping side of the bow and placed the soles of her boots solidly on the table support.

They'd come all the way out to the mouth of the fjord. The ocean came pushing over the flat spits of land out there. Nothing stood in its way anymore. Tora felt a little bit sick deep down in her stomach.

It was stiflingly warm in the cabin. The boat stove roared merrily. Between the rusty iron rings she could see a flicker of open flame now and then, when the fire got some oil from the tank.

Aunt Rachel had quieted down. She was almost as pale as Ingrid always was.

Tora looked at her aunt and wondered if she were feeling sick. It was strange, but she'd never considered the possibility that her aunt might have any weaknesses. She was equal to any situation. Cheerful, quick to answer. She could always straighten out difficulties and turn black to white. This was probably the first time she and her aunt had been on a boat together in a heavy sea.

Rachel was always rushing here and there on shopping trips and visiting all her acquaintances and family.

It was as if Rachel had more relatives than Ingrid and Tora, even though they were in the same family.

Ingrid and Tora seldom went anywhere.

In the summer, Tora would sometimes borrow a rowboat from one of the old men on the wharves and row out among the small islands.

Row and row until her hands burned and the open sea came at her like a troll. Shoving at the boat with broad, stealthy slow-moving ridges, even when the weather was calm. Eerie and magnificent at the same time.

Sometimes she sobbed for joy even though she was all alone, if the waves came at her too suddenly and she didn't dare row any farther out but didn't dare turn the boat to the waves either for the moment it took to turn around.

Her mother never knew about those trips. It wasn't worth the bother.

Oh yes, Rachel was sick. She leaned her head against the wall and swallowed heavily several times.

"I shouldn't have drunk that coffee," she mumbled and tried to smile.

"Are you sick?" Ingrid was concerned. She used the same whining voice as when something was wrong at home. Tora started to shake inside when she realized that her mother had brought that voice with her on the trip.

"Yes, you know how I am," Rachel said miserably.

"I'd forgotten." Ingrid was surprised at herself. "It's been so long since the two of us have been out travelling together."

Rachel managed to nod. Didn't have the strength for anything else. Seeing Aunt Rachel like that was completely contrary to nature.

Ingrid was sitting just as pale as always, her back straight and her hands holding her worn purse. She looked calm, almost happy, in spite of her concerned, whining voice. It was a long time between outings like this for Ingrid. But if Rachel absolutely insisted on having company and paid for the entire trip, then Henrik couldn't object.

Ingrid's eyes were a little blurred, but in a different way from Rachel's. Ingrid was at ease and a little tired. She was in Almar's boat and, unexpectedly, letting life surge within her.

Tora was becoming so full inside from looking at her. Felt like she was bubbling over. For a long time she forgot her aunt. Just sat there quietly and honed in secretly on her mother's face.

Rachel got to her feet abruptly and staggered up the three steps to the deck. She almost shoved Almar out of the way and hadn't come any farther than sticking her head out the doorway when everything that was in her somehow slid out. She vomited heavily and with a great many horrible noises. It sounded as if it were coming from another world, from some other Rachel.

Ingrid jumped up and rushed after her. Tora followed. When she came on deck, her mother was supporting Rachel, holding tightly on to her and the low railing. Rachel was nearly doubled over in her misery. Just involuntary retching noises were coming out now. She was empty, working her way through it, trying to calm her stomach.

Ingrid got her to sit down on the hatch cover. Grabbed a tarpaulin, and tucked it around her sister, as protection against the worst of the spray. Then she tied her own scarf around Rachel's hat and didn't notice that her own hair came undone and blew like spray around her head.

"Now, now, the worst is over. Sit here and rest a little in the fresh air. It'll be better now that everything's out. It's all right, it's all right. . . . "

Tora sat down next to them and put her arm around her aunt on the other side. They sat like that, the three of them, under the tarpaulin as the sea splashed over the small deck. Came in under the railing on one side and sloshed out on the other. Now and then Almar had to cut the speed and wait out a big wave. They heard it in advance and dreaded it for Rachel's sake. Ingrid sat there, thin and assured. Tora thought she could feel her mother's tough strength straight through her aunt's body.

They ought to sit on a hatch cover on a little boat all their lives, Tora thought. In a strong wind—like now.

The bow dug into the sea as if searching for something down there. Something it had lost or left behind, some other time.

Then, like a curious sea creature, it came up again, and got more slaps from the elements than it was prepared for. Turned aside first, then moved to the left, to the right. Wanted to turn its side to the storm and cover itself.

But Almar was also a force in there on his helmsman's step. He kept on the lookout for sudden gusts and anticipated them. Eased the helm and stayed down in the troughs waiting. That was enough. That was what was needed.

They were thrown up on the next wave but that was all right. The sea foamed over the deck. Over her aunt's new rubbers. Splashed on their legs and made dark stains on their knees where the tarpaulin was blown aside. Made their salt-stung eyes run and stiffened their faces.

Tora's hands were completely numb inside her new, thin gloves. They weren't meant for this. They were only for looks. But she was happy and warm inside anyway.

Mama had taken charge of everything! She was a different person from who she was at home. Here she even took care of Aunt Rachel! She was like a queen, Tora thought. Born again gloriously in the storm with her thick hair waging a battle with the wind.

Yes, that was exactly what she was: born again!

It had nothing to do with the prayer meetings. It was just a matter of being strong and invincible inside yourself and taking care of things without having to beg.

A heavy drop of water hung from her mother's chin. Tora noticed that she ignored it, just stared calmly into the distance and the storm. Tora sat there shivering but she was burning hot.

"It's getting rough. But you'll catch your bus, don't worry! You shouldn't be sitting out there in the storm freezing to death. Come back inside even if you have to throw up. It's safest with the women and children inside in weather like this!"

Almar had poked his head out the cabin door. He was shouting consoling words at them through the heavy spray. Sleet lashed at them in between times but they didn't notice. The spray was soaking them anyway.

Then! Right between the lighthouse and the strip of land, high up in the raging sky, Tora could see a single, blinking star in the spray. It was a miracle. A sign of change. An omen. . . .

She followed the boat and the motion of the waves with her whole body, let herself be thrown wildly along. The nausea was gone. The wind and the sea seemed to blow straight through her head. She felt it press on her eyelids, sting her cheeks, bite her earlobes. Her mouth was open and she could clearly taste the strange, salt taste of ocean. The strange, salt taste of death. But it wasn't frightening anymore.

Tora sat there and hoarded the certainty, the certainty that her mother had undergone a change. After this, everything was sure to be different. For Mama was stronger than Aunt Rachel when it counted!

Chapter Eighteen

"**I**F THIS WEATHER DOESN'T GET BETTER I'M NOT GOING back home today!"

Rachel fussed with her hat and brushed off wet snow as she climbed into the steaming bus. She looked pale and nauseated and picked up several of the little grey bags lying in the luggage net at the front of the bus.

The driver grinned. He'd seen worse than this and heard the same comments from people coming off the boat.

"Well," he said, "we don't rock nearly as much on board the bus, if that's any consolation."

He waited patiently as Rachel rummaged for her coin purse and counted out the correct change.

A bunch of boys on their way to the fishing station at South Fjord to work cutting cod tongues thought the line was moving too slowly. They kept bumping Tora in the back. Ingrid stepped between them.

Tora felt a sudden warmth for her.

And as she sat next to her mother on the wet seat and the bus rushed them on their way, she felt as if she'd been lifted from the earth and was flying to heaven.

Just her and Mama—and Aunt Rachel.

Rachel stuck to her guns. They weren't going back home today! Storm warnings were out.

They were sitting in the dentist's pale green waiting room and Rachel had just had her aching molar filled. That was enough for one day, in her opinion.

Ingrid tried to reason with her, the way you try to reason

with the children of your betters. Nicely but firmly. Coaxingly.

But now Rachel was her old self again. She hadn't been seasick for several hours. She made decisions and arranged things, the way she was used to doing.

Tora had to go to school and Henrik would be furious! And what were they going to do with themselves? Where would they stay? They didn't have any relatives here in Breiland.

"I'll get us a hotel room," Rachel answered calmly and put on her hat in front of the mirror.

Ingrid's mouth dropped open a moment as she stared at her sister.

"My God, Rachel! Have you lost your mind?"

"No, and I'm not going to, either," Rachel replied.

Rachel got her way. With Tora and Ingrid in tow she plowed through the storm to the town's only hotel. She planted one hand firmly on her hip, the way she liked to stand, and telephoned home.

Simon would just have to go down and tell Gunn and Henrik. Rachel tossed her red hair and with that was finished with the whole island. While she was on the phone, Tora and Ingrid sat on fancy chairs in front of the long reception desk in the lobby and waited.

Ingrid grumbled a little in a low voice about Rachel's crazy idea. Tora ignored her mother's whining tone. Wouldn't let it force its way in. It was probably just a little piece of her old mother still hanging on.

The woman behind the counter had thick glasses perched on the tip of a sharp nose. She was listening shamelessly to everything being said on the phone in the back room.

Tora thought she looked like the owl in the school reader. Her nose stuck out of her face like a beak and her eyes darted watchfully over them every so often.

As if she intended to make sure they didn't take anything and disappear. She watched them closely and mercilessly over her thick lenses. Took stock of their boots and the old coat. Studied the spots of snow and dirty slush and let her eyes rest on the loose strands of Ingrid's hair that were coming out of her kerchief, and on Tora's ravaged braids. Now and then she rearranged herself comfortably in her chair so that she could view the entire scene more clearly. The desk was high and she was short.

Nothing, though, could take away Tora's joy, the joy of knowing that Mama had changed.

Let the owl glare! All of a sudden she started to giggle, and Ingrid poked her in the side. The woman behind the desk jumped at the sound and shot a look at Tora.

"What is it?" Ingrid whispered nervously, as if she were afraid somebody would throw them out while Rachel was on the phone.

"Nothing, I'm just laughing."

"Stop being silly!"

The silk wallpaper and the painting on the wall across from them turned suddenly grey and faded in Tora's eyes.

"No, absolutely not, this will be much too expensive for Simon!"

Ingrid hung her coat and sat down perplexed on the edge of the wide hotel bed.

"For Simon! What do you mean—do you think it's Simon who's paying for this? Who says so?"

Rachel was bending over her large suitcase and getting out the little things she would need to freshen up.

"Well, who else?" Ingrid asked, staring at her.

"Me, that's who!" Rachel said, and straightened up.

They exchanged quick glances. It was as if they'd forgotten Tora was there.

"What're you saying? That you've got money of your own?" Ingrid whispered in disbelief.

"I should say so. I take what I've earned for this and that."

"Honestly, you don't know what you're saying!"

Ingrid had recovered from her shock and scoffed at her sister's arrogance.

"I pay myself what I'm worth for some of the things I do. At home I clean the house and keep everything in order. I take care of the sheep and the potatoes. I weave and sew. I even do the floors down at the fishing station and Simon's office too. Including those filthy hallways."

"For *that?*" Ingrid broke in, irritated. "The kind of work every woman does for herself and her family! That wasn't what I meant."

"But that was what *I* meant."

Rachel turned and faced Ingrid. One of her eyebrows was considerably higher than the other and her voice was almost angry.

"Can you tell me why I shouldn't pay myself what I'm worth for honest work Simon would have to pay some other woman to do if I didn't do it? If I weren't his wife? Can you?"

Tora looked from one to the other in bewilderment and wished they would stop arguing.

"Do you mean to tell me that you demanded a salary?" Ingrid asked, and laughed harshly. It was becoming too unbelievable for her.

"I didn't *demand*. I'm the one who figures out the budget and does the bookkeeping. Not down at the station, of course. I figure a certain salary for myself, depending on how much we have. And it's not a very big salary, either, I can tell you that! But I have to be able to have something that's mine. I have to be able to tell myself that I can afford this or that. I can't ask Simon for every penny. I'd go crazy. And so would Simon!"

Rachel was laughing now.

"So, that's what it's like to have enough money to...."

Ingrid mumbled the words into the air, as if she didn't mean for Rachel to hear them, as if she were talking about something she'd read in a magazine so unrelated to her life that she didn't want to bother her head with it.

"Well, we can't just stand here all afternoon talking like fools. We're going to have fun, we three women. Let's freshen up a little and go down and have dinner."

Rachel bustled back and forth in the room, getting ready. But Tora could see that Aunt Rachel had been stung by her mother's last words.

"There's a bathroom in the hall," Rachel said. "Before we go to bed tonight, let's all take baths, all right? But now I'm so hungry I could eat a horse."

They had meat. Chops! And dessert afterwards. They'd have coffee later.

They were alone in the dining room. Tora thought that the chandelier hanging up there from the ceiling was a fairy tale all by itself. Every once in a while she had to lean her head all the way back and really *see*. . . .

That's the way it must be in Berlin. . . .

The wallpaper, the lamps on the walls, all the doors, the colors, the prints and paintings. Tora took it all in and was deathly afraid she would overlook or forget something. She felt herself becoming new as she sat there, as though she saw and smelled things in a completely different way from when she was at home.

Then, in a flash, she saw her mother and herself in the middle of all this. Saw that they didn't fit. They were strangers here. . . .

And deep inside she felt a ripping, something she had to keep from tearing all the way.

She couldn't help it that she remembered, suddenly, the shopping trips to Ottar's store. Sat there and all at once felt shabby and dirty, even though she knew her clothes had been clean that morning before they left. People were different. Life was different *for* people too!

They ventured out into the storm again. That wasn't hard, when they were dry and full and they knew they had a place to spend the night.

Rachel wanted to buy a few "little things," as she called them. At one store she bought a pullover sweater and some yarn.

In a window Tora saw some jackets. Blue. They were fifty-nine *kroner* each. She looked down at her worn-out jacket, homemade out of cambric. The other kids called her the Ghost. Her jacket was white.

The other two chatted their way down the street so that she

had to run to catch up. They hadn't even seen the jackets. Tora knew better than to nag her mother about it. Oh, to be able to afford one of those! Not to mention a pair of new gabardine ski pants. A couple of the girls in the village had them. The sleek material glistened when they were at school and the girls moved under the lights. And such beautiful shadows fell across the material when you looked closely. And the snow fell off almost by itself.

They went into a yard goods store. Rachel wanted to buy some new material for a blouse. She discussed it with the clerk and decided on some green polka dot material. It looked as gauzy as a cobweb, thought Tora.

Ingrid was standing by herself at the end of the counter, holding some reddish-brown dress material. Her fingers were sliding carefully across the fuzzy cloth and she was lost in her own thoughts.

When her material was measured and cut, Rachel turned to her sister and started to say something.

It was as if she suddenly *saw* Ingrid.

A kind of tenderness rushed over her round face. Her eyes closed halfway and she tried to say something. For a moment her lips trembled.

"That's really nice material. It would look good on you, Ingrid."

"Twelve fifty a yard," said the clerk without being asked. She looked at them expectantly.

Ingrid looked away as if she'd been caught doing something illegal.

"Yes," was all she said, and she pulled on her gloves to go. Rachel stared at the material for a minute and then looked directly at the clerk and said, "It's hard to get hold of material you really like nowadays. I'll take three yards of that."

Ingrid didn't move—just stood there. She clasped and unclasped her hands, over and over. The bare fingers of her right hand in the gloved fingers of her left.

Then she cleared her throat and said, "You'd look better in something green, like that—up there.... "

She pointed randomly up at the shelves.

Rachel quickly looked up at Ingrid's face. It affected Tora

strangely that Rachel was so much shorter than Mama that she had to look up at her to meet her eyes. It was supposed to be that way, she thought.

The change.

"And thread and a zipper in the same color," Rachel said quickly to the clerk.

"Ingrid, let me use your back. . . . " She grabbed the tape measure on the counter.

"I'm so much taller than you," Ingrid objected in a low voice.

But Rachel didn't reply, just measured from the nape of her neck down. Then she told the clerk how long the zipper should be. Ingrid's eyes moved up and down the shelves, aimlessly, seeing nothing.

Once they were safely back in their hotel room, Rachel gave the package of material to her sister and said, "Payment in advance for the house cleaning you'll be doing for me this spring. And a little something for all the rags you've cut up for my rugs."

Ingrid's eyes filled with tears.

Tora watched the two women hug each other.

That's what they did when Grandma died too, she thought, surprised. But that was a long time ago.

"You're so kind, I'll never be able to make it up to you—all this. And it's so unnecessary and so expensive. Henrik is going to. . . . "

"To hell with men!" Rachel interrupted her cheerfully. "You deserve it. Besides, what you said today is true. It's easy enough for me to talk about spending and paying out and giving myself a little salary. Simon has a good income. That's the whole difference! I suppose that's the only difference. We're sisters, after all. And it's a pleasure for me to give this to you. Don't deny me this pleasure. And I don't have any children, either . . . I have only you two."

Rachel stopped abruptly. Got her handkerchief out of her coat pocket and blew her nose.

Tora was stunned. She didn't know what to do with her hands, even though nobody was looking at her or appeared to care what she did with them. It was as if something delicate and shining grew out of the walls and floor, came flying from the ceiling and spread over them. As if the whole world were made of glass. You couldn't move, you couldn't take a step because if you did everything could so easily break. She felt the twilight in the room like cotton around her body. She heard the two women talking quietly together about everyday things. Tora was standing by the window and she let their voices flow into her without understanding the words. They no longer meant anything, they were just voices—safe, low and trusting. She vaguely understood that the words had something to do with all they had in common—from before. The kind of things nobody else would notice about them: summer days and scrapes and bruises they'd shared. Walking to school on stormy mornings. Sorrows they'd shared and Christmas Eves together. The times when they'd hated each other intensely and wildly the way only siblings can and then, in the next moment, recognized that they were the strongest when they were together. It wasn't the words, it wasn't what they were saying, that told her this. No, it was the voices. The voices came up from a deep well of goodness that each had for the other.

Tora understood that even though her aunt could laugh as if she were going to burst, she had her sorrows. It wasn't always easy to spot them in someone who could afford to spend a night in a hotel and buy dress material.

One should always travel in stormy weather!

A flute was playing in the window cross. The music vibrated around and into everything in the room. Even into her. Of course it was only the wind, she knew that. But it was magic and turned into a real melody!

She was lying in the middle of the big hotel bed. All the lights were off. Deep within she heard the faint tinkling from the prisms of the chandelier in the dining room. They were playing a delicate and high-pitched song, a strange tinkling that blended with the flute.

She could barely see the outlines of the furniture because the lights from the other side of the street cast such a soft and yellow glow through the snow-covered window.

They were all three in the big bed. Three bodies. The warmth from the other two struck like a summer wind against her skin. Safely. Without hands. Without the danger.

No creaking across the floor, no fumbling with the door knob.

Only the flute playing and the light through the snowdrift and the fragile sense of safety.

Now and then she heard voices from rooms far away. Voices that didn't demand anything from her, that didn't even know she existed. Voices with nothing to hide.

Tora was sleeping behind a locked door for the first time she could remember. There was something magical about it.

"Lock the door," her aunt had said.

And Tora had gone across the room and turned the little key. So easy! To shut out the world.

Even the window cross, which could terrify her when she woke up in the night at home, seemed friendly here.

This cross was innocent and had seen nothing. . . .

And the warmth of the bed? There wasn't anything tense or disgusting about it. There was nothing that had to be dried off or folded over to the side.

It didn't smell of anything but skin. Like moss warmed by the sun. It was her aunt's hair spread out over the pillow. Out . . . over . . . it spilled over and tangled up in Tora's undone braids.

Deep inside Tora could still hear her aunt's cheerful voice as they were getting ready for bed, "How nice that you've in-herited my hair! Otherwise, I don't guess anybody would have. . . . "

Her aunt's voice was sad and happy at the same time. She brushed Tora's hair with long, careful strokes. Not fast and absent-mindedly the way her mother used to do before Tora could comb and braid it herself. So it wasn't because she was a German brat that she had red hair! The song the other kids had made up about her wasn't true: "Her hair's on fire, her hair's all red, her mother slept in a German's bed!" It was her inheritance from Aunt Rachel!

Tora wanted to ask about it, just to hear them say that was what it was, but she didn't dare.

Mama was so happy tonight, completely changed. She was smiling. Tora didn't want to ruin anything, so she didn't dare say anything about war or Germans. If she did, Mama would close up and wither like flowers in fall.

Cool, unfamiliar sheets. Mama's and Aunt Rachel's regular breathing. The room protected them, placed its boundaries around them and kept everything else away. The room let emptiness drown in its own meaninglessness and made the night precious.

Or maybe it wasn't just this room. Maybe there were lots of good rooms like this one in the world and lots of doors that could be locked.

Was it only in the Tenement that the nights were disgusting and the darkness terrifying?

Rachel and Ingrid didn't breathe the same. Her mother's breathing had little breaks in it. It sounded as if she forgot to breathe now and then, as if she weren't really sure it was right for her to let her lungs work freely. Rachel's breathing was always even and easy and that's the way it was when she was sleeping too.

Ingrid turned over in her sleep, turned her thin back to Tora. Tora could feel the warm pressure of her mother's body against her. Close, close.

Rachel turned toward Tora. Her breath flowed lightly over Tora's cheeks and her arm lay over the comforter like a seagull's wing. In it was both strength and tenderness. Even when it was asleep. It was white in the darkness.

They were sheep who found shelter together behind a boulder when the storm was raging. In a strange place they created their own safety and warmth, because they were allowed to be in peace.

They knew that the other's chill would break through and return to them straight through skin and flesh. It was important to spread all the warmth you had, then you would get tenfold in return. Here they didn't hide from each other as they did at home. Here they weren't interrupted by Mama having to go to work, or by *him* coming home. Here there was no one shouting down the halls or talking about the war.

But they had to go back tomorrow.

Then once again they would have to hush up and hoard what troubled them. Hide it so well that they'd have to forget it themselves. That's the way it was.

At home they weren't allowed to give each other the warmth they needed. They became frightened sheep again in the wild mountains.

For a little while, hopelessness seeped into Tora.

But she fought with it, right to the moment when she saw Grandmother brush by the edge of the bed with her white hair and soft wrinkles. She saw her friendly face and heard her talking about her father. The room became Grandmother's, the window cross—everything! She was in Berlin. She'd brought her aunt and her mother to Berlin with her. And Grandmother had made their bed and didn't want to awaken them to ask if they were all right. No, she just brushed past in her long, blue dress that billowed gently and made a little breeze as she moved. And Grandmother saw that they were fine and that they were far, far from the village and the island.

It was almost real. She struggled to make it real with every fiber of her body, to keep away tomorrow.

All the way into deep sleep, into that part of herself that she couldn't control, Tora held on to the smell of sun-warmed moss and clear, delicate flute melodies.

Once she almost woke up. Then Grandmother suddenly had Aunt Rachel's hair on the pillow and she'd settled into bed next to Tora. It must have been too tiring for her to float like that around in the draughty room and keep watch, Tora thought.

And the bodies in the bed floated over to one another and into one another and had no boundaries. Grandmother's, Mama's and hers.

Then she somehow had to go under the bed after her aunt too, and she struggled to get her body up into the bed. It was as if the bed were much too small. And she knew that her aunt had to be with them.

The wind whistled louder. You couldn't see through the window any more. The snow made small rivulets down the window pane outside. But the new, cold snow always kept the old snow from melting completely. The glass seemed to cry because it couldn't let the light in.

Suddenly wide awake, Tora stared out into the room. It had a greyish-yellow, blurred pattern. Like a landscape in fog. The window pane was covered over. They were snowed in. The night had warm feet.

God bless the storm!

Chapter Nineteen

"Everybody's looking at me so strangely," Rachel whispered to Tora.

They were watching the boat begin to move away from the dock. The storm was over, the dream was over.

For Tora, the reality began in her frozen feet down in her rubber boots, spread from there through her whole body like a kind of resentment, a tiredness she couldn't explain, because it hadn't been cold on the bus and she'd slept far into the morning.

"I can't see anything wrong with you," Tora replied.

She smiled, to get out some of the emptiness. Everything would be easier that way.

At the same time, it dawned on her that Rachel was right.

People were staring! Those standing on the wharf and those safely on board. Yes, even the little boy standing on the pier fender fishing for minnows was staring hard in Rachel's direction.

Tora studied Rachel's face and figure from top to toe to find a possible reason. Nothing.

They found seats in the lounge. Sat close together. Their handbags and Rachel's packages lay around their feet like obedient puppies. They had to rearrange them now and then, as people arrived who had to squeeze by to get to a seat farther in.

Rachel tried to start a conversation with the woman sitting next to her. But either she was unusually shy or else Rachel had offended her in some way, for the woman stared at the wall and wasn't about to chat.

Rachel was puzzled. Then she turned to Tora and Ingrid.

But something uncertain had come over her round, friendly face. Tora could see that her aunt was trying to understand all the sly side-long glances being aimed at her.

It was as if she had leprosy.

At last the three of them managed to create a kind of connection among themselves so that they could get through the short, but unending hour it took to cross the fjord arm, come alongside the two wharves, unload and load, let some passengers off and take on new.

The mail boat didn't go very fast, but it got them there.

The last stretch was left, into the bay, and then it would be over.

Tora waited for someone to explain what the matter was.

It had never been so quiet on the mail boat before when she'd been on it. It was almost spooky. Especially the stare of the old fellow sitting directly opposite them. He sighed and sucked his teeth. Continually.

Tora knew that he lived down in the village, but she couldn't remember his name.

"Been out and about, eh?" he finally said, sucking long and thoroughly. He stretched the right side of his mouth so wide and open that they could look right in at the chaw of tobacco tumbling around in there.

Rachel brightened, and her relief over the broken silence was written in every line in her face. She gave the old man a big smile and said that yes, she had. She was about to say something else, but caught herself. Each face around the five-sided table had its own unfathomable expression. The old man gave her a meaningful look and sucked some more— there was something he wasn't able to get out from between his stumps—and said, "Yes, that may well be. But now it's going to be hard to come home. But life goes up and life goes down here in this world. . . . "

His wife nudged him in the side without making any secret of it. People were sitting with their mouths open, leaning forward, as if afraid they were going to miss something.

The engine throbbed. The sea was calm. Nothing happened.

But Rachel got up abruptly and let packages be packages

and eyes be eyes. She snatched up her small purse and disappeared out the door.

Ingrid got up and hesitantly followed her out.

Tora stayed there, with plenty of room around her and eyes staring at her from all sides. They were a little ashamed now.

She stared out one of the sea-splattered windows and was brave. She'd promised herself to face the danger. She didn't know how, but there'd be a way.

So she could begin here.

She gathered her courage and flicked her eyes so quickly at one of the men sitting right across from her that he didn't have time to look away.

Tora stared at this one face, these two eyes. It felt as if her heart filled her completely, swelled up through her throat and head. Then she said, in a strange voice, "How come you were staring like that at my Aunt Rachel? Why is it hard to come home?"

The man she'd locked eyes with looked away first, and then out it came, "There's been a fire at Simon Bekkejordet's. The whole fishing station burned down last night. There was nothing to save. There was a heavy gale, you know. All we could do was wet down canvas and save the buildings around it. The Lord was merciful, for the wind was blowing out to sea!"

Chapter Twenty

SMOKE WAS STILL RISING FROM THE CHARRED EMPTINESS. Lazily, indifferently, it floated up from the rubble.

Fire!

That was something you heard about. Read about. Something you shuddered over. Something that happened somewhere else and to people you didn't know. Never to you.

In the middle of the cooling ruins, of the twisted iron rods and scarcely recognizable objects bearing witness to the fact that there had been a fishing station here once—in the middle of all this stood a single, rough, fire-blackened brick chimney and marked the burned-down building's ascent to heaven.

It was as if it stood there and said, "This far up rose Simon in his days of prosperity. This far. But now it is past."

Rachel, in her coat with the big checks, gripped the railing tightly as the boat docked. Calmly gathered up her bags and packages, moved slowly down the gangplank with Tora and Ingrid close behind her. And people made room. They retreated.

All the eyes that had stuck in her like nails back there in the boat's lounge were there again. She could feel them in her back, and she clenched her teeth. She understood that, for them, all this was a circus. Her eyes were looking for Simon's self-assured figure on the wharf. He knew she was coming. Would he be there? Would he understand what she would have to struggle with? He wasn't there.

All right! Then she'd have to save herself!

She didn't talk to anyone. But she nodded to those whose eyes drilled too shamelessly into her from the front.

She nodded to them, as if this were an absolutely ordinary day. Then she put down bag and baggage on the wharf and strolled around the site of the fire. Because she knew that was the last thing they expected her to do.

They'd get a circus, all right!

But not the way they'd imagined it. She'd cheat them out of the hysterics. Take it calmly, so they'd really have something to talk about. She'd show them it was possible. She didn't know the extent of the damage yet, but she knew that people had always envied Simon and her. Her most of all, probably. Envied them because everything turned out so well for them.

Until now.

She knew they thought this served her right.

To Rachel, everyone present was a malicious animal, on the watch for a sign of weakness in her misfortune.

Because she was by no means as modest and self-effacing as people wanted her to be. She despised servility, and that was wrong of her.

Now they were watching to see that she got her punishment for her arrogance. She seemed to forget the disaster for this one thing: to show strength.

But at Bekkejordet something else that had burned down was waiting for Rachel to deal with. Simon, who had locked himself into the weaving loft and wouldn't let anybody come in.

The fire had taken Simon, too.

EILERT DAHL
The Island
Fish purchased—all types
Processing - Export - Cod liver oil production
Fresh fish processing - Freezer
Diesel Fuel - Machine oil
Lodgings for fishermen - Net storage

"He's not wasting any time, getting fat on someone else's misery!"

Ottar spread out the *Lofoten Post* on the scarred counter top and read the ad with a wrinkled forehead.

Henrik stood there, his face turned away, and let the other

men jabber on. He was sober today. He'd been sober all week.

"Yeah, now Dahl's got it all to himself." Ottar scowled at Henrik's back. He wanted to provoke Henrik into the discussion. But Henrik just began swinging the tin buckets that were hanging from a hook on one of the ceiling beams. The bucket handles rubbing against the hook made a high-pitched screech.

"You'd think he'd wait at least until next week to print this goddamn ad, out of decency. He'd have earned just as much on it. What does Simon say about it?"

Ottar raised his voice, determined to get Henrik involved. Henrik didn't turn his head. Just stood, all eyes on him, studying the lowermost bucket with an expert's eye.

"I don't go visiting at Simon's any more than you do, Ottar!" he said suddenly.

"He's not still up in the weaving loft, I bet," Ottar speculated innocently, and he ripped off a huge piece of wrapping paper for Einar's coil of rope.

"They caught a lot of cod last week at Lofoten, there's fish for everybody," Håkon threw in, wanting to change the subject for comfort's sake.

Nobody paid any attention to him. Simon had to be discussed more thoroughly.

Several of them had decided that. Six men shopping. Pipe and cigarette smoke hanging thick under the low ceiling. The bell over the door was silent and there was time to gossip.

"Is it true Rachel's threatening to leave him, if he doesn't come down from the loft?" asked a thickset, insolent fellow with his cap on backwards. He was a young smart aleck who ought to shut up when grown men were speaking, but he was aggressive and a talker, so the others let it pass and played along.

"Oh, Rachel isn't going to run away, just because her skirt's got a little singed," Henrik sneered, and turned suddenly to face the others. He was hunched over, his bad arm leaning on the trap door in the counter. He didn't look at any of them. Said the words to himself, out into the air.

"No, she's not exactly flighty," Einar chimed in, and shook his head.

"They say the fire was set," Håkon said.

"If that's so, it wasn't for the insurance," said Einar with a grin, and opened his worn wallet so that the copper coins rattled.

"Too bad they had so little insurance," whined Håkon, wanting to sound virtuous.

"Oh, they're getting what they deserve," put in the smart aleck.

The window pane was heavily misted. A lot of men were in there breathing.

"Did he get anything?" Ottar asked.

"Don't ask me," Henrik answered harshly, grabbed his cap and started for the door.

"What's the hurry? I didn't mean to say anything bad about your kin. . . . "

The smart aleck all of a sudden remembered that Henrik and Simon were married to sisters.

"Yeah, you put your foot in your mouth, you son of a bitch!" Henrik hollered over his shoulder. "Keep that in mind the next time you start shooting off your mouth!"

The store got quiet. Ottar stood there open-mouthed and the men stared at the floor.

When the other men left the store at last, Einar couldn't help remarking, "Since when did he start making a big fuss over being Simon's brother-in-law? That's got to be a pretty sudden love . . . don't you think?"

They traded glances and chuckled a little.

"Yeah, he's usually quick to mention how easy it was for Simon, inheriting everything from his old uncle. The bastard kid from Bø, who came to the island and became a big shot overnight!" snorted a grey, oblong ball of wool sitting on a barrel over by the stove, who hadn't said anything up until now.

"The worst thing's the loss of the fishing station. There won't be much rebuilding if Simon doesn't get insurance money."

Ottar looked at them one after the other. He'd adopted Håkon's virtuous tone.

"They say Rachel's got him down from the loft," the ball of wool sitting on the barrel said.

"Some of the neighbors went straight into the lion's den and offered to help clean up the mess. Even Simon's workers said they'd help."

"Without pay, of course! Rachel treated them to waffles and stew, they say, every one of them. But Simon didn't show his face. Now that he's got the wind blowing against him and his money a little, it wouldn't surprise me a bit if he started to get delicate and a woman's nerves," the smart aleck sneered, and dug around shamelessly in his right nostril—the one with the polyps he was afraid to see the doctor about.

Oh, no.

It wasn't meant to be malicious. Not a bit of it was meant to be malicious. They were just words in a store, one innocent Monday.

It began with an attempt to get Henrik going, and then it took such an unfortunate turn.

But it was a good thing, Ottar thought, that nobody had come in unexpectedly and heard how they went to town on Simon.

He went on his rounds at dusk, locked the storehouse and the store. He could tell from the sale of rope and salt that Simon's fishing business was gone. But he wasn't going to mention it. It was too petty and wasn't at all important to a storekeeper who had his own steady customers. But the motorboat owners bought their salt and rope at his place now, since that unfortunate fire. Dahl didn't run a retail business, the way Simon had.

Mostly you saw them with their hands in their pockets and cigarettes in the corners of their mouths when times were bad. Shopping a little—two pounds of sugar, a pouch of tobacco—practically all day long. They were the ones who stayed furthest back lining up for work. Others were good at elbowing their way to the front of the line and didn't have time for that kind of thing.

But more and more of them were being shoved aside when work was given out and wages paid. Mostly it was those who didn't own house or land. All they had was a healthy bitterness towards almost everything, and time to shop but nothing to pay with. They lived in rented quarters and supported themselves with part-time work. Steady work was a dream that drowned over and over in the fishless sea. Or dangled from the crane at the end of the wharf. Only squealing in the storms or when other people's fish and cargo were being loaded and unloaded.

At home was a wife and kids with snotty noses.

Sometimes they got work and left. Everybody was happy. It was a strange sort of happiness. It had nothing to do with laughter or the joy of being alive. It was just a temporary end to the rumbling in the stomach and the long columns of figures in Ottar's book. That happiness was of a simple and concrete sort. It didn't require displays of emotion. It provided an opportunity to keep things going.

Those who owned a little piece of land and a motorboat, on the other hand, were free even if they did wear a yoke. Even if they were pale in the face during the worst of winter, at least they weren't completely blue.

God's uncaged birds were often overlooked. They didn't fly—didn't even hop. But they used their wings for support as they dragged themselves back and forth. A wing can be used for so many things.

One such bird lived in the garret above the porch and used a frying pan and honorably stolen pork. Einar never got the big chance, even if he'd wanted it. He was sentenced *before* he'd committed any crime.

And then there were Dahl, the pastor and the doctor—God help them through the needle's eye.

Dahl was an honorable sinner, however, for he provided work for many people. He maintained that he conducted his business democratically—whatever that was supposed to mean. Just like the bigwig he was, he took Sunday walks in the village with his dog, his wife and his two kids. He didn't consider himself above playing an occasional hand of cards in the fishermen's shacks either. Nothing like that had ever been heard of before from the likes of him.

You also had to have a doctor. He was entitled to almost anything. You gladly forgave both the fact that he was a bachelor and the rumor that he was stingy. He dispensed health in a drop of spirits, if someone was in real need.

The pastor was the worst. It was just hellfire and damnation with him, wisdom and holy thunder.

Oh, but the old pastor was a horse of a different color. Einar wasn't the only one who thought that.

The old pastor had worked like other people. He ran the parsonage himself. Sometimes the boats with bridal couples and wedding guests came up to the dock so fast, he didn't have time to do anything but pull his clerical robe on over his overalls and trudge to the altar. Especially during the haying and plowing seasons.

A bride might occasionally wrinkle her nose at the smell of manure and the muddy galoshes under his black robe, but by and large people considered the old pastor a first-rate work horse. And he died in his sheep pen too.

That's how it turned out. He fell at his post. Something snapped and sent him right out of this vale of tears.

He behaved like a human being right to the end.

Chapter Twenty-One

It looked like the season was over for Simon of Bekkejordet. He didn't even have a miserable desk to sit at. Not one salary to pay out. And as if one big disaster weren't enough, his crew boss caught his leg in the capstan and broke it clean through.

It was a Saturday night when Rachel received the telephone call about the accident. She took it standing up.

Afterwards, she didn't hurry, she put on warm clothes and went with the news to the unfortunate wife who was waiting for her husband with her three children. Rachel gave her enough money to tide her over for a week, then trudged back home and prepared to go up to the weaving loft and tell Simon.

He was pacing back and forth up there for the third week now, so this might be a good time to give his brain a little jolt, Rachel thought bitterly. She'd also received a shock. But it wasn't the fire itself that had caused *that*. No, it was that she'd been living with a man she'd never known, until now.

He wasn't the Simon she'd thought he was. The tall man was a child. First she'd threatened and nagged, then she'd left him in peace with his sorrow.

She carried food up to him and took care of everything else alone, but she fought a repressed battle with something inside that an observer would certainly have been able to name: contempt.

Rachel turned the handle and opened the door. Simon must have heard her coming up the stairs, because he'd sat down on the couch under two of the windows. He slept up here too, the few hours he let himself sleep. So Rachel had lived to experience that too: to be alone downstairs in their big bed.

"Are you coming down to eat today, Simon?" she asked without any greeting. She looked at the man sitting there, half hidden in shadow by the windows. He'd grown gaunt and hollow-eyed from his sleepless nights and brooding. But not much else had come of that.

He shook his head and made no sign that he was planning to say anything.

"Are you planning to sit up here until you rot, then?" she screamed. He barely raised his head, just looked at her as if she were a troublesome child.

"There's a lot I can put up with, Simon. All kinds of misfortune. But sitting up here like a spineless fool when I need you—I won't put up with that! Do you hear me?"

"It's all over, Rachel . . . I don't have anything left . . . I'm ruined . . . You know it too."

"Look at me, Simon! Take a good look!"

He looked with empty eyes at her standing there, her hands on her hips.

"How can you be ruined when you have a wife? I won't have any patience left for you if you don't come down. I'll slaughter the sheep and leave! Do you hear me?"

Simon looked at her in astonishment.

"Leave? You can't mean that you'd leave a ruined man. I need you, Rachel. You're just saying that to scare me."

"*You* need *me*, you say. What do you think *I* need? I suppose I don't need anybody, is that it? Oh, Simon, Simon, don't goad me into laughing in your face. Do you know the telephone call I got today? No, you don't! Because you're not downstairs long enough to take your own messages. And you don't do a lick of God's work otherwise, either. Everything would go straight to hell if I weren't here to do what has to be done! People are laughing at Simon of Bekkejordet. They're saying he's not taking this business of the fire very well. They're saying that the pants are on the wrong person up at Bekkejordet! Do you hear me, Simon?"

"Rachel, Rachel," he moaned, and put his head in his hands.

Then she took the two steps that separated them and sat down on his lap.

Rachel was a tactician. Just as naturally calculating as when she set the potatoes in the ground in the spring, just as carefully as she seasoned the sheep blood that she'd just cried over before making black pudding out of it—just that naturally she showed the side of herself that had to be shown *now*. She wrapped her arms tightly around her husband's neck and rocked him back and forth.

"Come down now, Simon, and Rachel will tell you all about another disaster. Come down, now . . . "

Simon really did come down to the kitchen that night.

Little by little, he let himself be fixed up, awakened from the dead.

After three cups of coffee and several slices of bread with sausage, he asked cautiously what sort of disaster it was she had to tell about.

"Erling's in the hospital with a broken leg!"

She could hear it herself, how brutal it sounded, but she no longer had the strength to spare her husband anything.

She'd known the business was poorly insured, but she wasn't prepared for *how* little there was to claim. She'd paid out what they owed the workers down at the loading dock, and now all she had left to fall back on was her own household money in the writing desk and a lousy insurance policy. It would probably take a long time before she got the insurance money. And she wasn't planning to beg anybody for a handout. They weren't going to have that to gossip about.

Then it was lambing time and she had to let the fire and Simon take care of themselves as best they could. Because now it was a matter of new life, new food and new money.

Turid and Anton came across the field one evening and offered to help clean up what was left of the fishing station. Rachel could have cried for joy, but she didn't. There wasn't time for anything like that. And Simon was up in the loft. She thought that was good enough reason to save her tears of joy.

"What're you saying? That I've lost my crew boss?" Simon became, if possible, even paler. "Then what am I supposed to do now?"

"You see! You thought you were finished with disasters here in this house, Simon. But let me tell you that if you don't go to Lofoten and earn a little money in all this misery, then you're going to find out how bad it is to be wifeless too."

"*Me* go to Lofoten! I haven't been fishing in years . . . not since I was a kid!"

"Then you can be grateful for the chance to start all over, this time on your own boat!"

The words she flung across the table were like frost. She was pale around her nose, which stuck out into the room defiantly.

"You're going to rebuild your business too, Simon."

A smile spread slowly over his face, a skeptical smile that made his whole face crack from the unaccustomed movement. It looked as if this were the first time he'd ever used those muscles. The corners of his mouth trembled.

"Rachel, Rachel, there are things women don't know anything about. Money, Rachel! Where am I going to get money from?"

"You're going to borrow it."

"You're talking. . . . "

"You borrowed money when you added onto the cow barn and replaced all the windows in the house. I didn't hear you say anything then about it being impossible."

"You're talking about things you don't understand. It's not hard to borrow money when you've got a whole fishing business for collateral, a boat as good as gold—and no debts. But it's as completely different story trying to get a loan when you don't even own the nails in your walls."

The light above the table cast shadows over his furrowed face. Helplessness was drawn in every line.

Rachel was on the verge of giving up. There was a burning behind her eyelids, and her head felt as heavy as lead. A strange feeling of loneliness threatened to overwhelm her, make her surrender.

But she mustn't do that. Not now, not when she'd finally

gotten him down to the kitchen.

"The sheriff thinks it was arson. Would that make any difference, if it's proven?"

"Oh, maybe. I was a fool for having so little insurance."

"Don't you wonder, Simon, who it could have been? Who could have started the fire?"

"Oh, I don't think anybody started it. The building was old, there was a storm, maybe somebody was careless. But set it? No . . . I don't believe it. People aren't like that."

There was a pause. At least they were sitting close together. Both were thinking about that more than about the fire.

"I think somebody set it," Rachel said harshly. "That's exactly how people are."

The next day, Simon went into the village.

Silence followed him wherever he went. He bought what he needed to take part in the Lofoten fishing. He made no secret of what he was doing.

Ottar asked no questions. Just filled the cardboard boxes Simon had brought with him and talked about the weather.

"It's the Devil himself who's responsible for the snow this year."

Ottar was certain of that. Nobody had seen so much snow. Winter, spring and fall would pass before it melted, in his opinion.

Simon answered. But there was no spark in his answers, and his skin hung remarkably slack on each side of his sad mouth.

Kornelius Olsa, who was the most experienced man on board the *Breeze* and had taken temporary command, shook his head when he learned that Simon himself would be in the wheel house. But he didn't say anything against it.

And Kornelius was all the support a desk fisherman would need. Later, the other crew members could tell how Kornelius Olsa shook his sou'-wester more than once and told the good Simon how he would have handled things if he'd been in command on board. And Simon would duck his head and do as the old sailor said without complaining.

The fishing went tolerably. It went better when Simon was able to forget the black hole back home on the bay. And it went even better as long as he was so far from home that he didn't have to go to Dahl's wharf to deliver his catch.

At home at Bekkejordet, Rachel began to sing in the barn a little and laugh without reason. As in the old days.

She'd taken over the weaving loft again and banged and beat every free moment she had.

She had some space around her now. Room to make noise, work and laugh.

But Rachel understood more clearly what a deep chasm life had always been for Ingrid. She went to visit her sister more often than before, and not just because she wanted consolation for herself.

Henrik left when she arrived.

That's what he'd always done. Rachel knew there might be many reasons why.

Probably the most likely reason was she'd never bothered to hide the fact that she thought the marriage between Ingrid and Henrik was another misfortune for Ingrid.

There was something about Henrik that Rachel couldn't comprehend.

She was unable to feel at ease in the same room with him.

Perhaps *that* was his curse—that so few people could feel comfortable in his company. He radiated something that aroused antipathy.

But she also had to admit that the island people didn't treat Henrik all that well, either. There was that arm of his, and a strange melancholy that came over him now and then. Ingrid claimed it came from the time he'd been torpedoed and got a fragment of steel in his shoulder.

Now Rachel had seen that Simon, too, could go under on account of a splinter of steel.

Apparently men weren't made as tough as women.

But there was something about Henrik's eyes. Granted that he went on a binge from time to time. Granted. But there was something else . . . She hadn't forgotten the time she ran into him behind the barn. He didn't give any explanation for why he was there. Just gave her that grin of his straight into her face and brushed by without saying a word. If he hadn't been Ingrid's husband and she hadn't known he only tolerated her on account of Ingrid, she would have thought he was out looking for what all unattached men are out looking for.

Simon went on a secret errand to Breiland. He went, a little more bowed down, on an even more secret errand to Bodø. Made estimates and wrote important letters, had deep furrows in his brow and crooked his aching fisherman's fingers around his pen. He spent several days on this, knowing full well that Kornelius Olsa could manage the boat and the business.

Over Easter he also spent his time writing and pondering.

The weather had improved enough so that the fishermen could use their hands outside their pants pockets now and then.

There were angry demands in the newspaper for investigations of the purse seiners' methods.

Simon scarcely had time to read such things, much less get angry.

But Rachel sometimes read the newspaper after her evening chores in the barn.

One day she read that the church authorities, with all due respect, had declined to have anything to do with the idea of women pastors.

Rachel snorted at the thought of grown churchmen having nothing better to do than respectfully decline such an idea, when there was so much misery in the world. They should be both sweaty and out of breath just from running around consoling and helping people in need. Jesus never said one bad word about women, not even whores. She'd read that in the Bible herself.

Then her eyes fell on the book review column: "Women are our hope," it read. "An American ethnologist, Montagu, has written a book that claims woman is, in fact, superior to man. She has greater joy of life, fewer physical weaknesses, fewer inherited diseases, greater power of resistance to physical pain and a more highly developed intellect! Women are even better at driving cars! Man is aware of his inferiority and therefore wants to develop his ability to rule in order to assert himself. The vulgar advantage of musculature is best developed in the man. As a consequence of that, we have war—which is man's special vocation because woman lacks the necessary qualifications. One must move the world forward an inch every generation. Women give life. If women fail, there will be no hope for mankind."

Rachel nodded as she read. So the world was finally beginning to use its eyes! Well, *she* certainly wasn't going to fail!

But what's an ethnographer? she wondered, irritated. Rachel was often annoyed at how much she didn't know, at words she didn't understand.

But the idea that women didn't have the qualifications for war—surely that couldn't be right. Rachel felt quite certain that she was willing to wage war if necessary. There were so many kinds of weapons.

Oh yes, from a rostrum—from a pulpit, if necessary—she'd be able to drive home a spear or two!

Chapter Twenty-Two

THE MAY SUN BAKED THE PEELING SOUTH WALL OF THE Tenement, so that heating with coal was a waste of money on cloudless days. That was a relief for others besides Ingrid.

She'd been able to reduce her debt at Ottar's. And her name was crossed off in the notebook at the milk store. It was as if spring held new meaning for her.

The burdens were still heavy enough. But it was like having a hundred pounds lifted from her shoulders after carrying two hundred pounds.

The shoulder straps didn't hurt *so* much now, because you could remember how much worse it had been. That helped.

Ingrid had scraped topsoil from a secret place behind the fields. The snow melted early there. It lay on a southern incline and couldn't be seen from the house or road.

She carried the soil home in a bucket on her old black bicycle. Let it dangle, heavy and full, from the handlebars as she wheeled the bike, because the bucket was so big and heavy that she couldn't ride.

Then she hauled the bucket up the steps, stoked up the fire in the stove in spite of the sun's warmth, and poured the soil into one of the bread pans. All the vermin had to be baked out. She would sometimes spare a grub and carry it back outside. After a couple of hours in the oven, it would be as stiff as a stick and couldn't be saved, poor thing.

Today she didn't have time to filter through the pile of soil so carefully. She had to be at work in a few hours. And she had to be finished by the time Henrik was expected home. He hated potted plants.

Every spring she had a potting day. It felt as if she were doing something illegal that day. As if her youth and her liveliness returned for one day.

The smell of soil... dear God! It sank deep into her mind and fed her something essential. Memories... of something else, something different? If only she could have her memories in peace! If only she could have the peace to sit down and make herself warm and happy by remembering a loved face, hands... a life that should have been....

Henrik *was*, and he didn't like her potted plants. He went his own way. But she held on anyway. And he held on. They were like the seaweed at low tide, stuck to the same bare rock, but carried in circles, always from one another, always away.

She added extra fuel to the stove to hurry the process.

Her face was red from the heat and she opened both windows. She looked for a moment at the dirty snow behind the shed in the yard. The roads were almost free of snow. The children mostly stayed there until the snow melted on the fields. She could hear the littlest of Elisif's kids squabbling out there. Poor creatures.

Ingrid should have started the bread too. There'd be just enough time. She had to use the heat for more than sterilizing soil. Otherwise, using so much fuel would be a luxury. Coal thrown away. Out the window, Henrik would say. He was down at Dahl's fishing station. Supposed to be helping out in the warehouse. Everything seemed to be turning out right today.

It was a good thing she had two bread pans, since there was soil in one of them. Tora was going to have to take care of the bread when she came home from school. She'd be able to manage it.

Ingrid felt the demands and the greyness in her growing less as she worked.

Next week she was going to clean the doctor's house. That would bring in a little extra money between packing. There was talk of layoffs in the near future, so it was best to take what you could get.

She'd felt such a strange tiredness recently. It bothered her and made her impatient, so she almost didn't dare speak to people. She was afraid of being too cross.

It wasn't worth it.

The pains in her stomach had been extra bad this winter. Days went by when she wasn't able to eat anything at all.

Tora had to have new shoes and a new skirt. She had to have new clothes for the 17th of May. Couldn't very well go in her old jacket. Besides, it was too tight.

Maybe she could ask Rachel for a dress she could alter.

Not that they were living all that high on the hog up there at Bekkejordet, even if they did have something to fall back on. But it had been a long time since Rachel had worn that brown jacket. Maybe she could spare it.

Ingrid made plans. Her hands tapped out a drum beat and her feet carried her lightly wherever she wanted to go.

Henrik had got them an old radio. It was on at all hours whenever he was home. It somehow brought life into the house. She had to admit that.

In the beginning she thought it brought only dread in, but that was probably on account of the war. . . .

Her opinion of Henrik improved as she watched him fix it and install it. And when he finally got a rasping contact with the outside world, with a quiet roaring like the ocean, then she understood that Henrik *was* competent. At last, sound made its way into the kitchen. They stood there, all three of them, and stared at the box on the shelf. Music came out of it. And that was Henrik's doing. It had been a good evening.

Shuffling steps on the stairs! She recognized them! It was him. Something had gone wrong. So he'd come home long before he was supposed to, if he'd even been at work at all. Ingrid steeled herself against the inevitable.

He wasn't as drunk as she'd thought at first. Mostly belligerent.

"What the hell! The sun's baking through the windows and you've got the oven on?"

"Well, I have to bake bread, don't I?" she replied, and tried to be friendly.

"Bread? Oh, sure! You're taking care of those damned flowers of yours that just get in the way so nobody can see out of his own window!"

"Shh! Somebody might hear how irritable you are today. Was the work finished at Dahl's?"

"Who gives a damn!"

"How you carry on! Do you want something to eat?"

"No!"

He threw himself down on the couch in the corner and Ingrid thought that maybe he would go to sleep. But suddenly he jumped up and stalked over to the counter where she was standing and slammed his fist violently down on it.

Now, it happened that the pan was on the edge of the breadboard. It tipped over instantly, and the burning hot soil and the even hotter pan ended up on the back of Henrik's hand.

Henrik screamed, swore and hopped around the room.

Ingrid turned on the faucet, tried to get him to hold his hand under it, but he refused.

Just then, Tora came up the stairs. She'd gotten out of school earlier than usual. She could hear that there was trouble and hesitated about going in. *Saw* that something was wrong, saw it in the way Henrik had taken off his boots. He'd just thrown his coat over in a corner.

She considered trying to think of a reason to go to the village or down to the wharves, but then she realized that her mother had probably heard her. She was hot in her thick sweater. She pulled it off out in the hall. It smelled of carnations again. Her armpits were wet.

Her mother looked up when she came in. It was as if she'd practiced; she just nodded and pretended there was nothing the matter. Tora sat down uncertainly at the end of the table.

Henrik was standing over by the couch and scowling viciously at his burned hand.

"Henrik burned his hand," Ingrid explained, and gave her husband a cautious glance. Tora didn't answer.

"You're home early, aren't you?" her mother tried again.

"Yes. Gunn thought the weather was so fine, she said we needed to get out in the nice weather and the sun more than we needed to be inside studying."

"Yeah, that gal knows how to get time off," threw in Henrik.

It was as if Tora woke up suddenly. She saw! Saw that Henrik had come home and didn't like her mother repotting her plants. Saw that he was mad about something and was punishing her mother, Gunn, her, for whatever it was. Blurry red dots seemed to appear in front of her eyes. The sunshine disappeared in them. Everything disappeared. Everything vanished in the black night, in the danger, in the hatred and the disgust. It was as if she were seeing him for the first time as something other than something that couldn't be changed.

Henrik turned into a human being, like everybody else. He shrivelled up there in his rage and wasn't so threatening now, in the light of day. Tora saw that her mother cowered at every word he said, all the while pretending that nothing was wrong.

Then suddenly it was as if Tora couldn't hold the words back any longer. She didn't know where they came from, she didn't think over what she was saying at all, it just ran out,

"I guess Gunn's not the only one who can get time off—is she?"

A strange stillness filled the room. The noises from outside sounded like thunder. The melting ice dripping from the roof sounded horrible, almost like a bad omen. Mama was the worst—Mama stared at her with wide eyes. Everything became unreal. Tora could hear a weak humming noise, coming from inside, from inside herself.

Ingrid stood there stiffly, both hands down in the greyish white dough covering her wrists.

A fat, hairy fly flew by below the curtain ruffle. Dizzy from its winter torpor and the sunshine.

Then he was standing over her. "What did you say?"

His face was distorted by rage.

Tora hadn't thought he would touch her. Not when her mother was watching, not like that. The shock turned her heart into a baby bird. She couldn't control it. It flapped wildly in there and her whole body got cold.

The pain wasn't the worst. It wasn't that he squeezed her so hard that she couldn't get the breath she needed until she was hanging, motionless, a few inches off the floor. It wasn't that he flung her down and went to work on her with his good hand. And it didn't really matter that there was a strange roaring in her ears and a flickering in front of her eyes.

It was his big hand against the skin of her neck. The touching, the nausea. The revulsion of his flesh on hers—while her mother was watching!

She was aware that Ingrid rushed up and grabbed his arm. The dough and the flour flew around in the room like a gale.

When he used the last of his strength to hit Ingrid on the side of her head with his fist, Tora seemed to fly out of her own body.

She forgot who she was. She'd never known she could scream so horribly. "Don't hit my mama! If you do, I'll kill you!"

But he'd already hit her. Several times. The blood was pouring fresh and red from Ingrid's mouth and nose.

Ingrid grabbed a dish towel quickly and held it below her face. When the blood seeped through the thin material, Tora got her a thick hand towel.

The fly had found its way out, and someone, irritated, was banging somewhere in the house. Apparently Gunda, on the first floor, was trying to take a nap in the middle of the uproar. Henrik stood in the middle of the floor, legs apart, bent slightly at the waist. His fist was half clenched. His head was thrust forward like an animal that feels threatened.

He was breathing heavily now.

Suddenly his face seemed to split. As if he were going to cry. He looked like a little boy who had destroyed a bird's nest without really wanting to.

Then he carefully wiped his nose with the back of his hand and moved slowly out the door without looking at either of them.

Ingrid sat down on a stool and wiped off the blood.

Tora wrung out a wash cloth in cold water and handed it to her.

Neither one said anything.

It amazed Tora that her mother didn't cry. She usually did when he hit her.

It didn't happen often—in all fairness. And never so hard that the blood flowed. He'd done that because Tora had suddenly let words out of her mouth without thinking. Of course, it was always her—Tora—who caused trouble.

Ingrid went to work the evening shift with a swollen cheek. She stood a little while at the mirror over the sink, looking at herself. Then she sighed and pulled on the worn wool jacket she used under the white apron at work, gathered up the things she usually took with her and was ready.

Only when she was standing in the doorway with her worn cloth shopping bag in her hand and scarf tied tightly under her chin, did she touch Tora's arm timidly and say, "When the oven's hot enough, put the bread in, and don't forget to take it out when it's done. And—then—you have to sweep up the dirt on the floor. After that, if you hurry with your homework, you can go to Aunt Rachel's, or meet me behind Dahl's warehouse. Is that all right?"

Tora nodded. Then her mother was gone.

It would be a long time before he came back. She knew that. That's the way it always was when something was the matter.

She took a deep breath and stoked the oven. Adjusted the dampers as well as she could. They were red hot. She poked at them with the stove jack, failed—and tried again.

Too bad she wasn't better at it. But she'd seen her mother fail too.

Especially when she was tired.

Tora wasn't tired, but she felt as if she'd been outside all day in bad weather. Her hands were numb. Feet too. Strange. Because it was so warm.

Tora put the bloody towels in a bucket of cold water, the way she'd seen her mother do with her underpants when she was having her period.

Tora hadn't started her period yet. She wasn't exactly looking forward to it, either. But Sol had prepared her. Thoroughly.

Her mother had also talked about it very briefly, her eyes never leaving the bloody water, one day when Tora had surprised her while she was washing the worst of it off her white underpants.

Strangely enough, this had nothing to do with the danger, although it came—from there. . . .

That was probably because she and Mama and Sol had whispered about it. Shut out the world and had something of their own. Something together. Something that had to be kept secret, of course, but still. . . .

It was both ordinary and, at the same time, deadly serious.

Sol told her that she'd cried the first time, because she didn't know what was wrong with her.

You had to live with it your whole life, almost—at least until you got old.

It was a little bit disgusting, Sol thought, but you soon got used to it.

Tora stood bent over the bucket and saw how the blood made funny stripes in the water. Slowly colored it pink.

Some of the biggest stains had already become hard clumps and threads that reluctantly freed themselves from the towels and sank to the bottom. There they stayed, rocking slightly as they slowly paled and turned the water around them redder and redder.

If she hadn't known it was blood, it would have been beautiful! It smelled sweetly of blood.

There wasn't much difference in the smell of blood, no matter where it came from. As long as it didn't get too old.

She suddenly remembered the stink up at Elisif's this winter.

Her mother never let blood grow old.

The smell of freshly-baked yeast bread! It wafted out of the draughty old cast-iron stove.

After that day Tora always associated the smell of bread and the smell of blood. Bloody rags and burnt fingers. Security and damnation.

145

She straightened up after putting the lid on the bucket and shoving it under the sink. Immediately after that she bent over again, peeked into the oven to make sure the bread wasn't burning.

She moved the pan higher up in the oven and put butcher paper on top of the loaves, as Ingrid did when they needed to bake fifteen minutes more. Then she began sweeping up the dirt.

Ingrid was a fanatic when it came to neatness.

She rarely worked at more than one thing at a time, as Aunt Rachel did now and then, unless she could manage it all. No, her mother stuck to one thing at a time and did it thoroughly.

But today everything was crazy.

Tora had a whole pile of dirt in the dustpan. She filled the fishball cans Ingrid had lined up in rows on the work table. Ingrid had carefully pounded four nail holes of the right size in the bottom of each can and lined the bottoms with pebbles, so the soil wouldn't turn acid. The hammer and the nail were still on the table where she'd left them.

Tora hadn't noticed the hammer, until now. A wild desire came over her to hit. Just hit! Use all her strength to smash something.

No—not just *something*. Something that would have to flinch away the whole time. Flinch away from her hammer! With shaking hands, she grabbed the hammer. Stood like that, without knowing what to do. Then she suddenly noticed that one of the biggest branches on her mother's nice impatiens had snapped off.

She took the hammer out to the box in the entryway, where they kept tools. It felt as if she'd escaped from something.

She had to prop up the branch with a knitting needle.

Nine cans in all. Tora stuck her hands down in the warm soil and filled the cans half full. One by one. It felt clean and good, even though her hands got all black.

The smell of soil. The smell of sun coming through the open window. Soil against skin. She felt so whole inside because of it. She forgot the hammer. Him. Forgot everything.

Did Mama feel that way, she wondered. That she only had to thrust her hands down into the soil to forget the awful things? It wasn't that all the bad things were gone, that they no longer existed. No, it was just that they didn't hurt. . . .

She could see her mother when she stood this way, her hands in the soil.

Pale face wreathed by thick, dark hair.

It had grown back out, Tora thought triumphantly.

The bun in back that was always threatening to come undone. Her mother didn't have a permanent, like the other women who worked at Dahl's.

Now she was down there in the cold packing plant, her hands in cellophane and fish.

Hands had so much to do. There was no way around it. Especially not for her mother's hands. They were never still.

Tora placed the plants carefully down in the new cans and nudged soil around them until there was just a small rim for the water.

She'd helped her mother, so she had the knack. And when she stood there like that, all alone and with nobody looking, she felt almost skillful.

Then the flowers sat there in their shiny cans and looked new. Even though there were ugly glue spots from the labels that had been around them.

Tora turned the glue marks towards the windows and tilted her head to one side to admire her work.

Something was missing. She looked high and low in the three rooms to find crepe paper. She finally found the green roll on the top shelf of the cupboard in the kitchen.

With a practiced hand she cut the paper to suitable widths and tied them around each can. She struggled to tie paper bows first but then discovered that straight pins worked just as well. That way, they wouldn't look so showy. Mama was particular about things like that.

Last of all she made a pretty scalloped border on top. No one would be able to tell that there were only fishball cans underneath. No one in the world!

Tora's head was tilted to one side and a little bit of the pink tip of her tongue stuck out of the right side of her mouth.

Mama was going to be happy! Tora would make coffee and pancake batter and set the table before she went to meet her. It was going to be nice!

Tora had forgotten the bread. She'd become used to the smell and didn't notice that it was getting stronger and stronger. Now she could smell it burning!

The loaves had an unappetizingly dark crust on top. Tora burned herself and got blisters on her palm as she was turning them out of the pan. She was suddenly on the verge of tears.

She'd thought everything was good again, and then she'd forgotten the bread!

Always, when you thought you'd come through a disaster and things were getting better, something tried to snatch the happiness right out of your body. Why did it have to be like that?

But Mama had burned breadloaves too. Tora had clearly seen her do it. Maybe not *as* much... but she'd scorched them!

Besides, they ate four loaves in a week, so next Friday they'd have to have four new ones anyway.

So who cares!

Chapter Twenty-Three

Tora THOUGHT SHE'D NEVER SEEN SOL WITHOUT THE smallest baby on her back. They seemed to be a single person.

Torstein had found work with the county, so as far as boots and bread went, life was better, but Sol didn't get much free time. Efforts had been made several times to place the children in foster homes, singly or together.

That latter possibility was a pipe dream, pure and simple. People could imagine having the hardworking Sol in the house, but no one liked the idea of kids in diapers, with snot and sleepless nights. So everything remained as it was.

Vanda, who lived near the river, came on weekdays and looked after the younger kids and did some cooking and laundry while the older ones were at school. People said she got paid by the county for her work.

But in the afternoon and evening, Sol always had to be there. Tora thought she was like an ant hill. Small children crawling and swarming on her, over her and around her. All the time.

But she didn't seem to let it bother her particularly. She just shifted a little, when it got too bad.

She did her homework on the tiny kitchen counter. With her legs crossed and the soft light streaming through the windows in the light time of year. But first she moved all the stools away, so the little ones couldn't climb up to her.

She sat there then, lost in her thoughts, high off the floor. It was as if she had the ability to turn herself off from the world. The way you turned off a radio.

But Elisif's kids weren't the worst when it came to causing a commotion, so things went along all right. A day at a time.

Children were always the women's. When the women failed in one way or another, it only meant trouble for the children. Nobody knew what to do with them.

There might be great piles of jobless fathers all over the place, but that was no help.

Tora had dreamed many times that Aunt Rachel would take in Sol and all of Elisif's children. She made up stories about it when she was in bed and wanted to put the danger at a distance. They were good stories that you could spend a lot of time on, similar to the stories of Berlin and Grandma. You didn't have to ever finish them.

Tora imagined all the children being at Bekkejordet. So much room! It would be so nice for them! Maybe she could be there too. In the weaving loft. There was room up there for all the little kids' beds. Then she and Sol could sleep in the little room with the green lampshade.

But that was just something she imagined. She knew that. Because even though her aunt couldn't have children of her own, she wouldn't want a whole flock of them.

And especially not now—after the fire.

One afternoon someone new appeared in the yard at the Tenement.

A thin, ungainly creature was suddenly standing over by the shed and staring curiously at the gang of kids coming from the wharves. He had unusually long arms and legs and his head looked much too big and heavy for the slender, graceful neck.

But it was his clothes they noticed most. They fit him perfectly, in every way. His sweater had neither holes nor darned places, as far as they could see. It looked almost new and had warm, matching colors in a fine pattern, like a girl's sweater.

"He was just standing there when we got here," Sol whispered, and glanced quickly over at the boy. He looked to be about her age.

They saw him swallow a couple of times. His Adam's apple seemed to be several sizes too big, and fluttered, scared, up and down. It looked as if his mother had used more sense in dressing the boy than the Lord had used in making him. But the kids at the Tenement didn't notice things like that.

"Where are you from?"

Jørgen spoke with a man's brusqueness, knowing full well he had the entire gang at his back. But he couldn't quite get the crushing tone that he'd heard Ole use whenever a newcomer appeared in their territory. He was too preoccupied with the thought that this was a real boy. At the Tenement there was a definite surplus of women.

Jørgen had "taken-borrowed" an old, black bike that had been leaning up against the wall of the shed. Now he started biking in circles around the shed and the newcomer. Tighter and tighter circles. Finally, when he was practically grazing the boy, he shouted, "Who are you?"

But the strange boy just stood there.

Jørgen stopped right next to him and repeated the question.

Then the stranger waved his arms and made the oddest flapping gestures that no one could figure out.

The gang's curiosity became too much for them. They came nearer and nearer, as if drawn by a magnet. All the little kids followed too. The youngest on Sol's back.

The boy by the shed looked almost friendly, even though the gang was closing in on him threateningly. He looked less afraid than curious. But he didn't say a word. Just stood there.

"Can't you talk, or what?"

Jørgen was standing on one foot, to keep his balance on the bike.

The strange boy shook his head energetically.

Jørgen snickered. The others stood there watching.

"What's your name, huh?"

Jørgen wouldn't give up. He usually didn't, although in other respects he resembled his father.

The boy opened his mouth but closed it again.

He made a helpless gesture in the air and went on staring into Jørgen's face.

"Are you crazy—or what?"

Jørgen got all the way off the bike because he heard the entrance door slam. He leaned the bike up against the wall next to the odd kid, in order to get really close to him.

"Leave him alone!"

It was Sol, who had shoved her way to the front of the crowd. Abruptly and commandingly, her words came out with an authority any educator might envy.

And it was Sol who first sensed the unusual. Who nosed out the fact that not everything was the way it was supposed to be. Of course it was Sol who first caught on that the poor boy was in fact mute.

He didn't seem to hear what they said either. He didn't cock his ear at them, which he would have done had he been hard of hearing. He just stared straight into their faces. Turned the entire upper part of his body, head and all, to whoever was speaking to him. It looked more than crazy.

Tora felt a kind of pain all the way from her chest down to her stomach. Yes, all the way down to there, to where the unmentionable was. A kind of crying.

She didn't really know why. It seemed as if the spring—all the pain, all the awfulness, all the shadows—flowed into her as she looked at the mute boy and understood. She felt helpless and stupid.

Tora had never met a human being who couldn't talk.

Chapter Twenty-Four

Fʀɪᴛᴢ ʜᴀᴅ ɴᴏ ᴏᴛʜᴇʀ ᴅᴇꜰᴇᴄᴛꜱ ᴛʜᴀɴ ᴛʜᴇ ᴏɴᴇ ᴛʜᴇʏ first discovered.

Except that it was confirmed that he was just as deaf as he was mute. But there were several people who could tell you that that's how it often was.

Oh, and sometimes he cried, the big baby. But Jørgen did too, if he got mad enough.

Fritz's father was Dahl's new chief machinist.

It didn't sit very well that Dahl brought an outsider to the island. At Ottar's store they stood along the walls and swore that more than one of them could have handled that job.

The kids discovered that Fritz could run even faster than Tora. He wasn't all that good with his fists, but he functioned well in the defense against the village kids, simply because he was mute. A kind of terror hung about him.

"Here he comes, the deaf-mute!" the village kids whispered among themselves and retreated.

And the Tenement kids made Fritz the standard bearer at every raid. They let the thin boy take the lead with his gutteral noises. Often that was enough to command respect.

Fritz and his parents lived in one of the vacant shacks that had once been a part of the Brinch fishing station. Now Dahl owned them and he used them to house workers who weren't residents of the island.

Fritz's mother had a permanent and her name was Randi. That was somehow a girl's name. She was as short and chubby as her son and husband were ungainly and tall. Her eyes sparkled with life and looked straight at people.

There was no moderation in that house. The father was

low-voiced and smiled a lot, if he wasn't exactly mute. All the kids liked him.

Randi wasn't content just to smile. She laughed, like Gunn or Aunt Rachel. And she talked like an avalanche. There was something so boundlessly free about people who laughed, Tora thought. Their laughter wasn't raucous like that of the men who gathered in some of the shacks on Saturdays to tell stories and drink, or the gangs of kids who came by on their way to the youth center. No, it sounded more as if they were so full of goodness and enjoyment that they couldn't keep it inside.

Randi had a low, cooing laugh. Almost like the sounds of grouse in the spring.

The shack's furnishings were more than a little strange, Tora thought. Of course there were the same spartan and practical things there that could be found in all the shacks: tables, chairs with spindle backs, kitchen counter, bunk beds. A stove with the indispensible clothes line above it. A nail for the stove jack. A nail for the ladle by the sink. A shelf on the wall for a radio, for those lucky enough to have one.

But at Fritz's there were newspapers on the radio shelf, because the radio was in a shiny, lacquered cupboard near one of the bunk beds. In the cupboard there was also a record player!

A radio cabinet, Randi called the cupboard. It was like a miracle.

Tora's eyes grew big the first time she saw it. Fritz was obviously proud of the cupboard, for he put a whole stack of records on the spindle above the plush-covered turntable, even though he couldn't hear anything himself. He kept the door open and watched carefully every time a new record dropped. Accordion, violin, guitar. Yes, even a flute. And songs! Tora sat and listened on the knitted bedspread on the bunk bed. Blessed Fritz, who didn't waste the precious minutes chattering! It was almost like getting a new warehouse attic. But it was warmer and brighter here.

Besides, the warehouse attic didn't exist anymore. When there was trouble, she was as homeless as an unwanted fly.

She was a snail on a wagon track. So there was nothing to do but hope nobody came driving along.

She always looked way up the side of the fire-scarred chimney when she was in the village.

Just *that* high the roof must have been, to judge by the marks. Tora felt powerless over what couldn't be changed. The defiance withered inside her. She too had become another person since the fire, just like her aunt and uncle.

The flames! She could see them, see her notebooks flying around like black, charred flakes in the fiery wind. See them disappear out over the ocean. As if they'd never existed. Taking with them the good solitude and all the blessed flute tones.

She'd been at Breiland when they needed her, just as her father had always been dead when she needed him. He couldn't help it, either. That was just the way it was.

But she'd got something in place of her notebooks. Something she didn't even have to make up.

There were lots of remarkable things at Randi's and Fritz's. The shelves, for example. Many shelves between the windows!

Several rows. Not full of bric-a-brac and flower vases the way they were at Aunt Rachel's and Uncle Simon's. No, they were tightly packed with books. Almost like a library. All kinds. Worn and new, thin and thick.

There wasn't room for all of them, so some were in cardboard boxes under the bunk beds.

Tora peeked into the thick novels. Glanced stealthily over at Randi to see if she disapproved of her looking in the books, or kept track of which ones she picked up.

But no, she just went on with whatever she was doing and didn't care.

Randi had a knitting machine that made a banging noise when she used it. And she used it a lot.

She made money knitting.

Sometimes she made cocoa when Tora was there. Otherwise, she stayed mostly over in the kitchen nook and at her knitting machine. Now and then she would turn and smile over at Fritz and Tora. And Tora, uncertain and surprised, smiled back. It occurred to her that the house was unique for a reason other than the books and the cabinet with a record player and radio in it: it was the smiling, for the sake of smiling. Strange.

Tora found a tattered and worn book without a real cover. It was about love. A young girl married a rich lord from England and moved with him to his castle. Then strange and unpleasant things started happening. It was unbearable. There was a housekeeper who tried to make the heroine leave. And then there was the rich man's dead wife, Rebecca! He was apparently unable to forget her. It was unbearable. Tora curled up on the knit bedspread and a thin skin formed on the cocoa. It slowly got cold, without anybody telling her she ought to drink it up.

Tora got to take the book home when she left. She didn't know what was better, the record player or the books. Or the room that didn't have the faintest shadow of the danger! Sometimes Fritz and Randi "talked" together. Then they used sign language. Let their fingers fly quick as lightning between them.

Randi was easy for Tora to understand too, because she said out loud what she tried to let her fingers say. She moved her mouth as if it were a funnel. Rounded it, stretched it and let the sounds out of her lips as if it were important to get out all the small sounds that otherwise disappeared so easily inside.

And Tora realized that Fritz could tell from Randi's mouth what she was saying. It was strange.

Tora tried to learn sign language too. It went slowly. But it didn't look as if Fritz let it annoy him. Nobody, in fact, got mad or annoyed at Fritz's at all. It was almost unnatural.

They talked to each other as if they weren't ashamed to show that they were fond of each other.

Aunt Rachel and Uncle Simon also loved each other, but now and then they quarreled anyway. At least her aunt did. If for no other reason than just to be a tease.

But at Fritz's quarreling was unthinkable and improper. Tora wondered if it could be because Fritz was a deaf mute.

The result was that Tora neglected Sol and the Tenement kids more and more in order to be at Fritz's.

Her eyes had someplace to be all the time. She didn't need to be afraid they were going to give her away. They were either reading or else she fastened them on the embroidered guest towel that hung over the wash basin. It had pictures of a mountain dairy on it, with flowers and goats. And a red-cheeked girl who was giving the goats something that flew from her hand like a cloud.

The music came through the room and carried her into the embroidery on the towel, where it was always summer.

When she started home, she felt sometimes a kind of tenderness for Sol. Knew that she was failing her. Because Sol couldn't go visiting and drag along all her little brothers and sisters to listen to the record player.

Sol was a prisoner.

Tora knew she was failing her. But it felt almost good to walk home in the strange, blue air and be sad because Sol was a prisoner.

It wasn't that she begrudged Sol a better fate. It was just good to feel sad in such a fine and melancholy way, without pain and torment.

One evening as Tora was about to go home, Randi followed her out into the big, cold entryway. "It's nice of you, Tora, to spend so much time with Fritz. And go to so much trouble to learn sign language."

Tora stood there. The blood flooded into her cheeks from embarrassment. She shook her head helplessly. There was so much she wanted to say, explain, say thank you for. But it would sound so dumb. It all disappeared through the grey-painted entryway floor. In a flash she understood how it might be for Fritz when she was sitting on the bedspread in the bunk bed and listened to music, or when the kids playing in the Tenement yard were talking and yelling without taking into account that he had to see their mouths to understand. And Tora tumbled out into the spring night.

She didn't go straight home. Wanted to have a little time to herself. Her legs seemed to walk up the gravel road to Bekkejordet by themselves. When she'd come so far up that the scrub birch took over from the heather, she was saved in a way. She stole in to the woods without searching for a path or an opening. The smell of birch shoots overwhelmed her suddenly and unexpectedly.

It made her feel as if she'd gotten well after a long illness. From up in the scree beneath Veten she heard the black grouse rustling and making noises.

Tora sat down on a mossy hill beneath a mountain ash tree. Strangely weak in the knees. The heather and the moss were damp. The snow was gone up here. She could glimpse the fresh green among all that was brown, withered.

After a while she had her face under control enough to walk down.

And Tora took the short cut under the fish drying racks, breathing in the pungent, sour smell of half-dried fish, fish that had fallen off the racks and begun to rot, and the strange smell of seaweed and salt air that was everywhere outdoors in the spring. It clung to everything and everyone.

The sea gull. The sea gull was free and afraid at the same time, just as she was. She looked at it. Listened to its sorrowing and piercing screams. She could afford to feel sorry for something that was less free than she. It felt like velvet behind her eyelids when the wind brushed past. Like that.

The small birds weren't as free as the gulls, and more afraid. There weren't so many of them down here in the village. But up at Bekkejordet they had nests in the underbrush. You began to feel good inside just looking at them. Wanted to hold each one of them, warm them in your cupped hands. Feel the tiny claws and the delicate feathers on the skin of your fingers.

And she thought of Fritz, who never said anything. Who just smiled and left people alone.

Chapter Twenty-Five

THE CONTRAST BETWEEN THE TENEMENT AND THE shack loft where Fritz lived wasn't so great on the surface.

The paint was just as faded both places.

There was the same kind of utility sink. Yes, even the rubber rim on the sink was the same.

There were more points of similarity than there were book shelves, record players and records.

But there was something in the air. At home it was sadder. Full of nervous soap smell and the lurking danger.

Tora felt bad when she thought like that, for she knew that her mother struggled so hard.

Above all, there was *him*. A kind of shadow. A dependency or threat that there was no use ignoring.

Tora taught herself not to think about it. One of the few times she remembered *he* was a human being was when he hit her mother this spring. The insanity that had made her talk back to him but made everything worse for Mama.

Tora had seen that his face had human features. But she didn't look at him often. It was too disgusting. And painful.

Tora's temper wasn't regular anger. It usually made things worse, she thought.

Sometimes she'd seen how it caused really big disasters.

It was that way with crying too.

You couldn't let people see you after you'd been crying.

Crying was by its very nature shameful. So completely incomprehensible and irrational to those who saw the traces it left.

After her uncle's fishing station burned down, Tora had to go into the woods to be all alone. And even in the woods there was sometimes a gust of the danger, now that it was beginning to stay light around the clock and she couldn't hide under cover of darkness.

Especially after the time she'd seen *him* come quietly and quickly around Aunt Rachel's and Uncle Simon's barn.

Tora had never imagined he walked around up there. Her heart still sank when she remembered that she couldn't be safe from meeting him in the woods either. . . .

"You shouldn't be down at the Monsens so much. You're just pestering them. They have only the one room, after all."

Ingrid was using her complaining voice.

"They're just happy I spend time with Fritz. That's what Randi told me this afternoon. That I was nice because I spend so much time with him."

"Why?"

"Because he's a deaf mute, of course!"

"As if you shouldn't spend time with him just because he's a deaf mute!"

Ingrid leaned wearily up against the wall and yawned, but a furrow had appeared between her eyebrows.

"That's what I think too. It's not me who . . . "

"No, no, but you mustn't be bothering them by hanging around all the time, anyway," Ingrid interrupted, irritated.

"The fish are in, I have to work tonight. No matter how tired I am. You'll have to take care of yourself, Tora. There's a big piece of baking chocolate in the drawer. Rachel brought it when she stopped by. We had some with our coffee, but there's lots left."

The words hit Tora like a fist. She'd been so sure that since her mother wasn't gone yet, this late, she wouldn't be going at all tonight.

She pulled off her jacket by the door and hung it up properly, to please her mother.

She'd already seen it in the entryway: his boots weren't there. That's all it took to make her happy. She thought at once of making tea for herself and her mother. Then they could drink tea and eat sandwiches and talk. Maybe she could tell her mother about Randi and Fritz.

Somebody was at the door downstairs and Tora felt a pain in her stomach like tongs. Was it him?

No! Her relief wouldn't last long. But it was a kind of breathing space, a postponement.

The night loomed in front of her like a whole winter. A cold and clammy wind with the door ajar. There wasn't any way around it.

She knew what she could expect.

She chatted with her mother about all kinds of things. Pretended she hadn't even heard that Ingrid was going to go to work. Didn't want her mother to feel she was a shackle on her foot when she had to go. She remembered all too well the last time her mother tried to get out of the night shift and had almost been fired. No, her mother had so many worries.

"They talk about everything you can imagine at Fritz's," Tora said. She was standing with her back to Ingrid, pouring tea into her cup.

"What d'you mean—everything you can imagine?" Ingrid was immediately on guard.

"Oh, just that they're afraid his dad's going to lose his job and they're worried Fritz will have to stay home when he graduates from the school for the deaf. They say he's too smart to waste himself like that. And they say there's a lot of gossiping in the village, too."

She stopped.

Ingrid stared at her warily.

"Well?"

"Don't you think it's strange they talk that way so I can hear?"

"What kind of people are they?"

"Fritz's father was at sea before, but he had to come ashore because Randi got too nervous being alone so much. Don't you think it's odd, her saying it herself?"

"Oh, she's just one of those gossips, I suppose. Can't keep her mouth shut."

"They don't talk about what other people do," Tora explained quickly and regretfully, when she realized that Ingrid had got a false impression of Randi.

"We listen to music. They've got so many records!"

Tora talked herself breathless because she was afraid her mother would believe she went to Randi's and gossiped.

"You'd better not spread it all over the island, if it's true that they tell you things that aren't meant for your ears or anybody else's!"

Ingrid's voice was sharp. Just a little. But enough. The room seemed empty.

"I don't tell anything to anybody but you, Mama," she said quietly and sat down at the end of the table.

It often happened that when Tora tried to talk to her mother, Ingrid hung a kind of curtain between them.

Tora's words stopped, stuck in the curtain. Never got through.

"Randi for sure comes from rich people in Bodø. She's got a knitting machine and a record player from her father, even though she's grown up and as old as you."

Tora didn't seem able to give up hoping tonight. Went on talking as if afraid her mother would disappear forever when she left.

"Well, it's time for me to be going," Ingrid replied. She began getting ready to go. With her checkered cloth bag in her hand, she gave Tora last minute instructions about the lights and the stove.

Tora was already listening for the sounds of someone turning the handle on the entryway door downstairs.

She felt sick and dizzy, her stomach tied up in knots. A kind of anxiety. No, emptiness after a wound. She wouldn't let Mama go! Couldn't! She had to think of something. Follow her into the yard? Yes!

Tora ran after her down all the steps. Wanted to walk with her part of the way. Then she remembered she didn't have her jacket on. She stopped and went to the outhouse instead.

Ingrid was already going out through the gateposts. She turned slightly when she heard the child behind her. She lifted her hand.

Tora stayed where she was, irresolute. Then she raised a powerless hand too.

For a little while she stayed there and watched her mother and felt that the night was meaningless.

Then she went slowly into the outhouse and closed the door. She was alone there with her face.

She discovered it as soon as she wiped herself.

The blood!

At first she refused to believe it. Her first thought was to run after her mother. But then she realized how dumb it would be to bother her mother when she'd just have to go to work anyway. The blood was there. Nobody in all the world could do anything about it. That much she knew, at least. The blood had come to stay. She'd suddenly become another Tora.

A Tora she didn't know herself.

Sol! Maybe she could call out for Sol?

No. Sol was putting the little kids to bed right now. Sol had enough to do. She'd heard the scrapings and the banging up there that meant the nightly uproar was in progress.

Tora wiped herself. Put a folded piece of newspaper in her underpants so it wouldn't go through until she got back to the house. It was bad enough as it was. The paper stuck to her skin, foreign and strange. She walked stiffly and slowly across the courtyard, up the stairs and into the kitchen.

All the while swallowing something that kept wanting to come up into her throat, she heated wash water. She washed quickly and anxiously, holding her breath and constantly listening for footsteps on the stairs and a hard grip on the door handle in the entryway.

Twice someone came. Quick as a flash she pulled down her skirt and rushed into her room. She couldn't take her heart with her. It didn't beat again until the threat was past and the steps continued past their door.

She finished. She burned the used newspaper in the stove. That part was easy. The pants themselves were more of a problem. She put them in a bucket to soak and put a lid on it. She found a soft, clean pair of cotton underpants. Put a wash cloth in her crotch and fastened it there with two safety pins, as she'd heard Sol say she did in a pinch.

Then she carefully removed all traces. It was as if the washing itself was shameful too and had to be hidden.

That night Tora didn't stick the knife in the door frame. It had turned out to be useless. All it did was give her time to wake up, to gather her strength and make herself numb to what she knew was coming, separate herself from her body like a used garment on the bed.

Tonight she didn't think she could stand it anymore. Everything had become too overwhelming for her. She didn't know if she'd be able to go on.

Powers she had no control over drove her to get her mother's big carving knife. It was long and sharp. Safer than the peeling knife.

She put it under her blanket. In her room. Ice cold against her skin. It got warm gradually. Hot.

Felt as if it had been in the oven.

Burned her under her arm when she bumped it.

Every time sleep started to come over her she woke up with a jerk. The knife!

She smelled the blood distinctly. Completely fresh blood.

But there was nobody in the room except Tora. The new Tora!

The moon came in through the window. Pale in the spring night and the clear sky, it stared at her. Asked about nothing. Didn't want to know, didn't want to understand. Didn't want to be part of it.

The curtains fluttered in the breeze from the open window. The angel was hanging over the bed, like a shadow afraid of the dark.

The smell of blood was there the whole time.

Tora shivered her way through the hours. Couldn't bring herself to shut the window.

Then the midnight sun came, with arrows of light against the thin skin of her eyelids. Tiredness and cold made a nest far down in her stomach and they spread to the insides of her thighs. She couldn't touch herself, not even to try to get warm.

The knife!

Suddenly she was wide awake. The door was already part way open! Life had become so overwhelming and so pitch dark. There was no other way out!

The knife!

At the moment of necessity, the sun lit up a red flower on the floor. That shield was safe, even though it was fragile. It had saved girls and women before, although Tora didn't know it.

A dried blood rose. A dark red flower in the blue gym shorts she'd made herself in home economics class. A top went with it. But she didn't wear that.

She hadn't had clean pants the day before . . . the day before yesterday . . . so she'd worn the shorts.

Neat, orderly stitches. Sewn by hand. Both her mother and Gunn had said she'd done a good job.

Basted and finished. Even homemade bias-tape.

She'd let them fall right by the bed. A rose of blood was in the crotch. To protect her from what she couldn't protect herself from. Brutal hands, the brutal danger. The night.

The reluctant door creaked a little. Then there was silence for the moment it took for the shield to stand guard and the sun to play its part. The door closed.

There wasn't any more creaking until she heard her mother's steps on the stairs. The running of water in the kitchen.

Tora stretched her legs. Felt the warmth flowing uncertainly around in her, as if it didn't really dare.

Felt the strange, hard cloth between her thighs. She hadn't bothered to feel it until now.

She heard her mother open the door to the living room.

Chapter Twenty-Six

Tora was never going to be a mother!

She'd made that solemn vow to herself. Never be religious, either. Like Elisif. Never marry someone like... like *him*. Never. She was never going down in some damp laundry room and scrub someone's socks and underwear.

The women of the Tenement were grateful that at least they had a laundry room. Its floor was concrete only where the drain and the hose were mounted, but it was a laundry room anyway. Good to have in the winter, even if it wasn't warm. They had the old stove with the illegal pipe going up to the cracked chimney. They could heat two laundry pans at a time in a pinch. If you dressed for it, and wore two pair of stockings inside your rubber boots, you didn't suffer all that much. That is, if you weren't lazy and didn't save up a month's washing and then have to stand there bent over all day and night. But people like that deserved what they got, in Johanna's opinion.

Each of the women in the Tenement had her own scheduled washday, and Einar up in the garret had his too. But his washing wasn't even worth the name, the poor old wreck. Sometimes Johanna pulled his clothes off the line and soaked them over again. Einar yelled at her when he discovered it. Stretched his neck out and stuck his face up into hers and cursed her and the Devil. But Johanna was accustomed to roguish men and took it calmly.

"We've never had shit butts and louse-infested bums here and we're not going to start now! You're just going to have to put up with me boiling your underpants, you old turd!"

But woe to whoever used the laundry room out of turn! She'd have to put up with being bawled out down the stairs. It was extremely rare that anyone ever tried and then it was usually by accident. The Tenement had its few, but inviolable laws, in war as in peace. One of them was the laundry schedule.

Tora was going to have her own house when she grew up. Like Aunt Rachel. She wouldn't take any lip from anyone. She swore to that as she sat on the stairs going up to Elisif's landing and consoled Sol because she'd got a going-over from Johanna for doing laundry out of turn.

She'd been down in the laundry room soaking diapers on the wrong day. So the wooden tub was full when Johanna came down. Sol hadn't been able to keep track of the days that week. Mistook Wednesday for Thursday, because she'd run out of diapers. That was the mistake in a nutshell. Sol wasn't married, she wasn't even confirmed, but she was stuck in a rut anyway that she had terrifyingly little chance of escaping.

But Sol had dreams that no one was allowed to share or take from her. She could sit at the kitchen counter with her legs crossed and stare out the window while chewing thoughtfully on her yellow school pencil. Staring and staring. Into some magnificence that was completely invisible to everyone else.

And Wednesday became Thursday without her knowing how it happened.

Away! Away from the island! That was the goal for both of them.

Sol sniffed a little and tugged at her shapeless sweater.

Tora agreed but didn't say much. Just nodded and gathered both braids into a point under her chin.

But she never wanted to be forced to run away! Someday Tora would be able to tell everyone she met that she, Ingrid's daughter, was going away for a while.

She never wanted to do anything so that she would have to go the way her mother had to once. . . .

She didn't want to be sent away either, like Elisif.

No, she'd go of her own free will and because she herself had decided it.

She didn't want to let the kinds of things that only grown women know the words for make her decisions. Never!

And she didn't want to run away like the father of Jenny's kid. That worthless bum!

No, she'd find a good reason. It would be just as natural as her aunt's trip to Breiland to get her teeth fixed. Yes, as natural as spring rain.

Because she should be allowed to return without anybody bawling her out! And she'd come back when she felt like it, just as naturally as the May sun and the buds on the trees.

Fritz had this kind of a reason. But he just longed for home when he was away at his school. Even though everybody was so terribly nice there.

He'd told her that himself in his sign language. Simply. Directly. But he'd signed it for her in his way. Tora understood it from his eyes, from his whole face.

They could sit for hours on his knitted bedspread while Tora practiced sign language.

It was fun. But it went slowly. She taught the other kids the simplest signs. But they didn't have the patience to use them when they were all outside playing. Tora had gotten a jump on the others and become unique in a way, because she had taught herself this. It felt good.

Gunn said it was useful to know, when she heard about it. And Tora thought this was better than when she and Sol were little and the first to learn Pig Latin. Gunn asked the children to bring Fritz with them up to the Manor, to be with them when they were in school.

But Fritz shook his head when Tora mentioned it and wouldn't.

In the fall, in September, Fritz would have to go back, Randi said.

And her eyes clung helplessly to her son when she mentioned that.

Tora sat on the stairs with Sol and thought about all this while

Sol vented her anger and humiliation.

But it must be nice to be like Fritz. To have a name for your misfortune. A name that gives you a reason to go your way and makes people long for you when you're not there.

Chapter Twenty-Seven

"IT SAYS HERE A GERMAN TRAWLER, THE *Heinrich Kaufmann*, has been fishing inside the limits off Finholmen!"
Ottar was reading aloud to the men.

He'd taken a short break, even though a couple of kids were standing there waiting their turn. They didn't need to learn any more bad habits. They, too, had to learn to wait.

Tora's mouth fell open. Her happiness over having eighty-five *kroner* with her from her mother was instantly forgotten.

"Sink the Devil!" said Håkon savagely. He shifted his pipe from one corner of his mouth to the other.

"There's more."

Ottar was in full swing now.

"They had ten tons of fish onboard. But now they have to appear in Hammerfest municipal court. Well, maybe that'll do some good. But I'm thinking about all the ones that *aren't* caught."

"Oh, well, they're probably not all from the Gestapo, those dogs, who are out stealing fish!" said Einar and sank down on a vacant chair by the counter.

"There's more," continued Ottar. Today it was Ottar serving up the great world to the simple Einar of the Tenement and the others. He enjoyed the role and completely forgot to wait on the children.

"Ten year's occupation of West Germany ends today! Uh-huh, just wait! In a few years we'll have them over our heads again. With bombs and rockets too. I don't know why the Allies didn't squeeze the life out of them when they had the chance!"

"Well, well, they're human beings too, after all," Einar said, and cleared his throat. "Not all of them were in on the slaughtering. And I don't suppose things have gone so well for them either, since the war. We have to remember . . . "

"What's wrong with you, did you just come from church?" Kornelius suddenly woke up at the counter, and grinned derisively.

"No," said Einar reluctantly, and smacked his lips, "but I think we have to start all over and give the Devil's children a chance."

"How quick you forget!" spat out Kornelius, enraged. "Maybe you're just like these fools they write about in the paper. Let me see, now . . . yeah, here it is: 'Ten year anniversary of Norway's liberation! Two minutes' silence at 12 o'clock noon, ten minutes ringing of the church bells. The war taught us to value truth, freedom and fatherland, and respect for the worth of human life.' Uh-huh! Kiss my ass! Two minutes of silence in honor of five years of war, huh?"

"I've never sided with the big shots," Einar replied, "not when it's a question of loud noises or those two minutes of silence as dignified as hell. And you know it! But you also know who it is who does the fighting when there's war. It's the common people! People like you and me! And it's in our best interest that the devilment and war stop! Don't you understand that, you fool?"

"Now, now, don't quarrel over it, you'll just make more trouble," put in Ottar and caught sight of Tora.

He cleared his throat and signalled to her with a nod to come up to the counter. And Tora walked slowly up and into the circle. She felt the back of her neck burning as all the men remembered who she was. But she steeled herself anyway and looked directly at Ottar when she handed him her mother's note and the eighty-five *kroner*.

The note read: "Send four pounds of flour (whole wheat) and a box of matches and a package of yeast with Tora. The money is to be used towards paying what I owe from before. Ingrid."

Tora raised her chin and fixed her gaze on the bundle of

paint brushes hanging from the edge of the shelf directly in front of her.

The store became completely silent.

Once she was safely out on the road again, she felt a strange, small wave of gratitude for Einar of the garret, who didn't like children, but who *saw* her the whole time.

He spoke in such a way that she was spared the worst.

And Tora understood that people aren't always the way they're rumored to be. She vowed not to believe a word of the gossip going around the village that Einar stole like a raven. Because Einar was the kind of person who saw and listened. That was the most important thing about people.

She defiantly kept kicking the same little rock all the way up to the Tenement, even though she knew she wasn't supposed to. Her shoes were too good for that sort of thing. They were brand-new and she was only wearing them that day so she wouldn't get blisters on the 17th of May.

There was a loud whistling and roaring inside Tora. Did it come from the sea? Or from the thin birch trees that stood there and didn't know if they dared burst into leaf? Or was it just the flute melodies in her? The knowledge that she dared look into Ottar's eyes when she handed him the money.

The waves! There was so much power in them, so much tenderness.

The ocean roared in a giant sea shell. Tora knew that she heard melodies that came from outside herself, from a larger context than the one she could get at Ottar's store. She knew there were more and greater truths than those they talked about there.

But she couldn't put them into words. She could only feel a kind of joy at it, a joy she could take out when it got dark and she needed it.

Chapter Twenty-Eight

THE KNITTED PIECES CREATED A COMPLEX PATTERN. ALL shades of red yarn next to each other.

Randi let the knitting machine run. She had already given Tora the afghan, even though it wasn't finished yet.

Tora had begged everybody she knew for red yarn. Even Gunn had given her a little ball.

But she didn't ask her mother.

The afghan grew bigger, and whenever Tora was in the village for milk, she found an excuse to go up to Fritz and Randi's to see how much was left before the afghan would be finished.

Randi always wanted her to stay a while.

The hours spent there were happy. Tora treasured her visits and looked forward to the ones to come. That way, she always had something good to think about.

Sometimes Sol came along, if she could bully Jørgen into looking after the smallest kids for a while.

And Sol took in everything she saw with awe and shining eyes.

The afghan and the radio cabinet especially.

Fritz just pointed teasingly at his own bedspread, so they'd understand that he thought it was fancier. Then they all laughed a little.

He let out the most remarkable throat noises, which he used whenever he laughed in front of people he knew. If strangers were present, he always laughed without making a sound.

The day the afghan was finished, Tora and the other kids were running among the fish drying racks playing hawk and dove, although they were really much too old for it. They had the littlest kids with them and pretended they were playing on account of them.

Then Randi opened a window and called Tora in.

It was as if Tora had imagined the afghan would always be unfinished, something Randi would work on for her forever.

Tora was standing in the door out of breath and hadn't even had time to take off her boots when Randi held the afghan up in front of her. It hung down from her outstretched hands all the way to the floor.

Tora just stood there, looking.

She wasn't able to get out a word of thanks.

"You can take it home with you," Randi said with a smile.

"Oh—no!"

Tora finally found her voice. Stared at Randi in shock.

"But of course you can! It's yours! You even got the yarn for it yourself. Take it! You're welcome to it!"

Randi laughed and wrapped it up in a big piece of wrapping paper. Tora stood there bewildered, playing absently with some yarn on the kitchen table.

"Oh, and take the yarn, too. You may need to repair it some day."

Tora shook her head. Then it came out hesitantly, "Can it—can it stay here? The afghan, I mean? It's good to have something to sit on—when I'm here. I mean because I read here, you know."

"But is that what you *want?*" Randi sounded disappointed. Had expected something else, apparently. Maybe expected that Tora would run straight home with it and show it off.

Tora understood. It was a torment she couldn't find words for. But there was no way around it! She couldn't spread this afghan out on her bed at home. Never!

She couldn't get the right words out.

Only a weak thank you.

Nothing more was said about the afghan going to the Tenement. It lay folded up at the foot of Fritz's bed.

The last thing Tora did before she left was to fold it nicely into a warm, woolly square.

Randi had given her another present too. She took that

174

home with her. *Bonjour Tristesse* was its title and it cost twelve and a half *kroner*. On the inside of the dust jacket was a picture of a young woman with an unreasonably strange name: Françoise Sagan. Tora stared at the picture, but quickly forgot the name.

As she read, she was aghast at how bad Cecilie, the heroine, was. Reluctantly she had to admit that this was a book that didn't have any "nice" characters. It was almost strange. Ugly! Tora didn't know if she liked the book.

At last she realized that if you were going to write books about people who really live, it couldn't be anything other than just that: ugly! And she thought about her grandmother in Berlin, and a kind of uneasiness came over her. That her story might not be ugly enough to be true.

When Tora was reading, almost everything else lost its hold on her. It was like rowing all the way out from Storholmen and the buoys. The islands far out there somehow came floating towards her on the broad, green back of the sea. Wanted her, wanted to subdue her, pull her out. And there was a never-ending motion. Heavy, but at the same time light. Powerful, flat waves that had neither beginning nor end but just flowed eternally in their own rhythm. Over and over.

That's why she always rowed backwards when she rowed.

Everybody laughed at her because she rowed that way.

But Tora didn't care. She had to *see*. She had to go into "it" with open eyes. She somehow owned everything as far as the horizon extended. Even knew a way beyond what she couldn't see. Could follow in her fantasy where the earth curved and plunged abruptly downwards. But it really wasn't so abrupt.

She knew that. Everything didn't happen at once.

She'd seen the mountains on the mainland look like they were floating in the sky, when the light was right. But of course she knew that they were in the sea, like all mountains.

Anyway. For her it was true: they were in the sky. They were a road to travel. Later.

In reality, the roads out in the world were gently sloping and endless. Yes! You had to give yourself time to learn the road.

You had to teach yourself to search and make choices.

It was like being in a labyrinth. You searched continually, you couldn't help it if you took a wrong turn. For in any case, you knew there were other roads. And you were sure that *one* road led out! It was just a matter of learning to wait, as silent as Fritz, without explaining anything to anybody.

All the steps, all the thoughts existed to be taken and to be thought. You could easily let them go a moment if you wanted to, but they came back. All the oar strokes were necessary, they were a part of the road.

It was that way with books, too. Tora always had a book she hadn't read yet. She was allowed to borrow them from Gunn and Randi. She trudged between the dusty shelves at the library in the shed-like building owned by the county and was as quiet as a mouse.

She found something to stare at while Dordi stamped her card and asked if she was borrowing for herself or for her mother.

Tora forced herself to stare at the painting above Dordi's head and answered, casually, "Both of us!"

And the farm in the painting had such sad, pale colors, the sheep were much too snow white, and the little pond at the edge of the forest was much too blue. And Tora thought that it was pretty enough, but it wasn't true.

And she recalled how her room could look on a clear morning in April, when the sun came in through the window and began to explore under her bed. Then it didn't make any difference that she'd washed the floor the day before. The sun showed her that there were millions of pieces of lint and bits of dust under there. The sun showed her that her bed was by its very nature shameful. Because it made her remember.

It was true. But it wasn't beautiful.

Sometimes she had to turn suddenly around on the road. Because the voices came into her from nowhere and swept her thoughts out. Or she had to turn her boat around because the waves from the open sea got too frightening and heavy, even though the weather was calm.

Even so, she could always know that it wasn't the end. Not

yet. Because the labyrinth kept going, turn by turn. She knew that!

There would always be days when somebody would loan her a boat again. There were millions of unread books in the world.

In the history book it said that Berlin was a bombed city where people still weren't allowed to be friends.

In her imagination Tora saw the bodies burned to pieces, the torn-off limbs, saw the flames that licked up over the faces which partly resembled her. It was agony while it lasted. But it made her thoughts so ugly and real that she could easily indulge herself in having a grandmother as large as life in the middle of everything.

Her mother didn't bring up the conversation about her father again. Tora understood that *that* was too ugly for her.

She would have to wait, she would have to walk the roads—alone. There was nothing else to do.

Even so, she forced herself out into the rain, forced herself to run off. Quickly, quickly. She took all her thoughts with her in her flight!

Tora could wonder how her father's bed looked, there in Berlin. Or how his doorway looked.

The dot on the map in her atlas sometimes grew in her imagination. She saw everything as in the crystal ball in the fairy tale. And Tora knew that what she saw wasn't ugly enough for it to be completely real. But she saw it anyway: a house in a big garden. Yellow light on one side, the side that faced the wide road and the high gate posts. A forest on the other side. The wind blew in the large branches, and ferns and flowers grew among the trees.

She saw the whole scene from high above in its wide expanse—and observed how it tapered off in the distance inside itself. The ferns grew in the middle of the picture. Lush, heavy and green. The landscape spread out from them. The church towers, the houses and the gardens on one side, the lake and forest on the other.

She always saw the same scene. In that way it became real

for her. Familiar, in a way. But she constantly discovered new details.

The house had a wide concrete stairway with a gilded bannister.

The house was painted white, with two stories, but it wasn't as tall as Dahl's. Because Dahl's house looked cold and arrogant, Tora thought.

No, her father's home had two dormers that faced the garden and rosebushes facing the street.

In a flower bed right next to the stairs, blue flowers like those she'd seen in a garden at Breiland last summer were growing luxuriantly, but she didn't know their name.

Of course her grandmother knew that it wasn't awful to be German. She knew that the ugly voices that came over the radio now and then, speaking German harshly, were intended to scare people into remembering the war that everybody really wanted to forget. Grandmother knew that Tora's father wasn't one of those terrible German soldiers, the kind pictured in newspapers and books, with leather boots and bayonets. Grandmother knew all that had been invented to torment her and give the other kids the right to tease and shout after her.

Sometimes Tora took Fritz with her to Berlin. But on those occasions, she never really seemed to arrive there. It was as if the thought of Fritz distracted her. She had to see everything with his eyes. And then she was suddenly able to see that it wasn't ugly enough—to be real. That could ruin a day that was otherwise nice.

Fritz!

She could sit on his bunk bed with the afghan covering her thighs and legs, pretend she was reading, and watch his long fingers when he turned pages.

He had such remarkable, strong fingers and palms. Strong hands that spoke for themselves. Sometimes she got mixed up when they were speaking sign language, just because his hands bewildered her.

And then, when he noticed she wasn't following him, he

bent as close to her as he could and stared straight at her with laughing eyes and did everything over again, slowly.

Or he took her hands and signed right against her palms.

It was so unreasonably sweet. She couldn't help it. Warm shudders ran all through her. From the hollow of her neck and all the way down in her thighs. She felt the faint soap smell of his hair. He already had a little down on his upper lip.

Strange: if he hadn't been mute, maybe his voice would already have begun to change, like some of the boys at school. So the girls bent double from laughing when they were trying to sing, and Gunn had to look at them sternly.

If only Fritz hadn't been mute. . . .

Strange that she never felt disgusting or embarrassed when she was with Fritz. Never felt ashamed that her sweater was tight and short across the chest, not even when he was looking straight at her. Was it because he was mute?

Chapter Twenty-Nine

THE BLOSSOMING OF THE CLOUDBERRIES WAS scandalously late on the islands.

People thought it had to be just a matter of three or four more weeks. They were waiting for the easterlies and the heat.

But in Oslo they were more occupied with Billy Graham, who had taken as his mission the unification of the Norwegian Lutheran Church, the Salvation Army, the Baptists and the Pentecostalists. Thirty-five thousand people filled Ullevål Stadium. It was so far away, and it couldn't be as important as the blossoming of the cloudberries and the sprouting of the potatoes.

Jealousy and sin were diseases of the soul, in the opinion of the great preacher. There was a picture of him in the newspaper. People nodded their heads solemnly and then went straight home and did whatever they felt like doing. That's the way it had always been on the island.

They didn't come by the thousands to be converted, the way they did in Oslo. This summer wasn't the season for conversions on the island. People had only just recovered from the last revival fever, the one that had knocked Elisif off her feet. Everything happened with a delay of at least five years. So Graham would just have to wait for a year when the cloudberries blossomed earlier. No hurry.

It was worse that the price of milk was expected to increase by fifteen to twenty øre. A poor creature would have to pay in blood for skim milk at the milk store, unless, of course, he had the time and means to feed a cow himself.

This spring the farmers had been forced to slaughter some of their animals. And there was talk of a bad year for the crops. The winter had been bad. The spring was like a forgotten paintbrush in the basement. It hadn't been cleaned. It just stood there and bristled in a cracked Mason jar, dry and useless.

Now the only thing lacking was a poor pollack season and a wet fall so the hay could rot in peace. So Billy Graham could save whomever he pleased down there in the south.

In the Tenement, Tora didn't have a rose in her blue gym shorts every time Ingrid had to work the night shift. Everything she'd said to herself about how she would just row, fly, disappear with the wind, all that made no difference when it came down to it. Her belief that her mother would be strong enough to save her—it meant nothing in reality.

Her will was constantly so shaky and so afraid of the dark. Sometimes she thought that she could run to Aunt Rachel and tell her everything. But no. Her mother's sad eyes. Mama had to be spared. Tora had no place in the whole wide world to put her "dirty" body.

The door creaking. Fingers that dug. Dug into her.

One night the door creaking came so suddenly that she had no time to go out of her body and let her thoughts run free out through the window. Tora was forced to be a part of it, experience everything that happened to her.

Then she began to wail and whimper and crawl around on the bed. Wasn't able to lie still and just let it come to an end, the way she did the other nights. That was an impossibility so great that she couldn't control herself.

It confused him and stimulated his hate. It could be used to arouse desire, to justify the use of strength and force.

Her resistance was soft, soft. You had only to press your thumb against its eye. It begged for its life and gave in.

Then something tore. Tora felt it someplace outside herself, didn't know where it began or ended. It didn't belong to the rest of her. But it hurt so much anyway.

Breathing and blood!

The blood came, but it wasn't supposed to. It was in patterns across the whole sheet because she wasn't able to stay in place under him. She understood that this was the ugly reality that couldn't be found in any book she had read.

God bless him if he would go now! She got her hands loose and hit him. She begged. Did it help? God bless him if it helped! He went away.

Her relief was so enormous that she couldn't get her breath. Lay there in a ball panting when she finally got it back. She was hanging over the side of the bed and was cut in half. She was somebody else below her waist.

Then he came back. With a rope.

Tora couldn't believe that she was being tied to the bed. Didn't believe it! The world wasn't that horrible. Things like that didn't happen!

Then he dug his way into her. Blindly. As if he had something to revenge. Just dug and dug. Held the pillow over her face and let his limitless will be done. It had taken a long time to reach his goal. Now he was there.

Everything functioned, finally, as it was supposed to.

Out on the kitchen wall, the clock ran in another world. In here, there was nothing to measure time.

The evening sun was beautiful. Yellow and friendly. It spread gently over the man in the bed. Infinitely gently. The sun in its mercy looks on—and warms anyone at all.

Eventually the creaking died away.

The night was long and light. The Tenement had its sounds. Now and then, crying could be heard in the night. But who could afford to give up a good night's sleep to investigate the crying? It was nobody's business and nothing could be done. Everyone had their own sorrow and their own work shift.

And under the harsh lights at Dahl's fish packing plant, a dark-haired woman was sitting with a kind of uneasiness about something for which she had no name.

But there were no reasons to worry, to imagine. . . .

She was just tired, that was all. It was late and the work tempo had been speeded up. They were in a rush with the packing. The ship was already on the way to load cargo. The fishing boats were already on the way with their roaring engines, ready to spew more piles of fish on the tables. She had her hands full.

There was so little room for two darting girl's eyes.

Dahl was already rubbing his hands. Everything was sold before it was packed. Just a matter of slaving away now. The pay was better than good. No one thought about dead cats.

At last, a grey line of women began moving towards the outer door.

Outside, it was fine early summer weather and the gulls were feasting at the edges of the fields.

Tora had put a clean sheet on her bed. Hidden the other one under the bed for the time being. She'd washed her torn crotch in cold water. She did it in the kitchen. It no longer made any difference somehow.

It was as if she were washing somebody else. She could wonder if the other one felt the same way she did.

The left corner of her mouth was drawn up. Her teeth were bared. Now and then, a twitching went through the stooped, unfinished body.

A kind of sigh spread across her contorted face and turned her mouth into an ugly grimace.

Otherwise everything was quiet. There will always have to come a day after, for the one who survives. There will always be a face for the one who dares to look at herself. Tora didn't dare. She was a half-naked human ball in a hated bed.

She had nothing to say, no one to turn to. If anybody had told her that she mustn't grieve because such things had happened before in the world, everything heals eventually—why, then she would have put on a sincere face and asked, "What things? What happened?"

And the sheet was well hidden.

Chapter Thirty

THE NEW SKIRT HAD LAIN ALL NIGHT ON THE CHAIR BY the bed. It had been a witness to everything. Her mother had cut it in a circle all the way around so that it would billow like waves around her hips. And Tora had been beside herself with happiness because of it. She'd gotten a green pullover sweater to go with it. Her mother had used some of her precious housecleaning money to buy Tora some dress-up clothes.

All the same, the skirt didn't seem to have anything to do with her. She wanted to throw up every time she looked at it.

She was very careful not to look down at herself after she put on the skirt in the morning. She knew she had to put it on, because today was the last day of school.

Fritz was unexpectedly hanging around by the fish drying racks when she passed that way. She was late because her mother had to iron the hem on the skirt before she went. Sol and the others had already left. She had to jog, if she was going to get to school on time.

Tora still carried with her the scent of the damp ironing cloth. She stopped in front of Fritz and tried to compose her face so that he wouldn't be able to see. . . .

It was harder with him than with her mother, for Fritz always looked her straight in the eye.

His stare clung to her so that the sweat sprang out in her armpits and on her back. He came right up to her and gently touched the skirt. Then he made the sign for pretty and smiled hesitantly.

It felt like something was breaking inside Tora.

He straightened up and smiled—that naked, worried smile

of his. Tora felt numb everywhere below her waist.

It was as if her legs were unable to support her any longer.

She wanted to force her way past him.

He raised his hand to point at her pullover—and it brushed one of her breasts. Tora rushed past.

She heard him using his throat noises behind her. But she ran. Ran and ran!

Her crying was stuck. It wouldn't come out.

Soon her pullover was drenched in sweat.

Not until she was in the schoolyard did she stop and breathe. She stuck her hands inside her sweater sleeves and tried in despair to dry away the sweat that wouldn't stop coming. It didn't help much. There were two big stains, one under each arm. She smelled of carnations and death.

Afterwards, as they were sitting and drinking cocoa and eating rolls that Gunn had baked for the big day, Gunn asked, as she filled Tora's cup, "You were late. Did you oversleep?"

Tora felt as if Gunn's eyes saw straight through her. She couldn't help it, she began to shake. "Uh," Tora mumbled, "Mama had to iron the hem on my skirt, because she didn't have time ... "

"That's all right, Tora dear. I was just asking. Because you're never late, you know."

At the word dear, Tora began to shake in earnest. She was barely able to get to the outhouse before she had to pee. It burned, hurt the whole time and she didn't dare wipe herself. Was afraid she'd start bleeding again, because she didn't have anything to use if she bled. She suddenly thought she was in Tobias's shack again, peeing on herself. She could hear the raucous laughter.

The old outhouse was cool and quiet today. Nobody was hanging around, because they were all eating rolls in the big classroom. Tora sat and pulled herself together, thought by thought, gesture by gesture.

At last she felt well enough to go back in to the others. When she came into the hall, she put her light sweater on over her pullover to hide the sweat stains under her arms. That helped.

Chapter Thirty-One

THE WOMEN AT THE PLANT WERE LAID OFF LATER IN THE summer. The fishing had been a disappointment and Dahl was left to chew on his pipestem. Ingrid was lucky and got work housecleaning.

She didn't complain.

Henrik went his own way. He was out of work again. He'd worked for a time at the site of the fire, getting it ready for rebuilding. But then he'd suddenly had a falling out with Simon and walked off.

One day towards the end of June, Simon had strolled onto Dahl's wharf. Talked to the men and was almost his old self again. He was hiring people, he said. To rebuild.

He was planning to go big and modern. He grinned crookedly and swore he'd probably go bankrupt, but it couldn't be helped. Since he didn't even have what it took to be skipper on his own boat, he might as well build a place where he could stay indoors and ashore.

The men forgot their scornful joking and the glances they would usually have exchanged.

They nodded, one after the other, for they spent most of their time looking for work, without any income at all for weeks at a time. Oh sure, they could lend a hand.

Summer was coming on strong, but of course you had to have something to eat then, too. They spat into the water, stood with their legs apart, and nodded. Deliberately and thoughtfully, agreements were made. Handshakes could be exchanged just as easily on Dahl's wharf as in Simon's old blue office.

But as soon as Simon disappeared, they rushed home to their families.

Had barely enough breath left to announce the great news.

They had work for several months! WORK! Not just begging and a few days' pay.

What a man that Simon was! What *wasn't* he capable of? He could even joke about going bankrupt on the business. And have you seen the plans for the fishing station? No? They were worth seeing!

Oh, that Simon! And wasn't that just what they'd said all along, when the jokes were flying their thickest about Simon's stay in the weaving loft, that Simon was a genius?

And geniuses were permitted to stew for a few weeks before getting down to business. And for that matter, wasn't he entitled to it?

"Mama's coming home next week! She's well again."

Sol was down with Ingrid and Tora, eating a late supper after Ingrid's day of housecleaning.

Ingrid leaned heavily on the table top. She let the words sink in.

Then she collected herself and said, "That's good to hear."

"I'm not so sure," Sol said simply.

"You're not sure?" Ingrid asked in disbelief.

"Well . . . Mama isn't made for this world."

A shadow passed over the face of the half-grown child.

"I wish she'd wait until confirmation was over."

"What're you saying, child? You don't want you own mother to see you confirmed?"

"Well, she's so religious."

Unexpectedly, Sol put her head in her arms and hid her face. They thought she was crying. But no sound came out. And when, in a little while, she looked up, she seemed absolutely normal.

"I'm not up to it. Everybody laughs at her."

"She's religious, but we have to put up with that in her. We all do. She is what she is, after all."

Ingrid said that with wrinkles between her eyes and an

angry blush above each cheek.

Tora just sat there and watched. Just think, Mama being able to talk like that! Get angry on Elisif's behalf, even when she was so tired.

"By the way, have you got a confirmation dress yet?"

Ingrid wanted to change the subject.

"No."

Sol sighed and pulled at the tufts of hair that parted in front of her ears. There was something stark raving mad about Sol's ears. They stuck out straight from her head so that you couldn't stop staring at them.

"But it doesn't matter. It's not the clothes that are important."

That sounded like something she'd memorized because somebody had repeated it so often to her she'd finally come to believe it was true.

"Maybe I can borrow a dress from somebody Johanna knows. She thought it might be too big, but . . . it's a pale yellow."

Sol sighed.

"It's short too," she added and took a deep and discouraged breath.

When Torstein came home, Ingrid climbed the stairs and talked to him for a long time.

The next day she took a few hours off work and went to Ottar's store with fifty *kroner* to buy material for a dress for Sol. She chose the white material that was cheapest. It was artificial silk. Really pretty. Ottar didn't bring out the most expensive remnants, because she'd told him right away that she was looking for material for Torstein's Sol.

That night it was almost a party down at Tora's and Ingrid's. Ingrid measured and cut. She'd made a pattern using wax paper that she'd fitted to Sol's stocky body.

The summer sun came diagonally through the newly washed curtains and made the scissor blades flicker like lightning as they snipped their way through the shimmering white material.

Ingrid was quick and deft.

This was something she knew how to do. She checked the measurements of every piece on the girl when she finished cutting it. Sol stood straight up with her gaze fixed on the dish towels above the stove, while Ingrid turned her around endlessly and made the material cover her body. At last Sol went into Tora's room and tried the basted dress on over her underwear. That way they'd get it right, Ingrid said.

Tora thought Sol looked like an angel as she stood there with the material flowing around her full hips. She was suddenly so grown-up, so foreign.

Sol was going to have a dream fulfilled: a long, white dress—and made for her alone!

She stood with her large, rough worker's hands above her head as Ingrid pinned the pieces of the bodice. She was almost graceful. Resembled a ballerina in a picture Tora had seen. She was so completely unlike herself that Tora had to think long and hard before she managed to be happy for her.

Long after the girls were in bed, Ingrid sat at her sewing machine. She had barely taken the time to make supper when Henrik came home.

However, he was having one of his good nights. Didn't curse the mess she was making with the sewing machine the way he usually did. He even praised her work. Ingrid was surprised by it. It felt like getting an expensive gift.

Otherwise he didn't say much. Like a tied up sack. A victim of his own thoughts and darkness.

He went to bed early. She heard him turning and tossing out there in the living room. But he didn't grumble, didn't call for her the way he often did. She was relieved.

Because she'd made up her mind to sew this dress for Elisif's daughter, that's what she'd done! Good deeds of that kind she felt she was up to.

Morning came before she had finished the last cloth belt loop at the waist. Then all that was left to do was gather the ruffle and put a zipper in the side. And the hem, of course.

She'd talked Sol into choosing a somewhat loose fitting fashion in order to conceal her large bosom. And Sol had given in, even though she clearly had a dream of how the dress really should look. But she was intelligent. She understood what Ingrid was trying to tell her, without the words being spoken outright.

Tomorrow night she could do the rest, and then Sol herself could finish the seams. Or maybe it would be best to let Tora do it. Tora did neater work with her hands.

Ingrid had felt such pleasure in the work all the time she was sewing. Tiredness seemed unable to find any foothold in her. Was it perhaps Elisif's God who arranged that kind of joy in work? Even Henrik seemed to understand that this had to be done.

When Ingrid got up from her sewing machine, it was bright morning outside the windows. She felt the long day of cleaning and the six hours as a seamstress burning in her shoulders and back.

One aching spot seemed to flow into the next.

She stretched and took the white dress over to the window. There she let the sun flame over the cheapest silk material in Ottar's store. Poor folks' material!

But Ingrid held it triumphantly in front of her and stuck out one of her feet. Turned slowly around and felt the material slide, nice and cool, across her leg.

For a moment she saw her reflection in the window pane. The white dress with the flowing skirt!

Ingrid let everything go. Something was singing inside her. Before she knew what she was doing, she was standing in the middle of the living room.

She turned slowly in front of the big mirror, holding the dress in front of her. Stood there a little while and just looked.

Then she put the dress on the chair by the door and took off her everyday clothes. Piece by piece.

When she stood with the white silk dress on and saw herself as a slender, white column there in the mirror, she burst into tears.

The long, forgotten years. The bitter role of being judged before you entered a room. The humiliating role of never having the right to be a human being with pride.

She broke down so unexpectedly that she wasn't able to keep the sounds under control.

Only when she became aware of the eyes of the man in the bed did she pull herself together and stop.

"What in *hell* are you doing!" he hissed between his teeth.

"I'm just trying on Sol's dress," she managed to say.

"What're you standing there bawling for, in the middle of the night? Have you gone crazy?"

She just stood there.

"It's also damned late to be putting on a white dress, for that matter. Brides in white aren't for Germans and day laborers."

The voice was distorted. She recognized it.

Ingrid took the dress off slowly, carried it out into the kitchen and hung it on the wall. Then she wiped up the silk dust from the kitchen table and picked up needles and bits of thread. When she went to bed, she was totally calm and empty.

Chapter Thirty-Two

SIMON WAS WELL UNDER WAY WITH HIS REBUILDING.
The framework was already roofed. Things were looking up.
The women put their heads together when they were out
shopping, thunderstruck at how fast it was going. But the un-
employed men who hung over the counter at Ottar's or
strolled around in the village spitting their way through the
long morning hours were of the opinion that Simon had bit off
more than he could chew and was going to end up in the ditch.
They smiled a little at the thought.

Those who were swinging hammers and singing up on the
scaffolding had other things to help them pass the time. For
them Simon's new wharf was nothing less than Solomon's
Temple as it stood there in the autumn storms and made hollow, lonely noises in the wind. It sounded like a badly
neglected organ.

The cause of the fire hadn't been discovered. It had started
in the bait room. Anybody, it was rumored, could come and
go in there. But Simon and Rachel didn't have the kind of enemies who would start fires, not as far as anybody knew. And
that same Simon was himself exonerated of the charge of insurance swindle. He hadn't grown fat on the little he got for
the building itself, and there was no insurance on the fishing
station and its contents.

Innocent, goodhearted curses rang joyously among the rough
bursts of laughter and the beams with their smell of tar.

As the builder, Simon had his hands full. Maybe he wasn't
losing as much on the fishing season he'd missed as he'd
thought at first. The fish weren't running and Dahl had to lay

people off. The women were especially hard hit.

Rachel was weaving. She went to Breiland on errands with thick rolls of woven rugs packed carefully in grey paper from Ottar's store. That was how everybody knew.

She'd almost doubled her flock of sheep and this year she took part in the haying herself.

That was a sign of hard times.

Simon had hired Henrik just to please Rachel. But he was a poor worker. And that was more because of the bottle than the bad arm, Simon thought.

When Henrik had failed to show up three days in a row without telling him, Simon lost patience and marched up to the Tenement.

There weren't many words to get out of Henrik's body that day. But late in the afternoon he came down to the building site and picked up his nail apron and hammer with incredible swiftness. He let the good arm help the other so that the men just stood there staring at how fast he was able to sweep everything up. And then he left without a word.

Simon felt sorry for Ingrid. As far as he was concerned, he had nothing to complain about, for there were three men who wanted to take Henrik's place before nightfall.

There was something inwardly crippled about the man, Simon thought. The heavy, hunched-over figure that only came alive when the bottle was on the table and he could tell one lying story after the other. But some Saturday nights he was left sitting alone at a table in one of the shacks. Then he talked to himself, gestured and hollered, asked and answered. Or just sat there dozing with naked, twisted features.

Simon wondered. He'd heard various stories about a different Henrik, before the accident with the shoulder, before Ingrid and the marriage. What he'd heard wasn't only bad, either. And Simon wasn't at all sure that it was just perversity and evil that made people that way. A bad shoulder or a fire—it could be that they were somewhat alike, Simon thought. And he shuddered whenever he thought of the long days and nights he'd spent up in the weaving loft, when he didn't even have the courage to go find a rope.

A certain someone had pulled *him* up by the hair. Ingrid wasn't the sort to pull people by the hair. It occurred to him that maybe that was more than one had a right to demand of a woman.

Simon regarded himself as a good-natured, simple soul. It made life so much easier. Nothing to brood about. Even so, he couldn't keep himself from puzzling over the hatred he saw in Henrik's eyes. It troubled him from time to time.

He discussed it with Rachel when he got home that night. She was washing lingonberries and glanced quickly up as she picked closely through them, looking for twigs or leaves that wanted to steal down into the wooden bowl she had on the bench next to the table.

"He's just jealous! Maybe he realizes that Ingrid has good reason to think she married the wrong man," she teased.

Simon laughed.

"Oh, you can come up with a reason for anything."

He began helping her pick through the berries but mostly ate them.

"Stop that! You lout! These are going to Breiland so I can buy new carpet warp for my weaving."

A shadow flew over Simon's face.

"It's not right that you have to work your fingers to the bone to make ends meet."

"Nonsense! Are you the only one who's supposed to work? Why shouldn't I, too? In the good days, I put money away in the desk. You never knew how much. And you weren't particular about things like that, either. I had everything I needed. Now the manger's empty. So why shouldn't I also have to sweep through the straw to find something to eat. It's only . . . "

She didn't get any farther. Simon bent his long, strong arms around her. Drew her close as his mouth searched over her entire face.

He drank her in like a thirsty man. Would never be satisfied. Would never have enough.

The next morning, stems, leaves and berries were still scattered over the kitchen table. Simon got up early and straightened everything up, lit the oven, went out for firewood, made coffee and was Rachel's errand boy. He didn't feel ashamed. Would have done it even if the entire village had seen him bustling in and out of the kitchen, being his own wife's maid. He was so happy that he had to do something.

Then he carried the tray up to the loft and served Rachel coffee and breakfast in bed, even though it was the middle of the week.

"I've been thinking," said Rachel, her mouth full of bread and cheese. "I'm going to get Tora to help me. We're going to begin keeping pigs."

Simon couldn't control himself. Rachel as swineherd! He laughed so hard it echoed.

Then he saw her face in the big bureau mirror, and quickly closed his mouth.

"I'll telephone this very day," Simon said. "I'll order two baby pigs and pay for them too."

"Nonsense!" Rachel said haughtily. "There's no time right now. I'll tell you when. And I'll want four. I have enough money myself!"

Chapter Thirty-Three

THE FALL WAS JUST AS CLEAR AND COLD AS THE SUMMER
had been wet and raw. The mountain ash tree outside the
Tenement slapped its red berry clusters against the south wall
whenever the southwest wind came blowing in like a strange
ghost but without any fog.

It looked like the potato crop would be better than the fishing. So you might just as well harvest ashore, and see what it
amounted to.

Tora helped Rachel dig up the potatoes. She would get half
a sack for every gruelling day she put in, said Rachel, all business. And a bucket of seed potatoes to start her own crop with
next spring.

During the noon break Tora sat on the peat box by the stove
in the kitchen at Bekkejordet and read while Rachel rested her
stiff back on the couch and dozed a little.

"What are you reading?" she asked, yawning.

"*Victoria*," replied Tora in a dreamy voice.

"*Victoria?* What kind of book is that?"

"You don't know—and you're a grownup?" Tora asked
amazed, and looked up.

She closed the book over her right index finger.

Rachel smiled.

"No, as things've turned out, I haven't done much
reading—of books."

"But you should, Aunt Rachel," said Tora eagerly. "You
can't imagine. It's so sad, so beautiful. . . . "

"Can something be both sad and beautiful at the same
time?"

Rachel got gingerly to her feet, grimacing, and tried to straighten out her back. Then she hobbled over to the stove and, with a clatter, poured three shovelfuls of coal into the black opening.

"Yes," said Tora earnestly. "It's so beautiful. It doesn't matter that they love each other. He's only the son of a miller and she's rich. It seems like the others want them to be enemies, just because of that. It's just like with Mama and ... "

Tora stopped suddenly. Two red blotches spread over her cheekbones and she didn't know what to do.

Rachel looked at her in amazement from across the room.

"Just like your mother and your father?"

"Yes," Tora whispered.

The low autumn sun crept in through the window and made Rachel's cat curl up, purring, on the rag rug. She licked herself lazily with her eyes closed.

"Do you think about your father a lot, Tora?"

Rachel walked slowly over to the kitchen window and stuck a finger in each of her flowerpots, one after the other. Then she went and got a pitcher of water.

When she didn't get an answer, she sat down on the peat box next to Tora, holding the pitcher in both hands absently, as if she had forgotten what she was going to do with it.

Rachel was so little. She dangled her legs like a small child on the tall box.

"Has your mother said anything more about him?"

"No." Tora hesitated, uncertain. She knew that her aunt was annoyed with her mother because she wouldn't allow any talk of her father.

"*He's* always there, you know."

"That shouldn't make any difference. Henrik knows everything about it. Nobody's tried to hide anything from him. He chose your mother because he wanted her. And besides, he got her in trouble too. But that ended badly.... "

Rachel sat and stared out the window, over the gently sloping fields. She didn't seem to be talking to Tora.

"What do you mean?" Tora asked cautiously.

It felt like rain after a long dry spell, that a grownup would talk to her about things she usually only thought about.

"You know about your little sister who died, don't you?"

"Like Elisif's?"

"Yes."

"Where is she? I mean, where's her grave?"

"She's in the churchyard. Haven't you been there?"

"No."

The cat got up and curled her long tail around Rachel's legs. Rachel picked her up from the floor and absently stroked her glistening coat.

"Then your mother must go there alone."

A strange, empty pain went through Tora.

But she knew that was how it was. One more thing Mama had that she wouldn't share with Tora. A little grave. She had the memory of someone who should have been Tora's father, whom she never talked about. It was as if she wanted to keep Tora at a distance. Tora suddenly felt all alone.

"Now and then it's hard, being a woman," Rachel went on. "It can be hard whether you have children or not. But maybe I've escaped a lot of what your mother's had to struggle with, just because I never had any. All I've got is a kind of longing inside. It never stops."

Tora didn't dare breathe. It was so strange, so solemn. Just think, her aunt was able to find the words for what she was thinking. And she'd say them to a young girl too!

Even though she'd never even heard of *Victoria*.

At Bekkejordet, meals were totally different from the way they were at home. Happier. Her aunt and uncle often laughed between mouthfuls.

Tora didn't laugh with them very often. She just sat there with her mouth open and the corners turned up, and felt happy all the way down to her feet. Nobody got mad if you dawdled, or if you couldn't eat all your food. Nobody even said anything about it. It was strange.

Mealtimes were so peaceful that you could eat a horse just to make them last longer. Tora almost forgot how it felt to hear heavy, dragging footsteps on the stairs when she was sitting with food in her mouth. Almost forgot how her tongue could swell so impossibly down there in her throat whenever *he* turned the door handle.

Her uncle never took a nap on the couch after dinner. She asked him why. He replied that he'd start that when he moved to the old people's home at Breiland. And then he lifted her high in the air, as big as she was, so that she banged her head on the ceiling lamp and he had to pinch both her cheeks so she wouldn't get mad because he was so clumsy. As if she could ever get mad at Uncle Simon!

Tora felt her body stiffen when he swept her up in his arms. She didn't think she'd be able to stand it.

But the nausea didn't come, as she expected it to. And Tora thought there must be something different about Uncle Simon's hands . . . Then he snatched up his cap lying on the peat box and rushed out the door trailing a big cloud of tobacco smoke behind him.

The potato digging was supposed to take four whole days. Rachel had figured it out. And they didn't have to hurry because this wasn't piece work, she said.

"We'll give ourselves plenty of time both to eat and clean up, and as a reward we'll take time off now and then to straighten our backs and talk a little."

On the third day they were in the field, the Old Jew arrived.

He made himself comfortable on an empty potato box and brought out his wares. It had been a long time since he'd made the rounds of the island.

Rachel laughed and said he might as well save himself the trouble of opening his suitcase for them, they were so dirty they wouldn't want to touch even the cheapest colored print. The bony old man sat there anyway, as if planted on the box. His brown coat with the enormous lapels and huge pockets covered him like a shell. It looked as if someone had placed his head loosely up there among the thick homespun material. In bad weather he turned up the lapels so they reached up over his ears and protected him from whatever the good Lord sent his way, whether it was rain or snow.

He carried his suitcase from farm to farm. Grownups could remember him from when they were children. He set out on the roads as soon as spring arrived. Late in the fall he seemed to disappear into the sea. Nobody knew where.

He was one of the few who remained from the old days. He knew just about everything, but wasn't such a gossip that it mattered. He didn't try to push his wares on anyone, just made himself comfortable and waited. If he was hungry, he stayed until it was time to eat—if he was lucky enough to have gotten past the door. If you bought anything, big or small, he usually left at once. That way you didn't have to offer him a bite to eat or a place to sit.

Everybody knew the Old Jew's ways but few knew his name. In some strange way he was invulnerable. You could try to drive him away or tease him. He just sat there. Or else he would get up and go on his way as if nothing had happened.

Once some of the boys in the upper grades had taken his suitcase and run away with it.

But the Old Jew—that was all they ever called him—sat down patiently on a rock by the side of the road and waited until the fun wore off for his tormentors and Gunn called them in to class.

Then he went, with infinite slowness, over to the stone quarry where they'd hidden the suitcase, searched and found it and went on his way.

Tora had watched him from the classroom window. Gunn was at her desk and didn't know anything about it. And that was a good thing for the backs that were supporting the sinners above their desk lids.

Tora had a strange feeling that the Old Jew and she were related. She wasn't exactly clear in her mind how. It probably had something to do with the fact that people thought they had the right to torment and bully the Old Jew too. He also came from bad people. There was a Jew smell, a smell of greed and money, people would say with a grin when he passed by.

It was the Jews who'd killed Jesus. Even Gunn said that. It

was the Germans who killed the Jews, during the war. Put them in concentration camps. Gunn told them that too.

Elisif thought that it was God's judgment on the Jewish people that Hitler killed them and hounded them everywhere. Tora's palms grew clammy just at the thought that God could be like that. But she was careful not to object. Nobody contradicted Elisif. It was the Germans who'd killed Pål Ingebriktsen's son and half of Norway too, that was certain. Tora had heard many horrible stories about fingernails that had been pulled out and gold teeth broken out of people's mouths.

Somebody had to take the blame for all that.

Somebody people could get to.

Tora understood that she and the Old Jew were among those who couldn't escape.

"You're hard at work, I see, digging up the potatoes."

The Old Jew sat there on the box with his clawlike fingers spread on his threadbare trouser legs. They moved back and forth, as if he were trying to get them warm. His coat was open and blew around him in the wind with heavy flapping slaps. The man looked like a huge bird who had forgotten how to fly.

"Oh yes, it's the same on all the farms. I don't sell much that way. Folk can't see that I've got fine embroidery. Christmas designs. I've got table runners with elves on them sitting in a circle. Mice and cats, spruce needles and twigs . . . "

"Yes, I know. But you can see how our hands are, can't you? So dirty I can't wipe my nose!"

Rachel sent Tora an amused glance over the pile of potato plants.

But Tora couldn't make herself return the grin.

It was as if she crept into the old man. Turned into him. Crawled into his coat, under his skin. She felt the helpless pain of having to expose yourself, humble yourself, beg for mercy. Beg for the least little thing. Throw all pride to the wind and clutch at anyone or anything.

And it no longer seemed to be day. Night came suddenly upon her where she stood. The potatoes' yellow eyes turned into spots of blood in the dark earth. Their small, scared eyes glowed. They were jumping up and down, wanting something from her. She warded them off by staring hard at something high above Rachel's head. She felt as if she were sitting in a swing that was going much too fast.

She couldn't stop it. It just went faster. Around and around, until the nausea was almost killing her. She heard her voice. She was crawling around in her room. Begging for mercy, holding onto the bed post for dear life.

And the yellow eyes stared at her from the dark earth.

It was no contest. Everything had already been decided by powers that were stronger and perfectly within their rights.

The German brat! The Old Jew!

Tora dug in the damp soil. Dug and dug until the soil burst its way under her nails. All the way in to where the nails were attached to the skin. Farther. She felt her nails tearing and had to stop. Something pulled apart. It hurt. But it was obvious. There was always something that had to be skinned and nailed to a fence. Might as well get used to it, get it over with.

NO! A kind of shout came out of her. She couldn't help it. It didn't belong in the fields, in reality, at Bekkejordet. It was a shameful and hoarse sound. Incomprehensible. But it came out of her anyway. Like a great defiance.

She picked up a large potato. Looked closely at the small pink hollows in the yellow-white skin. Then she got up, leaped up as if her life depended on it. Stretched her right hand, holding the potato, as far back as she could. Stretched all the way up on her toes, found her balance and gathered all she had of trembling resilience.

Then she threw the potato. Higher and higher it flew over the black, dug-up rows.

Her dirty hand hung at her side. In it there was still a little of her trembling strength. Then it was over.

The two grownups watched in astonishment as the potato disappeared somewhere behind the barn roof. Then they turned simultaneously and stared at Tora.

A hot blush spread over her face and neck. She'd thrown a large, good eating potato far into the woods!

She went meekly down on her hands and knees again and

dug potatoes as if her life were at stake. So she didn't see the expressions that passed over Rachel's face. They shifted from astonished disbelief to admiration before finally breaking into a dazzling smile.

"Why, Tora! I didn't know you were so good at throwing! I've never seen anything like it. You're just the way I was when I was your age. I also needed to run, jump and throw. Oh Lord, that was a long time ago! Well, it's time for a break now. Let's go in and wash off the dirt. And we'll make some waffles." She turned to the man on the potato box. "Would you like waffles too?"

"Praise the Lord and thanks!" The old man was on his feet in an instant. Shuffled his feet in his eagerness and held onto his suitcase tightly.

And Tora ran to empty the buckets of potatoes. They thudded and bounced into the box when she dumped the potatoes out.

The dirt fell off, revealing the small red eyes. They stared up at her. Hundreds of them. Tora covered the box with a sack and went quickly to the house.

How strange it was that Aunt Rachel invited the Old Jew in. Almost nobody ever did. Could her aunt guess that Tora felt she was related to him? No, she brushed that idea aside.

But she shouldn't have done that with the potato. Now it was just lying there behind the barn someplace, of no use to anybody.

Rachel almost had to force the man to take off his coat and shoes. Then she placed a wash basin with water in it in front of him.

"Wash your hands!" she commanded him.

Tora looked at the Old Jew. Shame made his face appear empty, for his hands were so dirty.

Tora hid her dirt-caked hands behind her back until it was her turn.

The Old Jew spread out the printed runners and doilies on the kitchen table. Rachel went back and forth and prodded and turned everything this way and that, held a piece up and asked Tora what she thought. Now and then she was over at the stove, pouring more batter in the iron. It sizzled and steamed and covered over what had happened out there in the potato field.

"Do we have time for embroidering, Tora?" Rachel wondered, and raised an eyebrow. She held up a guest towel and looked at it critically.

The design was a cottage, birch woods and lots of flowers. Tora nodded with her mouth full of waffles. She had coffee to drink, too. She looked at the colors that Rachel held up to the pattern to decide what went best with it.

The man smiled only with his eyes. A close network of wrinkles puckered the skin around his eyes and gave him away. But his mouth had no expression. He ate slowly and carefully, without slurping his coffee from the saucer the way old people, in Tora's experience, did. Everything he did was almost silent.

It was as if he were afraid someone might notice he was there. He forgot his manners once in a while and wiped his moustache with the back of his hand. Only to remember, a moment later, that he was sitting in the kitchen of one of his betters. Then, embarrassed, he would pull a handkerchief, not very clean, out of one of those deep pockets. And, with a dignified gesture, slowly wipe the spot on which he'd just used the back of his hand.

This was an entirely different Old Jew from the one Tora had seen dragging his suitcase through the village, a trail of kids behind him and his coat flapping in the wind.

This one was somehow—a human being.

The plate of waffles was empty. Tora couldn't understand how anyone could be eating so slowly each time you looked at him, but still eat so much so fast.

The sale of the embroidery was concluded to both parties' satisfaction and then the Old Jew quickly made ready to go. There were so many more places he had to visit. He didn't attempt to sell Rachel anything else, just hesitated in closing the lid of his suitcase. Moved the dress material and ribbons a little, as if by accident, let his crooked fingers run absentmindedly over a bunch of broad lace.

When he was gone, a strange odor of spice remained after him.

Rachel said Tora could embroider the runner. She said they'd had enough potato digging for one day. Now they were going to embroider. And they turned on the big light above the kitchen table and got busy choosing colors.

At first Tora couldn't get her fingers to do what she wanted. The potato digging had made them stiff and uncontrollable. Rachel handled the needle skillfully and showed Tora the most difficult stitches, so she could take the work home with her. She'd get thirty *kroner* for the runner when it was finished. That was an unbelievable sum and almost shameful to accept. But Rachel snorted and said that, in return, the runner would have to be embroidered properly on the back side or else Tora would have to take out every single stitch. And now she'd have to borrow a flashlight and see about getting home before they started to worry about her. Potatoes again tomorrow morning, eight o'clock sharp!

Tora hesitated, once she had her coat and boots on. Didn't seem able to get the little table runner wrapped properly in the big piece of gray paper. It kept sliding out. Rachel finally had to tie twine around it, then handed Tora the package with a smile.

"Could I stay overnight?"

The words came out of Tora's mouth without her even knowing she'd thought them. Rachel gave her a surprised look.

"Are you afraid of the dark, you big girl?"

"No, not exactly. . . . "

"You can stay overnight tomorrow," Rachel decided and gave one of Tora's braids a tug. "That'll work out fine, because Simon's going to Bodø. Ask your mother if you can. All right?"

"Yes!"

As she trudged her way home on the gravel path, Tora could already feel the next day as a soft, warm baby animal in her lap.

She pushed away thoughts of the rest of the evening, and of the night, and let the flashlight beam dance over the fields and the ditches on either side of the road. It was as if she didn't need the light to see. Even though the sky was dark and the scrub forest close, its twisted branches reaching out after her.

Chapter Thirty-Four

SHE SAW IT THE MOMENT SHE CAME UP THE STAIRS, although the hallway was dark because the light bulb on their landing had burned out.

Her mother's shoes and coat were gone! *His* shoes and jacket lay in a pile under the peg on the wall.

Tora hesitated at the door. She didn't seem to have the strength to push down the handle tonight. She could hear scraping sounds inside.

She turned around and found the bannister with her free hand. She held the flashlight and grey-wrapped package tight against her body with the other. Like a thief in flight.

She closed the front door as carefully as she could, but it made a small complaining noise anyway. Then she was outside in the biting cold again and let the darkness hide her.

She didn't want to go through it tonight!

A small, hunched figure with a package under one arm. Avoided the road. Found the path up to the moor and through the bogs. The alder thickets stood in her way like startled ghosts.

Once she sat down on a rock, out of breath, and felt saved. She was Tora. She was on her way—*away*.

The stone quarry! She'd go there. She could sit there, protected from the wind. It must be late. No one must see her out now. For then Mama would hear about it and be ashamed because people would say that Ingrid couldn't even keep track of her only child, out wandering around in the pitch black night. And people would wonder. Tora had learned that people shouldn't be given the chance to do that.

Because they let unpleasant and accusing truths grow out of their wondering. The more they wondered, the uglier the truths became.

When she'd almost reached the cart path that led to the quarry, two figures appeared up on the hill. They seemed to come from nowhere. She didn't recognize them.

She crouched down in the ditch and felt the ditch water trickle over the tops of her boots. Coldly and mercilessly it enveloped her calves and ankles and finally her toes. But she stayed crouched there until the men were gone. The quarry no longer seemed safe. She stood up, uncertain, and no longer knew which way to go. If she only had a warehouse attic now!

Then it occurred to her that the new warehouse was roofed now and had walls with many snug corners. Maybe she could find a hiding place there. Just so she could sit there a while until she was sure her mother was through working. She could meet her outside Dahl's. She could put up with getting bawled out for being out in the dark so late at night. Yes!

She darted across the road and found the edge of the beach, so she could go down into the village unseen. The water in her short boots squished coldly and sadly.

She should have left the embroidery in the hallway at home, then she would have had both hands free, so she could warm them in her pockets. Now she had to warm up one at a time. That didn't help very much.

The wind was strong. Her braids stuck out like twigs behind her in the dark, and it was impossible to keep her jacket closed in front. The cold crept up her legs and thighs and she bitterly regretted that she hadn't kept her "potato pants" on when she walked home. Her skirt was short and her stockings thin. Besides that, something was wrong with one of her stockings, so every now and then she had to stop to fix it.

Once she wasn't watching where she was going and ended up on her head in the rocks. She felt a sharp rock rip through the knee of her stocking and into her flesh. She sat down and let her fingers feel around the injured spot. They came away warm and sticky. Blood. The stocking was ruined. She'd lost the package and the flashlight. But she had plenty of time to search, wasn't afraid of not finding them again. Everything seemed so far away. She felt as if she'd have to spend the rest of her life crawling around on a dark beach.

The waves glittered as they washed up the shore. The foaming came afterwards. Rhythmic undertow. Came and went. Tora sat there without moving until she couldn't feel her feet. She'd stuck her hands between her legs, it wasn't so bad for them.

When she finally turned her head, she saw the lights of the village. She seemed to wake up then. She stood up shivering. Groped around until she found the flashlight and the package.

She didn't turn on the flashlight. The darkness was good. It left no tracks. The darkness always had a hiding place for a girl's body. But in that case there mustn't be walls surrounding it. Had to be the way it was here: boundless. Even so, a kind of desolate fear of the dark came over her. It was like moving in a dead world. She was the only survivor. Alone with herself. She forced herself to forget why she was walking here. She didn't have a reason. It was just a way of existing. To wander between dead, cold rocks in a world where only the wind, the ocean and Tora were alive.

She crept around in the scaffolding, found her way into the darkest corners in the shadow of the immense structure. It was so much more frightening now that she was there. At last she found a ladder that went up to a work platform. She climbed up to it, rung after rung, and collapsed with her back securely against the wall.

With every move she made, the wind screamed desolately in the unoiled block and tackle. The pain wasn't so very bad in her cut knee. She could stand it.

She tucked her skirt around her as tightly as she could and tried to make the sleeves of her sweater reach below her wrists, pulled off her wet boots and dumped the water out. She was swinging high above the earth!

Slowly she began to feel her feet. Wiggled her toes, amazed. Strange to feel your own toes so painfully near. She wedged her boots and the package tightly in the space between the planks so she wouldn't lose them in the dark. She got dizzy for a moment, when she realized how high up she must be. As high as the warehouse attic had been.

She made up a game with the rule that if she only kept track of her boots, then everything would turn out all right.

Once she thought about the Old Jew. She seemed to feel his coldness as well as her own.

It had to be very late. But she mustn't fall asleep. Not because she was afraid of falling down, but because nobody must find her up here when morning came. She pressed her back even harder into the wall and wrung out both socks. That helped. It really did!

She leaned her head back and felt the rough, unfinished wood dig into the back of her head.

If *he* disappeared, she thought. Then everything would be different. *Him*. If he died—or just went away? Yes. She sat and let the thought sink in. And she became aware that it tasted salty and slimy and was difficult to swallow.

"Dear God! Don't you think you can do without Henrik here on earth?" she prayed quietly. She could just barely hear her own words and she forced herself to name him by name so that perhaps the prayer would have more power.

After she had repeated the words a few times, Aunt Rachel appeared. She could smell her aunt's waffles and bread. Tora gilded the bitter, gray night with the thought of all the best things she could remember.

At last she thought that she was lying in the white bed in the tiny dormer room at Bekkejordet. Over there was the glass cabinet with the ancient tea service from Grandma! At the same time, she was where she was and saw how a delicate red color spread across the sky just where the lighthouse island stuck out into the ocean. It was almost a miracle. The Old Jew came, his whole lap full of yellow potatoes, and complained because the colored print he was going to sell had been taken up to heaven.

And the embroidered runners hung on the rusty clothes rack in the Tenement's courtyard and were just as dirty as the clothes Tora had worn to dig potatoes in.

Tora rose into the air like a balloon.

Higher and higher. It was so easy to breathe! But the heap of potato plants grew so fast and thick and came rushing after her.

All of a sudden she was the potato she'd thrown herself. She felt the strength of her own throw. It was perfect. She was climbing so lightly and so fast. She rose high above the clouds. Above all the buildings and the people far below. Nobody could reach her. Nobody!

Then she saw *him* standing in the doorway at home, his arms spread out over the door to her room.

She began to fall. Fall and fall. Tried to steer away from the doorway and the door, but he came closer and closer. The door was suddenly so close she could see where it was worn around the handle and scratched on the middle panel. He didn't have a face. Then she realized that nothing had changed. He only had the disgusting words he usually grunted out. And the strong fingers. There was no way to escape!

For a moment she saw that Fritz was hiding behind the doorjamb and trying to tell her something. But she couldn't figure out the signs he was making. He was holding up his arms and making many strange signs with his fingers. But she couldn't understand any of them. Then he disappeared. The door was so close, so close. She saw the man's rough, dark hairline.

She recognized the acrid smell of the danger and she braced herself.

She sat up with a jerk so sudden that her stiff neck felt like it was broken. It was the smell!

It was light. Dear God, so she'd fallen asleep anyway!

Her mind struggled out of sleep with her body following reluctantly. Then she saw it: fire under the scaffolding! No, under the wharf. The acrid smell of smoke and tar. The flames sputtered a few times before they caught in earnest in the newly-tarred beams that supported the warehouse.

Tora was on her way down the ladder before she really knew what she was doing. Fast and easily, keeping pace with the fear that was making it difficult to breathe.

She didn't know if she was dreaming or really climbing down the ladder. But when she felt the boards of the wharf under her stocking feet and remembered that her boots were still up there, she had no doubts.

She paused, uncertain. Who could she run to for help? Because her uncle's new wharf had to be saved! She took a couple of quick steps towards the stairs to where the rowboats were docked, to see how bad it was.

Then she saw him!

The man on the crossbeams under the wharf!

She would have recognized that figure anywhere!

The door! She'd fallen down on the door after all.

So it wasn't a dream, as she'd first thought.

She didn't want to, but she was drawn towards the stairs anyway. He was coming towards her with his head down, carrying an oil can. The fire was crackling and flickering down there. It came after the man, as if it had something to avenge. Spread more and more swiftly. When *he* got to the foot of the stairs, he raised his head. His face was white against the flickering, red background. The flames were alive and writhing behind him. Tora was standing on the edge of reality. The edge of nightmare. Standing in wet stocking feet, her boots forgotten high up under the sky. She'd run away in vain.

Then came the scream.

It echoed through the crackling and the sounds of the sea, felt like a great ache as it flew out of her. It cut straight through. Through the fear and everything else.

The man below her stood there a moment, swaying. He hadn't yet put his foot on the bottom step.

To her amazement, Tora saw that he had a face. A hunted and frightened face! Terror was etched deeply in each feature.

And again the scream came rushing out of her. This time it carried so much farther because she was aware she was screaming. He swayed once more, and then he fell. Heavily and with flailing arms. His body hitting the crossbeam. It sounded like the coal truck when it tipped the sacks off against the cement steps at home: soft and hard at the same time.

Then came the splash. But it was smothered quickly by the crackling from the huge blaze and the rhythmic smacking noises of the sea against the pilings. The oil can flew over to the rocks and lay there, banging in the wind. As if it wanted to tell the whole world where it was.

The fire was flickering and glowing down there in the restless, dark water. Came to life, in a way. Ate its way up and licked around the dry, new framework. Spread outward like a giant fan. It's getting warm, she thought, astonished. It was like a friend. Shining for her.

His hand was yellow when it came up for a moment. Then his head came up too. His cap was floating all the way over by Simon's rowboat.

In daylight, the boat's gunwales were blue, Tora remembered. The entire harbor was stained yellow now. And his cap was floating, all alone, over there. Maybe it felt a little happy. Like her. Because he certainly couldn't save himself.

Happy!

If he'd been over where his cap was, he could have reached the gunwale. But he wasn't! He was too far away! And everything was burning. He was going to drown and burn. Drown and burn. In all eternity. Amen!

"Get the boat, damn . . . !"

The shout was choked off as the man swallowed sea water and went down again. There was a red flickering in front of Tora's eyes. It felt as if a lid were being pushed up with great force. There was such a whistling in her head, as if she weren't entirely herself. She was outside of everything. Each time the man went down, she became a little freer. Finally she wasn't able to keep it inside any longer. It got too big. The gasping started, as a warning of the bubbling laughter to come. It poured from her mouth without her expecting it. And then the shaking started.

The right corner of her mouth pulled down and showed her teeth. Her mouth was like a trembling, ugly grimace in her white face. The laughter couldn't be stopped.

She couldn't reach him. She *shouldn't* reach him. That was certain. At last, no sound came from the man when he came to the surface.

Soon he would go down for good into the seaweed far below. The jellyfish and the crabs would settle on him quietly, eat up his huge body bit by bit. Would bind his hands and feet and pull him down in shame. Own him and cast him aside. But come back. Always! His clothes would rot until at last he wouldn't have anything to hide behind except the cold, whispering ocean.

Tora would never swim in the ocean again!

He would open his mouth all the while and holler and beg for mercy down there. But it wouldn't do any good. The stars would see and hear nothing. Everybody would be too busy to notice anything. It would be so quiet in her room.

Finally the tides would rock him and carry him out into the depths where nothing left any traces any longer. And there were currents too.

"Oh God!"

The jubilation poured from her mouth like a howl.

The huge blaze was crackling.

The fire was beginning to climb onto the wharf deck. Licked between the boards with countless eager tongues. She was surrounded by a lovely, golden glow. She'd never seen anything so beautiful. It was like being inside sunshine. It smelled of tar and summer. But this was even better, this was in motion. It was dancing!

Then she remembered that it was Uncle Simon's new wharf that was burning. Suddenly she saw the difference between dream and reality. And it felt as if someone slapped her in the face. Was she supposed to be so cruel, in order to bear reality? No! She realized that she was standing in the rowboat.

Worked quickly with dead hands. Untied the hawser knot. As if she'd never intended to do anything else. Shoved off with an oar. Quickly. Done!

She was holding him safely out of the water when they arrived. By the hair. He floated remarkably easily on his back. Face up. She'd managed it as easily as anything. Even though she could tell that he had a kind of strength in him that wanted to turn him over on his stomach and plunge his head under water. But she twisted him back. She gripped his ice-cold chin and held tight. His eyes were wide open. But even so they didn't see anything. She was absolutely sure of that. They looked like the eyes of a fish you've pulled up fast and gutted. But there was a difference. His body was sluggish and still.

His cap was still floating by itself over there. It had floated all the way over to Peder Larsa's rowboat.

Carefree, it bobbed and set its course according to the way the wind was blowing. As if it were thinking of flying. But it had become too wet and heavy, when it came right down to it.

Metal-clear voices. Orders. As if forged in steel in the dense grey morning. They were coming from everywhere. Through the smoke.

The whole wharf was hidden in the smoke. But the smell of tar tried harder and harder to spread a reconciling cover over the destruction. Rolls of tarpaper crackled and burned. As if the fire had undertaken an impossible piecework job. It went at it blindly, in a rage.

The rowboat rocked. Tora felt a sudden gust of breath against her face and a large, warm body close to hers. Big hands took over where she'd been holding on. A heart beat. Was it Uncle Simon's heart or her own?

The dead body was hauled over the gunwale like a giant octopus. It seemed to be just cartilage and skin in a bundle of clothing. His tufts of hair! Only when it was no longer touching her did Tora feel it on her hands. Like rotten fish netting—forgotten at low tide, left to drift haphazardly with the tides and winds.

Simon Bekkejordet let the others take care of Henrik's lifeless body and of putting out the fire. He carried the child up to

Tobias's shack, where she could be safe.

"The oil can's lying under the wharf where he dropped it," she said firmly.

He understood in one incredulous flash and asked no questions. But he held her close, close to his wild heart. And salt ran from both of them.

Then he pulled off his jacket and put it around her before he looked around and found a barrel.

When two men came in carrying the body of Henrik Toste between them, Simon had taken the door to Tobias's shack off its hinges and laid it on the barrel. They put the body on the door and Simon forced his hand far down in Henrik's throat.

Tora sat crouched on a fish box and wondered how a heart could have the strength to beat so terribly hard. She could feel it all the way up in her ears. It was like a machine. When they rocked him back on the door, she saw his face. Suddenly it began growing right in front of her eyes and came towards her. Tore itself loose from the dead body and came!

"Dear God, I only had stockings on, don't you remember? I couldn't do it any faster. Could I?"

She felt she was about to be choked. But suddenly it was as if she were up there again and on the way down to the door. He had the door under him now, but it was just the same. She'd thought she was saved, and now she was falling, and nothing was going to be as she'd thought. Nothing ever turned out the way you thought it would, for everything was determined in advance. He could reach her even if he was dead!

Yes. That's how it was. She would never escape.

She made a gesture with her hand, wanted to say something. But nobody paid any attention to the girl on the box. They worked to get the vomit and the sea out of the man on the teeter-totter.

Why didn't Uncle Simon understand that it was too late! He was dead! They'd saved him from the loneliness down there. That ought to be enough.

Finally the men could see that the sunken chin was starting to move. Henrik began retching again and again. Simon turned him lightning fast on his side and forced his hand down his throat once again to hasten the process. The men jabbed him gently and firmly in the belly to help.

All eyes were on the white-blue face on the door.

Then his eyelids fluttered and in confusion he tried to focus his gaze on the man standing closest. The sharp light from the wharf competed with the flickering light from the fire. The man blinked at all of it and looked like a boy who is forced to wake up much too early. A little under the weather, a little cross.

Then something happened inside the man that he hadn't counted on. Something in there fighting for his life without his knowing. All at once he doubled up and let out a rattling sound before he threw up over the old, peeling door.

It seemed he would never be finished. He curled and twisted like a giant crab.

Tora saw it all. And she remembered that she'd forgotten her boots on the scaffold after all. Felt indifferently that it didn't matter. She didn't have the strength to go get them.

She had come back to earth. The dream was gone. Both the good one and the bad one.

The bucket handles clanged rhythmically. The shouting of orders had died down. Everything was going the way it should.

"Heave and heave and heave!"

Suddenly a voice cut through the smoke. It belonged to no one she knew, just came from nothing:

"That's far enough, far enough! Turn on the water, goddamit!"

Then came the thick, liberating stream from the wharf hose. It hissed and threw itself over the flaming mass. The smoke and the steam forced the men to retreat quickly away from the wharf. Tora coughed without noticing it.

She saw the buckets gliding from hand to hand down there. The men's backs bent in time to the chant. Now and then a bucket pumped against the edge of the wharf so that the man who was supposed to take it got the whole bucketful in the face. But there was no more cursing. For everything was going just as it was supposed to, and the fire would have to give up.

Rhythmical and echoing, the men's voices rose in the air like a roaring in unison. There was a kind of triumph in them. Tora had never heard anything like it.

"Heave and heave and heave!"

And high above the men and their buckets rose the wild gush from the wharf hose and drenched the whole world.

Rainbows, coming and going quick as lightning, flickered in the stream of water. But as the fire was forced to give up, the colors disappeared in the smoke. The sky and the sea were tangled up out there. There were no more boundaries.

Morning came. The wind blew from shore in God's name this time too, people said.

Chapter Thirty-Five

THE DAY LAY LIKE A SHROUD OVER THE MARSHES WHEN
Nas-Eldar drove up the hill with the soaking-wet body of
Henrik Toste bundled in a tarpaulin in the bed of Dahl's
truck.

Tora had been lifted into the back of the truck too, because
the passenger seat was old and worn out. So they had Ingrid's
whole family in one bed.

If they'd had any understanding of a child's psychology
they could have written coarse ballads or tender poems about
life's brutal paradoxes. But no one thought of anything like
that.

Tora's hands were tightly clenched around her knees. She
stared at the road behind them and went backwards into the
new day.

She'd made a small, powerless protest at being put up in the
back of the truck with him, but nobody paid attention. The
girl said something about a pair of boots, too.

"Neither one of you has any boots and you don't need any
either," somebody replied impatiently. So that was settled.

No matter how much she tried to look away, she could still
see *his* legs sticking out of the tarpaulin. So she had to fix her
eyes on the gravel road. That wasn't so easy when the truck
was lurching at its worst.

Ingrid had been notified. She was standing on the steps when
they arrived. Her arms were crossed over her chest and she
was clutching the opening of her knit sweater. Tora thought it
looked like somebody had poked her mother's eyes out.

Then there was only the clock, Mama and her.

They'd put him into bed, rubbed life into him and got a stiff drink down him for his health. That didn't present any great difficulties.

Ingrid went back and forth with burned-out eyes and offered Nas-Eldar coffee and bread. But he didn't have time. That was true. She just nodded dumbly but didn't forget to thank him for the lift by giving his rough hand a firm shake.

Ingrid knew it didn't pay to forget what you had to thank somebody for. The old man looked away for a second, then he opened the door and was outside in the hall. His steps made a hollow echo through the sleeping house.

Ingrid's eyes were not there for Tora. So many unspoken words lay between. So many questions the grownup couldn't bring herself to ask. Not now. Maybe later. Maybe as early as tomorrow morning. Ingrid dried her wet hands on her apron and brushed some of her dark hair back behind her ears.

"Eat, Tora, so you can go to bed!"

Her voice was unfamiliar. It seemed as if Tora had never heard her mother talk before. But she didn't have the strength to feel anything about it. Instead, she took three bites of the bread to appease her. But she quickly realized that it was a wasted effort because her mother's eyes were turned inward and had no room for her.

The angel above the bed looked as if she wanted badly to fly out the window and join the gulls. The curtains weren't pulled. The wind had blown the fog away and the sky was remarkably new and gleaming all the way into the dark blue ocean.

A freighter was making slow headway out there.

It was so strange that everything just continued. Nothing had ended.

Tora undressed in the grey light. The arms of her sweater were wet far up to her elbows. Her mother hadn't noticed the ruined stocking. Tora stood undecided a moment, when she saw that the cut on her knee had started bleeding when she took off her stocking. She couldn't get under the covers with a knee like that.

She found a handkerchief in her chest of drawers and tried to make it go all the way around. It was much too tight when she tried to tie it. For a moment the world seemed about to fall apart because she couldn't make the handkerchief fit. It felt as if she had sand under her eyelids.

The angel still looked as if she wanted to fly away. Then an avalanche came raging through Tora. Sharp ridges tore away. Wild forces in her were struggling to break loose. She snatched a clean stocking out of a drawer and pulled it on over the bloody knee. It helped a little but not enough.

She climbed up on the bed and took the angel down off the wall, opened the window and threw her out. The picture flew straight over the overgrown garden and behind the large mountain ash trees on the other side of the stone wall. The glass glittered cheerfully when it reached its highest point. Tora felt as if something had torn in her right shoulder because she'd thrown so hard. There was still a throbbing, angry power in her that she kept alive with clenched teeth.

Lying in bed, she saw that a dark square was left after the picture. Nothing could be erased. Nobody was supposed to be able to fly away without leaving marks behind. That's how it was.

Then, suddenly, as she was cradling her arms, still covered with goose pimples and damp from the sea water, the warmth of Uncle Simon's body came flowing into her. She could smell the tar and the smoke strangely close to her, as if she were still in the rowboat.

Uncle Simon's heart! Beating all the way into hers. He was so warm, Uncle Simon!

"My poor little girl!"

Is that what he'd said? His voice seemed to come from deep within his chest. The words had swung trembling from his warm body to hers.

Strange.

Tora stared at the dark square left by the picture until the sun made its way in and with gentle fingers caressed the unpainted panelling covering the walls. The knots showed clearly. Emerged from the walls somehow and came alive. She could have created a fantasy in that landscape to make the day a good one, but somehow she couldn't keep track of her own thoughts. The wall was like an old, abandoned magpie nest. No order in it. Dry knots sticking out everywhere without rhyme or reason. But cutting right through everything she could feel the beating of Uncle Simon's heart.

They didn't come for him until late in the day. The sheriff had another man with him.

There wasn't a lot of excitement. But you could hear that it had to do with Henrik.

Windows, doors and landings had ears and eyes.

Forces had decided to tug at the piece of yarn sticking out until there wasn't anything left of the sweater, even though winter was on the way. Still, you wanted it at a little distance. It was safest to stand behind something you could hold on to and just observe what went on. Because one thing was certain: Ingrid was going to freeze for a while. You had to be allowed to whisper—in strict confidence, of course—and speculate on how she would make out.

But it's true. People like her, who'd once committed a great sin, couldn't expect to feel secure in their destiny.

Tora got out of bed and put on the other stocking, and the skirt and blouse from yesterday. Felt how the clothes fitted her body nice and tightly. It was as if she'd never really known how it felt to have clothes on her body until now.

She knew there wouldn't be any potato digging at Bekkejordet today. She couldn't ask permission to sleep up there tonight either. But that didn't matter anymore. That was so far away. Because Tora had heard the men. The doors that slammed and the footsteps that disappeared. She could scarcely believe the wild joy she felt.

She went out into the kitchen and put on the heavy wool socks lying in front of the stove. Her mother had taken away the wet, dirty rags from last night and put clean socks in their place.

Tora felt comforted when she saw what her mother had done.

Ingrid was standing over by the counter, her back to Tora. The sun was gushing in through the window like a big shining surprise.

When she turned, Tora's face broke into an uncertain smile. But she saw that Mama had disappeared for her in every way.

The important thing was not to give up now, Tora thought. Her feet had jumped into the rowboat by themselves. She couldn't do anything about it. He was saved. But Mama had gone away. Now she'd have to take whatever came. She'd said almost nothing to her uncle, but the sheriff came anyway. Mama couldn't blame her for that. She couldn't! Tora wanted to scream it at the slumped back. But no sound would come out. Had she said anything to Uncle Simon anyway that her mother had found out about?

Ingrid had turned back to the counter. Her narrow shoulders sagged. A shadow lay over her whole defeated figure.

Tora saw it. For an instant she felt her mother's pain as if it were her own.

Then she looked over at her bedroom door. And a feeling of security enclosed her, swept everything else away and made her strong, strong. They'd taken him away with them!

She took the few necessary steps and stood at her mother's side. Barely touched the sleeve of her mother's blouse and said, "I'll mop the floor today, Mama. I don't have school, you know. And they say there's lots of lingonberries up on Veten this year. Shall we go up there together?"

Her mother stared out the window for a moment.

Then she turned slowly to Tora.

About the Author

Herbjørg Wassmo is currently considered one of Norway's most important writers. *The House With the Blind Glass Windows* is the first volume in her trilogy about Tora; she was recently awarded the Nordic Prize, the prestigious annual Scandinavian award, for the third volume.

About the Translators

Roseann Lloyd is a poet whose first collection, *Tap Dancing for Big Mom,* appeared in 1986 (New Rivers Press, Minneapolis). Allen Simpson is a professor of Norwegian at the University of Minnesota.

International Women's Writing from Seal Press

EGALIA'S DAUGHTERS by Gerd Brantenberg. $11.95, 1-878067-58-3. A hilarious satire on sex roles – in which the wim rule and the menwim stay at home – by Norway's leading feminist author.

NERVOUS CONDITIONS by Tsitsi Dangarembga. $10.95, 0-931188-74-1. A moving story of a Zimbabwean girl's coming of age and of the devastating human loss involved in the colonization of one culture by another.

CONSTANCE RING by Amalie Skram. $10.95, paper, 0-931188-60-1; $18.95, cloth, 0-931188-61-X. A stunning turn-of-the-century feminist classic from Norway.

CORA SANDEL: *Selected Short Stories*. $8.95, 0-931188-30-X. Masterful short stories by the Norwegian author of the acclaimed Alberta Trilogy.

EARLY SPRING by Tove Ditlevsen. $8.95, 0-931188-28-8. The classic memoirs of Denmark's beloved poet and writer.

NOTHING HAPPENED by Ebba Haslund. $8.95, 0-931188-47-4. This moving story is one of a handful of novels with a lesbian theme ever written in Norway.

TO LIVE AND TO WRITE: *Selections by Japanese Women Writers, 1913-1938*, edited by Yukiko Tanaka. $12.95, 0-931188-43-1. An important collection spanning a twenty-five year period of change in Japan, during which women writers emerged as major voices in the country.

A WEEK LIKE ANY OTHER by Natalya Baranskaya. $9.95, paper, 0-931188-80-6; $18.95, cloth, 0-931188-81-4. This enthralling collection features the work of one of the Soviet Union's finest short story writers.

WORDS OF FAREWELL: *Stories by Korean Women Writers* by Kang Sok-kyong, Kim Chi-won and O Chong-hui. $12.95, paper, 0-931188-76-8; $20.95, cloth, 0-931188-77-6. Three of Korea's foremost contemporary women writers explore powerful and important themes in this landmark collection. *Winner of the 1993 Korean Literature Translation Prize.*

ANGEL by Merle Collins. $9.95, 0-931188-64-4. This novel from Grenada follows young Angel McAllister as she joins her country's move toward political autonomy.

SEAL PRESS, founded in 1976 to provide a forum for women writers and feminist issues, publishes many other books of fiction and non-fiction, including books on health, self-help and domestic violence, sports and outdoors, mysteries and women's studies. You can order the books listed above by writing to 3131 Western Avenue, Suite 410, Seattle, Washington 98121 (please add 15% of the book total for shipping and handling). Write to us for a free catalog.